THE BODY UNDER THE SANDS

a historical murder mystery with a stunning twist

JAMES ANDREW

Paperback published by The Book Folks

London, 2018

© James Andrew

This book is a work of fiction. Names, characters, businesses, organizations, places and events are either the product of the author's imagination or are used fictitiously. Any resemblance to actual persons, living or dead, events or locales is entirely coincidental.

All rights reserved. No part of this publication may be reproduced, stored in retrieval system, copied in any form or by any means, electronic, mechanical, photocopying, recording or otherwise transmitted without written permission from the publisher.

ISBN 978-1-7905-6063-9

www.thebookfolks.com

To Jennifer

PROLOGUE

You stop. The tang of sea is strong in the nostrils, the summer afternoon's breeze light on the skin. You're alive to everything: the give of sand as you shift your feet, and the sound of a gull cawing. You're particularly aware of her.

She's a young woman in her late teens, with dark hair worn short, and a curve of leg that draws. Her skirt is cut just below the knee in the latest way. Before the war, they didn't dress like that, but that conflict changed everything, didn't it? She paces along her stretch of beach by the dunes, four strides forward, three strides back. You don't know if she's counting or not, but you are. Why should the number of strides matter? Why does she? But you are drawn to her, to this fever in her pacing, and the whiteness of anger in her face.

It was her voice that seduced you: it was light, like something fluttering in the breeze; and melodious, like birdsong at dawn. When you fought your war, that was something you missed – the sound of a woman's voice. You heard male ones, moaning about the taste of the bully beef, the night patrols, or the sound of guns. This had none of that muddle. This was a voice simple in its call to you.

She's by herself on the beach, defenceless, and she doesn't know it. You do. You know the briefness of the moment between life and death; you remember the space beside you that a comrade had occupied.

When you came across her, the lightness in her walk and the curve of her breasts under her top held such appeal to you. You could almost feel the softness in her skin under your fingers. You liked her youth and you liked her innocence. She isn't happy now, but you want to fix that.

Watching her fascinates you, and you know when she's calmed down she'll go. You want her to stay. You can help her through things.

She doesn't hear you creep up behind her, doesn't know of the marlin spike raised, till she turns around and fear takes over her face. You swing, so she steps back, but you swing again and hit her. Blood spurts and she spins, then falls to the ground with a scream, her arm out to break the fall. As she tries to scrabble off, you take in the terror in that face. You want to make things better for her. That rock will do it. You lift it with an effort. Her face is upturned and she raises her arm to stop it, but this is futile. When you drop it onto her head, more blood spurts as the rock rolls off and something leaves her face as she falls back. Her eyes are still, and you feel relief. You watch the body twitch; then it also becomes still.

You become conscious of your breathing, short and heavy, and even more aware that she no longer breathes. You stand and study her. She's gone to wherever it is they go, and you are glad of her quietness.

You listen to the sound of the breeze in the marram grass. Another gull screeches. Waves rush and fall. Your breathing is still hard and you stand till it has settled. You look around but there is no one.

INTRODUCTION

Sunlight shone into the courtroom, a reminder that somewhere it was bright and optimistic. The dark wood of the court reinforced the scowl on the coroner's face.

It was noon on 24 September 1920.

Bob Nuttall fidgeted on the mahogany-stained bench with its uncompromisingly upright back. He glanced at the man seated beside him, noticed the affected nonchalance with which Harry was leaning back, and wondered how he managed it. With that half-smile on his lips and the boldness in his eyes, his friend made Bob even more aware of how sick inside he felt. Bob eased the knot of his tie in the hope it would help him breathe more freely.

He and Harry Barker were attending an inquest into the death of a young woman on Birtleby Beach, whose name was Anne Talbot; they were attending at the request of the police.

From his seat, Bob looked up through tall windows to a turret. Across from him, in the courtroom, the coroner was seated under a plaster canopy of medieval symbols beneath a ceiling with sweeping stone arches, awesome in height and effect.

The courthouse was one of the grandest buildings Bob and Harry had been in: it was a castle. The original one in Linfrith had been burned down in the nineteenth century and, though there was no longer a need for defensive fortifications, a benefactor had provided funds to have another built – for use as a courthouse and a coroner's court. Bob thought it looked as if it ought to have graced more auspicious occasions. With its gothic, arched windows with their tessellated stained-glass, it added a touch of melodrama to this one.

Bob looked at the thin face of the coroner with the gold-rimmed spectacles perched on a long nose. Bob thought the man's white, curlicued wig ridiculous but there was nothing clownish about the firm manner in which he banged the gavel, or the precision and authority in his enunciation. His black gown added to the severity. He had introduced himself at the beginning of the inquest as Mr Edmund Archibald, the court-appointed coroner in this case, and he was now proceeding to begin his summing up.

There was a jury seated opposite Bob and Harry. The coroner had stated one was necessary in this case, as it might lead to trial. Bob noted they were all male. The coroner must have assumed this case didn't suit the delicacies of the female. They were even now little more than rows of faces to Bob, who had steadfastly tried to avoid looking at them properly, but he'd taken in an assortment of ages and shapes, some looking criminal themselves with low brows and crafty eyes, others of that respectable class with dapper suits and gold watch chains that always seemed to look askance at him; which everyone on that jury was doing now.

'This case is one that should be considered as a whole.' As his voice rang out, Archibald's eyes peered through his round spectacles. 'It is one built on circumstantial evidence. The nature of such evidence suggests to some people less reliability. But circumstantial evidence is often more sound than direct evidence. Circumstances cannot lie, though people often do.'

He paused to allow the significance of his statement to be grasped by the jury, whose gaze in return was intense.

'Circumstances don't lie?' thought Bob. They did in this case. He and Harry had been on the beach with Anne Talbot, but they'd left her alive. Bob shifted his legs but his right knee joint, hit by shrapnel in the war, continued to annoy him.

Archibald stopped to sweep a look across the jury, one that held challenge and authority, then continued, 'When we consider the evidence of Pulteney, the sailor who came forward as a witness, the jury may rely on it. The two prisoners were seen walking with a girl along the East Sands. And there were other witnesses, the workmen on the railway amongst them. Evidence of identification could be stronger, but you have to look at a number of small circumstances before considering whether there is any doubt the girl they were with was Anne Talbot.'

And who was this Pulteney? He and Harry hadn't noticed him.

'The character given of the girl is quiet and particular. But she was young and holidaying alone.' Archibald's voice stumbled as if the vulnerability he was describing upset him. 'She was the daughter of a humble housekeeper, the type of person who might be easily impressed by young men like the prisoners, who are known to meet on the beach, chat with girls – particularly girls on holiday – visit hotels and entertainments.' The reproachful look he aimed at Harry and Bob held the cynicism of years on the bench. 'You know how these things go on, particularly at the seaside. And we know from the way he presented his evidence, how plausibly Harry Barker can conduct himself.'

Bob was annoyed at that because he had thought he could rely on Harry to talk them out of this.

'Dealing with the evidence from Linfrith prison, we know the prisoners tried to get a fellow inmate to help them concoct another false alibi. There is no need to cast doubt on this evidence just because it is the word of someone who has committed a crime. He has no motive for coming up with a false statement.'

That was said with certainty but, oh yes, convicts did, Bob thought. What did the coroner know? He had never been in prison. The only power left to prisoners was the possibility of tormenting fellow inmates, though no lie was being told here. Harry had been stupid enough to try and get someone to say they'd seen the girl struggling with a sailor.

'No motive has been presented for the crime but, obviously, the persons who committed it did have one. It's true no one saw it.' Bob thought that a pity because then they would be sure he hadn't done it.

'Most of the evidence consists of witness statements. And sometimes they contradict each other. One witness is sure of the identification of the men but not the girl. Another witness is sure of the identification of the girl but not the men. There is only one photograph that can be used to identify the girl and that was of her after she was dead. But there is such a weight of witness statements, there are no doubts these two men were with her when she was murdered.'

When she was murdered? No, Bob thought. Just before it, which was unfortunate.

'On top of which they were spending more than usual afterwards, and Miss Talbot's purse, which was said to contain several pounds, is missing. Note that Nuttall had to change clothes when going on to the theatre in the evening, which suggests that, in the scuffle during the murder, his suit had become dirty or bloody.'

Bob could kill Harry for larking around in the way he had. If he hadn't, that suit would never have become so dirty that he had to change it.

'There is evidence here, though the jury does not need to consider whether it is conclusive, as this an inquest. A verdict of guilty would only lead to a trial at which this would be examined more fully.'

Bob envied the smugness in the summing up. He didn't remember ever feeling so self-satisfied about anything, and he had no doubt the jury would find him and Harry guilty; which they duly did. After which he allowed himself to look at them again. They seemed glad to have got rid of their big decision, so that they could go back to their homes and families, three square meals a day, and beer on a Saturday night. When the constable stepped forward to lead him back to his cell, Bob found it difficult to stand up. Then he managed to recover composure before stumbling off. He looked across at Harry, who was strutting, but whose eyes held fear.

CHAPTER ONE

Bob thought back to the aimless day they had led when they were supposed to be murdering Anne Talbot. As was often the case, they'd been drifting from one thing to another – to fill in time with things that would help them forget what they needed to. They still hadn't managed to put their war behind them.

At least they lived in a good place to loaf about. Birtleby was a northern seaside town popular with tourists. The seafront was famous for its long beach; the grassy Links overlooked by the Victorian bandstand with its brass cupola; the cricket club; and the indoor seawater swimming pool in brick and glass, known for its health-giving qualities. People had travelled to Birtleby for years to enjoy the waters and, since the arrival of the railway at the end of the last century, the population of the town had quadrupled every summer.

It was early afternoon on Thursday, 19 August 1920, and Bob was with Harry, strolling along by the Links. They were chasing women. Though the war had been over for a year and a half, they hadn't been demobbed till almost a year after it ended; now they often paraded about in the throng of the visiting crowds, looking out for the company of young women.

Bob was slightly taller than Harry and had a broader build, but walked with a limp, which was why he carried an ash stick with a brass top. Harry's walk held a cockiness mirrored by his perennial grin. The two men were tall and spare. Both were broad in the shoulder and narrow at the hip but they also had the pale skin of the undernourished. They wore dark-grey suits in the current fashion; Bob wore a cloth cap, and Harry sported a felt hat.

There was a young woman with them on this occasion, less brassy than their usual sort, though she was dressed to attract. This was Anne Talbot. Her skirt, typical of those of the day, was the opposite of the Edwardian prim, though elegant, long sweep, and hung just below the knee. Her black hair was in a bob. She had a slight but deliberate sway to her hips, more the equivalent of a male swagger than anything.

Bob considered she looked classy, and he wouldn't have dared try to pick her up on his own, but Harry was bold enough for anyone. They'd first met Anne the day before.

This was her third day in Birtleby. She worked as a secretary in Leeds, which allowed her the luxury of a holiday by herself, which would have been unheard of for a young lady before the war even if she could have afforded it. She was staying in one of the better boarding houses along the seafront. Bob could only imagine what that was like, as the cottage he lived in was basic, damp, and full of the sprawl of his family: his parents, brother, and sister.

They were walking on the cobbled pathway along the seafront. To their left was a sweep of grass and wildflowers leading to the beach and its straggle of pools, sand, and rock, with the expanse of sea behind. To the right was the area called the Links, with its broad, grassy area, and a cricket pitch and cricket pavilion. There was a match in progress with its panoply of whites against the green. A bat thudded a ball, which sped towards the roped boundary. The crack of bat against ball was compelling and Bob's eyes turned for a moment towards the batsman and the aggressive angle of his bat, before being drawn back to Anne. They strolled to make the most of the day but also because of Bob's limp.

'Did it happen in the war?' Anne asked him.

'Yes.'

She gave him a sympathetic smile. 'I've no brothers, and my father was too old to go,' she said. 'But I knew plenty who did.'

Bob hated it when girls asked questions about his leg; the next thing they asked about was the work he did. He had had none since he came back, and neither had Harry. And look at her with her office job and her fashionable clothes.

'Shrapnel,' he said, his head turned away as if from shame. 'It's still in there.'

She glanced at the leg. 'Does it hurt?'

He grimaced, and they walked on in silence further onto the track along the beach. He thought back to the pain after the shrapnel hit, and to the relief of morphine injections, then of his attempts to walk again after the operation. He hadn't liked the world's habit of going awry with every step forward of his right foot, but he had in time regained steadiness on his pins.

'You ought to talk about the war,' she said. 'I'm always on about that.'

He frowned, said nothing for a while, then asked, 'And do people open up?'

'No.'

'We'd like to forget,' Harry said.

'If we could,' Bob added.

'There's a film on at the theatre tonight,' Harry said with a light tone in his voice and a grin on his face. 'Fatty Arbuckle.'

'Fatty Arbuckle.' Anne giggled.

'All the soldiers in our regiment liked his movies,' Harry said.

Anne's eyes shone with pleasure at the thought of him. 'He's a card but that Buster Keaton's better looking. Though my mum prefers Charlie Chaplin. He might be a tramp but he always gets the girl. They feel sorry for him.'

'What does your mum do?' Harry asked her.

'She's a domestic in a big house in Leeds, but if she was my age she'd go in for being a secretary too. You get a life of your own. No way would she have let me go into service.'

'Tell me about it. My mum was a maid before she married and she's never stopped groaning about what all that washing of floors did to her back,' Harry said, then put his arm around Anne's shoulder.

Anne looked questioningly at the arm but didn't push it away. 'Fresh, aren't you?' she said.

'Nice though?'

Anne giggled. 'Nice enough.'

Harry stared in Bob's direction, then nodded slowly. Bob nodded back, then slowed down, and Anne and Harry walked on ahead. Harry was always the one who attracted the girl; he had a smile on him and laughed easily. Bob rued he seemed to have forgotten how to.

Bob trudged on, his head down as he kicked at a bit of sand, began to whistle, then stopped. He had been one of the lads before going out to the trenches but now he was a hanger-on with a hang-dog look – and he was aware he was too quick in taking offence. He remembered the first Christmas after the war, which he had expected to be a cheerful occasion, but he'd managed to spoil it. They had been trying to 'take it easy', but when an arrogant cockney had sneered about northerners, Bob had forgotten himself. The problem was he had been trained to kill and had to do it often enough, so he had only just been able to stop himself. Killing had been his allotted goal, that and avoiding shrapnel, and he was supposed to switch that off and relax?

Bob hoped his touch with people would come back but he found girls, particularly girls like Anne, difficult; he had no concept of what they might be thinking and feeling. His thoughts could fill with the sound of a shrapnel burst, and the sight of Eric, a soldier beside him, being hit in the face. Not only were all his lower teeth knocked out but his whole bottom lip was torn off. Bob couldn't imagine what it would be like going through the rest of his life with half a mouth. That was all Bob could think of when he was kissing one girl: what she would look like minus a lip. When he had pulled away from her, she had kicked him on the shin.

Bob manoeuvred himself onto a rock, took out a cigarette, lit it, and stared out to sea. He thought back to life in the trenches. It hadn't been all dodging bullets. There were days when nothing seemed to happen, and that was when he had gorged on his smokes. As he relaxed into the sound of a wave crashing against the shore, he did so again, savouring the cigarette. A gull cawed. He reached down and ran fingers through sand, as he luxuriated in the lack of puffing shells and the absence of zinging bullets. Then he heard the swish of limb against grass as someone strode towards him, and he looked up, half expecting a German helmet, but saw the scowling face of Harry instead.

'Bitch,' Harry said. 'C'mon. Let's go.' He strode past.

Bob leaned on his stick as he pulled himself up and winced at a spasm in his knee. 'Why the hurry?' Bob asked.

'No hurry. I'm fed up. Some of these grand ones put on such airs when they turn you down. If they've shown interest, they ought to put up.'

'It's not like rest camp,' Bob said. 'Not every second girl you meet is a prostitute.'

'Bloody bitch.'

As they walked on in silence, Bob fell further behind. When Harry looked back and saw this, he slowed down. Bob caught up and Harry gave him a cigarette as a peace offering. Bob didn't know why Harry always felt so entitled to succeed with women. He had the chat and the look, but women suited themselves. Didn't he know that?

CHAPTER TWO

The best time for Bob in the war had been his worst – when he was wounded, when at least he had escaped the fear he'd known in the trenches. Lying in his bed in that field hospital, he could still hear the sounds of war but the guns were distant. There was no thought at the back of his mind that this could be his last breath of air, or mug of tea, or cigarette. Reading was brought to him, the trench newspaper *The Wipers Times*, magazines from Britain, and books. Sometimes you could play cards with other patients, and the nurses brought tea or chocolate from a Red Cross parcel.

Adjusting to the wound had been traumatic. When he had woken that first time and explored his body, he'd been terrified at what he might discover. But he was pleased to find all his limbs, although his right leg was raised on a wire contraption and bandaged.

A voice spoke to the right of him and told him he was in a field hospital. He looked across and saw a nurse in a white dress, wearing a white cap. He thought of angels but the look on her face was pained.

'I'm glad you've woken,' she said. Her voice was soothing and she smiled. 'You were hit by shrapnel – in the right knee. They've got most of it out, and you should be all right unless infection sets in, but it shouldn't.'

Bob had attempted to shift his leg, which responded, and when he tried to move his toes, he was pleased to see they wriggled.

In a bed next to him, a man lay prone with a bandage round his head. A moan came from him, with a smell of flesh rotting. On the other side lay a twitching mess of bandages from which sprouted a bald head, with a pair of eyes above a mouth that moaned too.

Bob's brain struggled with the effort of trying to remember what had happened. There had been a huge noise and a blow, and he had been thrown forward. There was the smell of cordite, the wetness of mud as his fingers scrabbled through it, and a scream. That hadn't been his own, had it? He could remember nothing after that before waking in the field hospital.

There was pain. When he asked for morphine, the nurse disappeared and returned with a syringe. As it entered his veins it reduced the agony within minutes, and an exultation pulsed through him.

'Thank God,' he said. 'And thank you, nurse.'

But he would find the pain wouldn't go entirely, and it was difficult to watch what his wounded comrades on either side endured.

He had worried at first about losing the leg as he didn't know how easy it was to operate on shrapnel in the knee, and he was told they hadn't managed to take all the metal out, for fear of damaging the knee itself, but the shrapnel must have been clean because no infection set in.

Bob realised he was lucky as, two bunks down, a soldier with a shrapnel wound had lost his leg, though he didn't seem to think it unfortunate. This was the longed-for Blighty wound, one which would send him home and end the war for him. He was even cheerful about it, chatting about the girl he was going back to, and all the things he was going to see again: the traffic in Piccadilly Square and the music hall.

Now the war was over, Bob was back in Blighty, with only a limp that wasn't too bad; and he and Harry took their chance to pursue the moment. Later that same afternoon, they were drawn by another piece of skirt. Nancy Harland was a servant in a big house with one afternoon off a week, and Harry knew she often went over to Blackforth Bay for a walk, so he led Bob there on spec and they met up with her near Blackforth Castle.

There wasn't much left of the castle, only crumbling walls, one of which could have held battlements. It was on a headland with a view over the bay. They met Nancy walking on the shingle below. She had an easy smile, which she flashed at them, though Bob noticed the primness around the eyes.

'You haven't asked her if she has a friend?' Bob asked Harry, but he only smiled his properly charming smile. 'She'll have one. Take it easy. We can have fun with her.'

Nancy's grin struck a chord with Bob, so he didn't mind her opening jibe. 'You two not found anything useful to do, like work?'

'There isn't any,' Harry replied. 'Women are doing it all.'

Bob gave a half-laugh, then stopped himself.

'You can have my job as a maid in a big house if you like,' Nancy jeered.

'You know what I mean,' Harry replied.

'Women did their bit in the war,' Nancy said. 'All that munitions work. Some of them ended up with yellow skins. And it was dangerous. Shells blow up if you didn't know it.'

'We do,' said Bob.

'And we were glad our lot had shells to use,' Harry said. 'But we'd still rather have been making them ourselves.'

Nancy grimaced. 'And they've paid off those girls. They don't need munitions now.'

Bob respected women's point of view. The ones he talked to made sure he did, but he still found himself envying them. When he and Harry boarded a bus, they were ordered around by an aggressive bus conductress, while the man who used to be the conductor in that bus sat with his wooden leg in the seat laid aside for the disabled.

In doing their bit, women had taken on the jobs men had left, and now so many soldiers had come back from the war all at once, a lot couldn't find any. Not that he could blame women for improving their lot, but he was jealous. And he thought Nancy could do better for herself than life as a lady's maid. He was surprised a girl like her hadn't gone for a job in a mill, as the girls earned so much more there. But now they'd started to lay off women to make jobs for returning soldiers, so perhaps there was less for Bob to be jealous of; not that he and Harry had managed to find work.

'You've no idea what life's like as a servant, have you?' Nancy said.

'Of course not,' Harry replied. 'We're the shiftless unemployed.'

'In a morning, I've to whiten the doorstep, black the stove, make fires, do beds, fetch water, dust, polish, and do anything else it occurs to anyone to ask me to do.'

Bob thought back to digging trenches while German soldiers aimed machine guns at them.

'You just walk about, talk to girls, drink in pubs, and go to the theatre. I don't know how you manage it.'

For one day every so often, yes, they did, Bob supposed. The rest of the time they spent tramping after jobs advertised in the morning paper, or lying around with no money to spend even on that because everything had to go on food and basics for the house. Just as well he was able to stay at home, like Harry. It had brought him down to earth, back from being one of the men in the trenches to the room he shared with his brother at home, and to avoiding his mam's wrath, but it made it possible to have spending money. Not that he felt like explaining any of that.

Harry made a joke about Charlie Chaplin. Nancy laughed. Bob liked her laughter. It jingled like the lightness of coins in his pocket, though it felt just as temporary. Despite his resentments, he adored the laughter of innocent girls who knew nothing about men holding their guts in their hands while whizzbangs zipped around them.

They took the bus back and Harry bought her an ice-cream from a shop in Birtleby. He and Harry had one too and enjoyed the coolness and smoothness.

CHAPTER THREE

Others would later wonder how Bob and Harry could spend so much time in one day chatting up so many women, but it had made sense to them. Dancing. It felt as if they were dancing through the days, Bob thought, the man leading and the woman following him into the flirtations. There was something soothing in the ritual of the same moves, something rhythmic and hypnotic.

Of course, as it was the day of the murder, they would have to scramble through the jumble of it in their minds, to make enough sense of it to come up with alibis, and that was a frantic job. And they would attempt to predict who would appear as witnesses against them – but that was for later on.

When they walked into the Victoria, another young lady, Elspeth, flashed a smile at them. They'd just entered the bar she worked in, and she was behind the counter. When you were with Harry, you never did walk into a pub where there was a barman.

The Victoria was a hotel with a tap-bar and a parlour bar, and Harry and Bob stood in the parlour bar. This was small with comfortable chairs, a fireplace, and a large mirror. The dark green of the fern-leafed wallpaper pattern complemented the dark of the polished wood and the leather on the chairs. With the low gas lighting, the coal fire and limited natural daylight, there was an intimate effect, if a gloomy one.

'You're back,' Elspeth said.

'Obviously,' Harry replied.

'We couldn't stay away,' Bob said.

Harry ordered a Guinness each for them, then asked Elspeth, 'What would you like to drink?'

Elspeth considered this for a moment then said, 'I'll have a port wine for later.'

'And your friend?' Harry gestured to the other girl near Elspeth.

'Oh, put by a whisky and splash for me. Thank you kindly,' Hilda said with a simper.

When their drinks had been served, Bob and Harry sat in chairs by the bar, ready to chat. Bob contemplated Elspeth, who was a young woman in her twenties with short, shingled, auburn hair, and a blouse cut to give a fashionable, straight look to the chest. The top was brown with large diamond patterns. Elspeth was attractive but, when she was not blasting her impression of a dazzling smile, a natural downturn to the lips was clear. The two men sipped at the white froth on the black Guinness.

'Lovely,' Harry pronounced, 'as yourself.'

Bob admired his friend's gall but Elspeth raised her eyebrows.

'You're in a good mood. Spending money too. Did you do well on the horses today?'

'I never back a horse, only myself,' Harry said.

'A difference from this morning,' Elspeth said. 'You could only afford a half of shandygaff.'

'Would you hold that against a friend? And there's nothing wrong with shandygaff.'

He took a cigarette packet from his pocket and offered a cigarette.

Elspeth looked at the pack with wonder. 'Turkish, huh?'

'A rich, dark aroma,' he said. 'You breathe it in deep.'

'Sounds lovely,' Elspeth said, helping herself to one, 'and not much like the gaspers you usually smoke.'

'Now, now,' Harry replied. 'Woodbines are all right.'

Bob supposed Harry would be broke again tomorrow morning and so might as well enjoy the unemployment money Bob assumed he'd drawn. Elspeth laughed and Hilda giggled. Of course, young men didn't tell young ladies that was what they were spending because that wouldn't impress them.

Bob was studying Hilda. With her exuberant curls, she'd have been no good at the fashionable, straight cut of hair, and it would have been a waste of time for her to attempt the flat-chested look, but Bob liked her ample femininity. He attempted a smile and she smiled hesitantly back.

'Would you like to go to the Hippodrome?' Bob asked.

'I like a bold one,' Hilda replied, 'but I'll tell you later.' Though she did simper. Then she frowned as she noticed his suit. 'Messy clothes for chasing the ladies.'

Bob looked down at himself. 'Oh, that. A bit mucky right enough. Harry pushed me when we were larking about on the beach. I haven't had time to change. But I will,' he added, 'before going on.'

Hilda sipped and looked at him. Elspeth drew in smoke from her Abdullah, and said, 'I suppose you did get this money honestly?'

'I have thought of robbing a bank when I've been desperate,' Harry said. 'But that's as far as it's ever got.'

Elspeth said nothing, but from the glazed look that appeared in her eyes Bob could see her thoughts were starting to wander.

'Has anyone told you that you look like Greta Garbo in *The Silver Siren*?' Harry asked her.

Elspeth looked at him for a moment, then replied, 'No.'

'They should've done.'

Elspeth snorted. 'Maybe they can't afford to go to so many picture shows as you.'

Hilda giggled. 'A man once told me I look like a film star.'

'You do,' Bob said, seizing his chance.

'I asked him if he was pretending to be a producer.' She leaned back and roared with laughter.

Bob noticed Hilda's laughter was a bit of a bray, but this didn't put him off her.

'One of this pair would be happy to do that,' Elspeth said.

'How do you know we're not?' Harry said.

Elspeth frowned at him. 'Common sense,' she said.

'You're definitely not common,' Harry said. 'With those high cheekbones and that silky hair, you'd be a cameraman's dream.'

Bob gazed with admiration at him. Hilda giggled but Elspeth frowned. 'You two aren't half a laugh,' Hilda said.

'Have you had your eyes tested lately?' Elspeth asked Harry.

'Twenty-twenty vision,' he said, his expression modest. 'That's why they picked me out to be a sniper.'

'Trained killer, huh?' Elspeth said.

'Definitely.'

'You're killing me,' she quipped. Elspeth enjoyed her own bullets. Hilda guffawed.

'Seriously,' Harry said. 'We could give you a camera test.'

'I'd need my head tested if I agreed to that,' Elspeth said.

'It's the head we'd concentrate on, how it would show from different angles.'

Elspeth restrained a laugh, and her look remained one of disinterest.

Harry's flirtations were full-on. He often went on from there to act so fresh he put girls off. When he did make a conquest, he swaggered with superiority, as if it was all a game. But there were other occasions when women glimpsed an undercurrent in him and acted as if there was danger in it.

'We'll see you at the Hippodrome tonight then?' Harry asked her.

Elspeth drew on her cigarette, then flicked ash into the brass ashtray beside her before looking back at Harry with a look almost of contempt.

'We're going. You might.'

'I'll see you there,' Bob said to Hilda. The words came out in a rush and she blushed, hearing them, but smiled at him.

'A quiet but a bold one, eh?' Hilda said.

'Still waters run deep,' he replied.

'That's what worries me.' Hilda giggled. She flicked hair from over her eyes and paused before replying. 'But I'll take a chance. See you at the Hippodrome then?'

Bob's fingers clenched on his stick as he replied, 'It's a date.'

Harry and Bob drank up, Harry with obvious relish. He tipped back the glass to make sure he had every drop. 'We'll have to go home to smarten up,' he said.

'Good,' Hilda said as she glanced at Bob.

Bob and Harry walked off.

CHAPTER FOUR

Perhaps if he'd had a poetic streak, Bob could have explained his feelings for women. Something he often did was watch dolphins in the bay just off Birtleby – there was something he envied in them. He supposed it was the cheerfulness in the way they turned their fins into air. If you were out in a boat, you could watch them rushing along in the light just beneath the waves. Bob thought this was maybe what he and Harry were attempting to do with girls – race along in their light and sparkle. Dolphins don't understand what they're doing just as he and Harry didn't, but Bob thought it must be thrilling, skimming along just under, and over the waves.

And so, as the day of Anne's murder continued, Harry and Bob continued in their predictable ways. The Hippodrome was the entertainment theatre of Birtleby. It showed its music hall origins with its tiered seats, gaudy columns and draperies, but also doubled as the film theatre now that the silver screen had become so popular. The two-shilling seats Bob and Harry bought tickets for were in one of the posher tiers and had the best view. Harry and Bob went over to Hilda and Elspeth, who were seated there also.

'Two such pretty girls,' Harry said. 'And two handsome men. Why don't we sit beside you?'

Hilda giggled. 'Go on then.'

'I came to watch the film,' Elspeth said.

But they sat by them anyway. Hilda put Bob's arm round her shoulder, while Elspeth pushed Harry's arm away when he started to put it round her. They watched the pianist setting the mood with thunderous flourishes of music and a dramatic use of the arms and hands. The theatre darkened and a black-and-white image flickered onto the screen as the film started. 'Buster Keaton in *Convict*,' the screen read. Harry put his arm round Elspeth's shoulder again and she pushed it away again.

'C'mon,' Harry said, to which again Elspeth replied no.

'Try to behave like a gentleman,' she said.

But Harry persisted. 'C'mon,' he said again, and replaced his arm on her shoulder, manoeuvred her head back and tried to push his lips down on hers. She squirmed.

When she managed to pull her mouth away, she said, 'Fucking cut it.'

'You don't mean it,' Harry said.

'I bloody do.' Elspeth gave him a slap on the cheek.

Remarks were made by others. 'What are you up to?', 'Quieten down,' and 'We want to watch the film.' Bob pulled at Harry's arm and Harry pulled his fist back to punch him, then changed his mind.

'Let's get out of here,' Bob hissed. 'Let's go for a smoke.'

They trudged down the aisle and pushed through the curtains, then strode out of the door, walked down to the shore and sat on a seat to light up.

'What did you do that for?' Bob said. 'I was in with Hilda.'

'We paid two shillings,' Harry said. 'When we've finished these fags, we're going back in.'

'That film's supposed to be good and it hadn't started.' Bob waved his cigarette towards Harry who stared at it.

'We'll see it.'

'It'll have started.'

Harry frowned. He snorted, then said with an attempt at patience, 'The second one's supposed to be better.'

'We'd better not sit near them,' Bob said. 'They'll be on at us.'

When they'd finished smoking their cigarettes, Harry and Bob returned to the Hippodrome and sat in the two-shilling seats again but well away from Elspeth and Hilda. Bob noticed Elspeth turning around to give Harry a warning look. When the show had finished, they went in their different directions.

CHAPTER FIVE

The police-inspector noticed everything: the half-light of evening; the rhythmic sound of waves; the give of the sand underfoot; and the rustle of the marram grass in the slight breeze. It was seven o'clock on 20 August, and Inspector Blades and Constable Hodgkins had just arrived at the scene of the murder they had been called out to.

Blades was thirty-seven, tall, and broad, with the clear complexion of the physically fit, and a frown. He would rather not have been there. He had been painting a fence, and he'd been getting around to do that for a while.

Constable Hodgkins was only eighteen, though tall, and with a self-important manner beyond his years. He'd been the one on duty when the call had come in. He'd taken the report and sent for his Inspector.

Blades admitted his nervousness to himself. Though he'd been fifteen years on the force, this was the first murder he had been involved in. Despite the stream of visitors to the town, major crimes had happened elsewhere.

There was a man on the dunes who appeared to be poking around with a stick in the sand. Blades took him in:

grey-haired, angular, and grunting with the effort of what looked like a search.

Blades supposed the man read crime novels and was being the amateur detective. He had often cursed those books and the ideas they gave people. He expected this was the Mr Allen that Hodgkins had told him of, the owner of the boarding house where the mother and child who'd discovered the body were staying. He frowned. He would rather have been dealing with them. What was this Mr Allen doing here? He noticed the man's face lighten up when he saw them.

'The body's over there,' the man said, waving his arm in a general direction further off, normal greetings forgotten.

Blades forced himself to be polite. He wanted to get as much as he could out of Mr Allen. 'Would you show us, please?' he said.

Mr Allen led them away from the path and into a dip between dunes where they saw a mound of sand out of which protruded a young woman's foot. Fortunately, Mr Allen hadn't been poking about here. Or had he?

'Once I'd uncovered the body enough to ascertain that's what it was, I didn't touch it,' Mr Allen said, as if reading Blades' mind.

Blades glanced around the beach looking at marks. The sand was quite firm between these dunes and there might have been helpful indications, but Mr Allen had been doing a lot of tramping around even though he had left the body itself alone. Blades tried to work out what the scene might have looked like before Mr Allen turned up. He tried to catch a look at the soles of Mr Allen's boots to ascertain the print. He could have him hand those in, but he wasn't sure there would be helpful footprints here anyway.

'And look,' Mr Allen said urgently. 'Look at that rock.'

Blades had noticed it, as it would have been difficult not to. It was solid sandstone and must have weighed at least ten pounds. He wondered if darker patches he was looking at were traces of blood.

'I suppose the rest of the body's there?' Blades said to Hodgkins.

The constable looked at him, then back at the body. After a pause, he began to clear sand away, then stopped. 'No doubt about that,' he said, looking at the extended leg he'd uncovered. Blades saw Hodgkins' lips were tight, his face white.

'Keep clearing it,' Blades said.

The arms, upper torso and a head emerged. Blades managed a smile. Hodgkins had been adept and uncovered the body without moving it. Blades studied the corpse, which lay on its left side. The left arm was fully extended from the shoulder, and the right arm lay under the left armpit. The head was on the left arm. The body appeared to be fully clothed. Blades nodded to Hodgkins to continue clearing away at the sand. Blades was able to see the right foot had no shoe on it and wondered where that had gone. The coat and skirt were turned back, disclosing her leg from the thigh downwards. As the hat was turned down over her face, Blades bent down and pulled it up, but the mouth was still covered by the fur on the collar of the coat. He lifted the collar and looked down at the bloodstained features. He studied the damage to the mouth. Two of the teeth were broken and the jaw looked slack.

'A young woman,' Blades said. 'She could have been pretty.'

'Didn't help her much, did it?' the constable said.

'We could consider the stone as the murder weapon–' Blades said, then paused for thought. 'I don't know,' he said. 'It couldn't have been used quickly unless the assailant was enormously strong but, barring Hercules, it's not likely, and if anyone saw anything that size being lifted, you wouldn't think they'd hang about.'

'Perhaps she was hit and her head fell against the rock.'

'We'll have to wait and see what Dr Parker says when he gets here.' Inspector Blades looked around. The path they'd come along stretched further. 'They must have walked along this track. Which is about fifty yards from the railway line.'

'There's a hut over there by the line.'

'I wonder whether anyone was in it then.' Blades looked down at the woman's head. He bent down and scrabbled at the sand. 'There's a lot of blood underneath that head, it's spread to quite a depth, and there's none anywhere else. The body hasn't been dragged here.' Blades continued to stare at the corpse as he thought things through. 'We'll need to get lights set up for the police surgeon.'

'Sir.'

'And we'll need a constable on constant guard so no one else disturbs evidence.'

'Sir.'

Keeping others off would help, though things already looked bad. Blades thought back to the fence he had left with its clean lines and pristine green paint. Some of that clarity would be helpful. He looked at the girl. Another wasted life. You'd think enough people had been killed in the war without more of it happening in peacetime.

'I'll need to interview the mother and son,' Blades told Hodgkins.

'They're at the boarding house,' Mr Allen offered.

The inspector stared around him at the beach. Hadn't he visited here as a child? He had memories of digging in the sand and building forts over there. Or had he? He felt his innocent memories had been bludgeoned away.

CHAPTER SIX

Dr Parker didn't arrive till nine o'clock. He was a thin man in his early thirties, his mouth set with annoyance.

'The body's in East Birtleby,' he said. 'I'm the West Birtleby police surgeon.'

There was precision and authority in the way that was said, and Inspector Blades glowered at him. Like suspects who'd met Blades' wrath, Dr Parker looked elsewhere.

'Do a few yards make much difference?' Blades said.

'Some would say so,' Dr Parker replied but not with much conviction.

'We need a surgeon's report on this body. When the next corpse turns up in twenty years' time or whenever, we'll endeavour to make sure it's a bit further east.'

'If you did, it would be convenient,' Dr Parker replied, then sighed. 'But all right. You need a report. Has the body been moved?'

'No.'

'The sand's been shifted.'

'But not the body.'

Dr Parker's eyes swept over the footprints, before settling on the girl and studying her. 'You don't get a natural light from acetylene lamps,' he said, 'but they'll do.'

He continued to look at the body. 'Not the common type you'd expect,' he said.

'Why d'you say that?' Blades asked.

'The style of her hat, and the fashion of her blouse.'

Blades looked back at the corpse. He wondered how good Parker's understanding of working-class women was. Parker's background was middle-class, his schooling expensive, and his further education would have taken place in what Blades thought of as a cloistered university. Though he must have worked with all sorts of women daily in surgeries, Blades supposed. Blades didn't presume to know whether this young woman was common or not going by clothes, as he knew it could depend on how they were worn. He doubted if this girl had led a sheltered life though, or she wouldn't have ended up lying dead on this beach.

Parker reached down and turned the head to reveal more of the damage to the skull. He winced at the sight, but his voice became brisk. 'There are two possible suspects for cause of death: the blow to the lower part of the head, or the blow to the upper. It's not a natural death. We will need the post-mortem.'

Blades had already worked out that the death was suspicious, but he just agreed.

Parker touched the girl's arm. 'Rigor mortis has set in.' Then he felt her skin. 'Absolutely cold.' He paused, then continued, 'If you're looking for an estimate of time of death, which I suppose you are, the girl's been dead about twelve to thirty-six hours. Not that you can tell, really. It depends on weather conditions, the depth of sand covering her and so on.'

'But if you've any idea, it might be helpful,' Blades said.

Parker looked at the girl's face, then reached in his bag for one of the bright, steel instruments there, and used it to investigate blood that stretched from a nostril. 'Maybe twenty-four hours,' Parker said, his voice hesitant.

'Thanks,' Blades said.

Parker studied the girl's face. He took out a glass and peered through that. 'The damage to the mouth looks as if it's been done by a narrow object.'

'Thanks,' Blades said.

'Possibly with a blunt edge, though there are lacerations that confuse the issue.'

'Any idea what kind of object?'

'No.'

The inspector stared at the face as well, wishing it would speak and tell them something. The doctor speculated. 'Could have been a stick, I suppose, one with a knob on it even.'

'Any idea what type?'

'No. There are nobody's initials helpfully imprinted on the skin, though I did read that happened once.'

He studied the body. 'Or it could even have been a pointed stick,' he said.

The inspector gazed at the body.

Then Dr Parker pronounced, 'But the cause of death was probably the blow to the temple with a stone, possibly that one.' He indicated one nearby. 'It does have blood on it.'

'It's convenient to find that there,' the inspector said.

'Hard to believe she waited around for a stone that size to be dropped on her,' Parker said. 'We'll analyse stomach contents to see if she was drugged.' He continued his study of the corpse. He turned the head with his hand. The analytical tone left his voice as the same thought Blades had occurred to him. 'She could have been attractive.'

'Just give as many details about the death as you can,' Blades said.

'I doubt if the post-mortem will tell us any more than we can observe here, though we'll find out. The blow to the lower head area probably caused unconsciousness, followed by the blow with the stone.'

'Definitely murder?'

'It's difficult to see how this could have been done accidentally.'

Blades grunted. It was his opinion too, and he was glad it had been established. 'Any chance she was hit on the jaw, fell back, and then her head just hit the rock?'

'She'd have had to spin right round, and, in any case, it wouldn't cause this scale of damage to the skull.'

'How many deaths caused by violence have you been asked to give an opinion on?'

It was a pointed comment and received the natural look of irritation from Parker. 'Two or three,' he said.

'We'll need the second opinion, then.'

'This shouldn't be my case anyway.'

Parker scowled at Blades who couldn't stop himself frowning back. Each was expressive with this look, and Inspector Blades found himself glancing away this time.

'I'll write up my report,' Parker said.

'I'd be grateful to you.'

The inspector found himself talking to Dr Parker's back. 'Do you think–' he stopped in mid-sentence. He looked back at the girl.

'How did this happen?' he said to her silently. 'Who could have been this malevolent to a girl like you?'

CHAPTER SEVEN

Blades left Hodgkins guarding the scene, walked back along the path, and drove along to the boarding house, which was a large, stone house on the seafront near the Links. There he was shown into a sitting room with hunting prints in thin gilt frames; a mahogany sideboard; brown velvet curtains; and high-backed chairs. There was a deep-piled, red, Indian patterned rug on a dark-wood, polished floor. The mother and boy that Blades saw were incongruous there. Tommy slouched on his seat with a peevish expression on his face, and Agnes held herself erect but spoiled the lady-like impression by chewing the thumbnail on her right hand.

Blades showed sympathy as he asked his questions. 'You're the ones who found the body?' he asked.

'About three hours ago,' Agnes said, flicking at an invisible piece of fluff on her skirt. 'We thought you'd have been over before now.'

'Due process,' Blades replied. Agnes had a manner that made him feel like apologising, but he would make a point of retaining authority. He sighed and allowed his gaze to wander from the woman to the boy and back again. 'Tell us about it,' he said.

'There's not much to tell.' Her look was dismissive. 'It was lying there.'

Blades tried to stop his look at the woman becoming a glower. 'How did you come across it? It must have been a surprise.'

'Tommy fell over it when he was chasing after his ball. It was a shock to him. It was a horror to me when he told me about it and I went to look. A young boy shouldn't have to see that.'

'No.'

Blades waited for her to continue. She wrung her hands as she looked pityingly at Tommy.

'A body buried under the earth. You've no idea how many nightmares I've had about that. That's how his father died. Not that it said so in the telegram. "Died instantaneously of wounds," they said. Liars. I found out from other soldiers in his regiment. I had to go on at them, but they told me the truth eventually.' She scowled. She bit her lip. 'He was buried alive when the trench he was in collapsed under shelling. He suffocated under all that earth and mud. I wake up in the middle of the night thinking I'm suffocating.'

Blades didn't know how to respond to this. 'So many dreadful things happened,' he said. 'I'm sorry.'

'So you should be,' the woman said. She paused and continued wringing her hands.

'It didn't happen to the woman you found,' Blades said, keeping his voice deliberately calm, 'if it helps. She was dead when she was buried – to hide her. A bit of a shallow grave too. It must have been done in a hurry. Did you notice footmarks?'

'I saw Tommy's, and the sand was all sort of scuffed over. There might have been others. I don't know, I'm sure.'

'They looked as if they'd been hiding their footmarks then?'

'Yes. That could have been it.'

'I don't suppose you saw anybody?'

'Near the body? No.' She looked askance at him as if being asked a foolish question.

'A pity.'

'I suppose. I took Tommy straight back to our digs and told the landlord. Mr Allen said he would go over and check what we'd said. He didn't believe we could have found a body. I told Tommy to fetch a policeman. You can always rely on Tommy even if he is young. He's the man in the house. That's what I've always told him. Though he insists the woman must be sleeping.'

Tommy, who had been watching and listening in silence with a frightened look on his face, now spoke. 'The lady under the sands? She is asleep, isn't she? Can I talk to her when she wakes?'

'He is a bright boy,' Agnes said. 'He knows. He must do. He is a clever boy. He doesn't want to believe it. And neither do I.'

Blades supposed he'd found out as much from her as he would.

CHAPTER EIGHT

Next morning. Saturday. There was a light breeze and, despite a grey sky, it was warm. Blades walked over to the railway line with Hodgkins. Someone else had the task of guarding the crime scene now, and the constable was free to accompany him. The railway line was set back from the shore on gravel behind a wire fence, and there was a workman's hut there. Shrubs and rosebay willow herb straggled the area, but there was nothing to spoil the view of the dunes, though the spot where the body was found was hidden in a dip. When he and Hodgkins reached the hut, Blades looked over. Someone standing in the spot where he was now would have seen anyone walking along the path leading up to that dip. Blades knocked on the door but there was no answer. He tried the handle but the door was locked, so he looked around.

'There's somebody on the line up there, sir,' Hodgkins said.

Blades looked in the direction he was pointing and saw some men, bent down, working at something. He and Hodgkins walked over towards them. As the two approached the workmen, the men stopped what they were doing and laid down tools. There were three of them, and they gave ingratiating smiles to the two policemen. Blades wondered why this lot looked nervous. They looked like an ordinary bunch in their blue overalls and caps, though they were on the rough side, and not overly clean.

The oldest, the foreman Blades supposed, said, 'We thought you might be along.'

Blades frowned as he began to try to work the man out. 'You heard about the incident?'

'Yes.'

Blades noticed the man shifted his feet as he spoke.

'A young lady, I understand.'

'News travels,' Blades said, trying to look non-committal. 'And your name is?'

'John Sinclair,' he replied, then added quickly, 'but none of us saw it.' And there was firmness in the way he said this.

'Did you hear anything?' Blades asked.

John looked back helplessly. 'No.'

'How long were you here?'

'All day till six.'

Blades wondered why no one ever heard or saw anything. He often thought half the population must be blind and deaf. He looked across to where the incident had taken place. 'You must have noticed people going up and down?' he said.

John looked flustered but replied quickly. 'At this time of year? You see a lot of them.'

'Would it have been too far away for you to recognize anyone?'

'Probably.'

Blades reached into his inner jacket pocket and took out a photograph of Anne Talbot, which, as it had been taken after she was dead, he knew might have limited use. 'I don't suppose,' he said, 'you recognize her?' He held it out, and John took it.

'Poor girl,' he said. 'Who would do a thing like that? Alex, you'd better look at this,' he said to the man next to him, a tall young man. 'This is Alex Herriott,' he said to Blades. After studying it, Alex said, 'It looks like her. It's hard to tell but I think so.'

Blades' heart leapt. 'Like who?' he said.

'The woman with the cat,' Alex replied.

'I wondered about her,' the foreman said. 'About three o'clock a young lady went by with two young men; they had a kitten following them. The young lady brought it over and tried to get rid of it by giving it to us.'

'So she came close?' Blades said.

'It was a lovely cat,' another of the men, the youngest, who looked about sixteen, said. 'It was ginger and very friendly. It tried to steal my sandwich.'

'And your name is?' Blades asked.

'Ian Morrison,' the young man replied.

'I'd seen that kitten before,' the foreman said. 'It lives in Rose Cottage. It must have followed them up from there.'

'It's not the kitten we're interested in,' Hodgkins said.

'How close did she come?' Blades asked.

'As close as we are,' John said. 'She came right into the hut.'

'That's right,' Ian said. 'She said here's a present for you. It's been following us for a mile and we can't get rid of it. Have fun.'

'Did the two men she was with come into the hut?' Blades asked.

'They stayed on the path,' Alex said.

'Could you look at the photograph?' Blades asked Ian. 'Was it her?'

'I think so,' Ian said, then showed it to the others again. They studied it, nodded, shook their heads, then nodded again.

'I could be wrong,' Alex said, 'with that blow to her face, but it does look like her.'

'It's definitely her,' Ian said, to which John also had to agree.

'Could you describe the two men?' Blades asked.

'We didn't see them close,' John said.

'I think the nearest they came was about a hundred yards,' Ian said. 'After she left the kitten and went back to join them, we were too busy playing with it to pay attention to anything else.'

'I did notice they walked further along the path,' John offered. 'They were having a good time. They were joking and laughing.'

'I wondered if they'd been drinking they were all so merry,' Alex said.

'They might have been,' Ian said. 'And then one of the men put his arm around the girl, and she giggled as if she were loving it. I looked after them, but I lost sight of them in the dunes.'

Blades tried again. 'Can you describe the two men?'

They had been almost speaking at once, but now this stopped.

'They were young,' Alex offered. 'And tall.'

'Two tall men,' Ian agreed.

'But we only saw them from a distance,' John said.

Then the men started to interject with each other quickly.

'They were both wearing suits. They were grey ones,' Alex said.

'I'm sure one was wearing a blue suit,' Ian said.

'And one of them had a stick, a thick one, with a brass knob on it,' John added.

'He didn't look like someone you'd want to argue with,' Ian said.

'Build of a boxer,' Alex agreed.

'And you didn't recognize them?' Blades asked. 'You'd never seen either of them before?'

'I don't know,' John said.

'They were too far off,' Alex said.

'Would you know them again?' Blades asked, pursuing the point.

They made various replies that weren't helpful. 'Maybe.' 'I don't know.' 'No.' 'Yes.' 'No.' 'I wouldn't.'

'We could get you to confirm your identification of the girl. We'll get to you view it, if that's all right.'

'I suppose so,' Alex said.

'There's a thought,' Ian said.

'All right,' said John.

None of their replies were enthusiastic, but they'd agreed to help.

Blades had eyewitnesses, but ones that weren't much use on the face of it. They'd said they wouldn't recognize the two men she was with, and clear identification would be needed. The workmen would recognize the kitten, and Blades thought it a pity it wasn't suspected of anything.

CHAPTER NINE

Bob watched Harry stare at the newspaper. They were seated on the seafront outside a café, a small place with rickety wooden seats and wobbly tables with well-worn tablecloths, but it had a clear view of the sea. It was also cheap. When they could afford it, they often sat here looking at the water over tea and a cigarette. Bob noticed Harry's concentration didn't waver as he read, and wondered what article interested him so much. A girl walked past. She had auburn hair, a pretty if pointed sort of face, and excellent legs, but Harry didn't even glance in her direction.

'That must be some newspaper story,' Bob said.

Harry pointed at the headline and Bob peered at it.

'I forgot,' Harry said. 'You don't read much.'

Bob could read, but slowly, and it wasn't something to dwell on.

'I can read a headline for heaven's sake,' he said.

'They've found a body,' Harry said.

'Someone's dead?'

'In Birtleby, here, on the East Sands. I'll read it.' Then his voice became clear, and steady. 'A boy and his mother were shocked yesterday, Friday afternoon, when they came across the body of a young woman lying in the dunes on the East Sands. She had been killed by a blow or blows to the head. The young woman was about 17 or 18. She was about five foot seven, with black hair cut in a bob. She was slim, and well-dressed in a green coat with black fur trim, white blouse, and black, short-cut skirt. If anyone has information about this, they should contact the police station.'

'But that sounds like Anne.' Bob's voice had become querulous.

'Doesn't it?'

'But it can't be,' Bob said. 'We saw her the other day. How can she be dead just like that?'

Harry folded the newspaper and put it down. He reached for his cup and sipped tea with a thoughtful expression.

'It happened often enough in the trenches. Now you see them, now you don't. Does it still surprise you?'

'That was war.' He stared at Harry for a moment. 'You saw her last.'

'After you,' Harry replied quickly. 'And not last. She must have met someone.'

Bob's expression became thoughtful. He looked away, then back at his friend. 'She must have done,' he replied. 'D'you remember those soldiers on the seafront?'

'That pair selling lavender? She did talk about them. Why?'

'She said one of them was a right sod.'

'So she did.'

They thought about this.

'For a woman on the refined side, she was open,' Bob said.

'I'll bet those soldiers tried it on.'

'They try to get off with them all,' Bob agreed.

'Hilda complained about one of them to me. When she took up with him, he did nothing but get fresh and didn't half get annoyed when she slapped him.'

Bob thought back to Hilda. 'You have to mind your Ps and Qs with her,' he said. 'She's a good laugh though, if she feels like it.'

Harry sipped more tea. He took out his pack of cigarettes and offered Bob one.

'Dead,' Bob said. 'A good-looking girl like Anne Talbot.'

He looked at the cigarette and shook his head. Harry put one in his mouth and reached for a match then lit the Woodbine, drew in smoke, and leaned back.

Bob frowned. 'You called her a bitch.'

'Did I? Yeah, well, they're all like that when they want to be. But she didn't deserve anything like this. She was a nice kid.'

Bob watched him draw in more smoke. 'You know,' he said, then paused.

'What?'

'When you think about it—' he stopped.

'Go on then,' Harry said.

'You had a quarrel with her and then her body turned up where you had the fight.'

'Argie bargie, not fight.'

'But you know what they might think. It could be bad.'

Harry snatched up the newspaper and opened it. 'It just says the dunes. There are a lot of dunes out there. It might not have been anywhere near where we were.'

'Maybe, but it was the same beach. It doesn't sound good.'

'You really reckon they'll think I did it?' Harry's face showed fear.

'You know how suspicious the police are. They're bound to want to follow it up.'

'Damn.' Harry crumpled the newspaper up and threw it onto the pavement.

'Maybe if we went to the police and told them what we know,' Bob said.

Harry looked at him askance. 'We're not bloody doing that. We don't tell anyone we were anywhere near the place. If the police want to ask me questions about that, they can look me up.'

'If someone tells them we were there and we haven't gone to them, it could look suspicious.'

'Who would tell them?'

Bob thought. 'We walked all the way over there from Birtleby with Anne past plenty of people. We're from Birtleby. Use your brains. Someone will have seen us. That bus conductor. What's his name? George Blackwater.'

'Yeah. He did. Would he remember?'

'This is all over the papers, and you think he won't?'

'Then they'll suspect us, whether we tell them or not.'

Bob stared at him. 'Us?'

'You must have worked out you're in the frame as well.' Harry stabbed his half-smoked cigarette in the ashtray. 'We've got to lie quiet,' he said.

'It wasn't me that was on my own with her.'

'But you were there as well. I know you didn't do it. I didn't either. But it's what it looks like. D'you see?'

Bob pulled a face. He looked at Harry's cigarette butt. They didn't always have the money to smoke which was why fags were precious, and he was surprised at Harry. Bob sipped more tea but it had gone cold. Come to think of it, so had he. He was reminded of how he felt in the trenches when they were expecting a barrage.

Harry had an urgent look on his face. 'We don't tell anyone we went near the place,' he said. We say we went straight to Blackforth Castle. We've got a witness that we were there that afternoon.'

'Later.'

'They won't know exactly when she was killed.'

'It makes sense I suppose.'

'Unless you want to hang.'

'Survive those whizzbangs and get hanged for a murder someone else did?' Bob's face looked incredulous, then became wary.

Harry leaned forward and spoke with intensity. 'I wonder if that sergeant's still recruiting for Ireland.'

'For Ireland? The best thing that ever happened to me was getting out of the army. I don't want to go back in and I don't want anything to do with the Troubles in Ireland.'

'There's no work here. There are too many ex-soldiers chasing anything there is – and it would get us away from here.'

'The army.' Bob snorted with disgust. 'And we didn't do it. Why should we have to run away?'

Harry clenched his fist, then unclenched it. A decisive look appeared on his face. 'Blackforth Barracks. That's where that recruiting sergeant said he was based.'

'And I like it here,' Bob whined. 'Lots of people do. They travel miles to get here for day trips, and for holidays. It's a nice place. A lot nicer than I bet Ireland is.'

'Blackforth Barracks.' Harry finished his tea and stood up. 'Are you coming?'

Bob looked up at him. 'We must have better ideas than that.'

'Before the war you were an apprentice boat-builder. I was an under-gamekeeper. Neither of us finished learning our trade because we went off to France. Soldiering is the only thing we're qualified to do.'

Bob looked thoughtful. 'My grandmother was Irish.'

Harry leaned his face close to Harry's. 'Everyone knows we chat up all the visiting women. The police will ask around and that's what they'll be told.'

'It's not illegal.'

'It's what they think that matters, not what we've done. They're looking for someone who might and could have done it, and then they'll look to see what can be proved.' Harry's face was white.

'They can't prove we did it if we didn't,' Bob said, but didn't sound convinced. He looked at Harry and thought he seemed as scared as if he'd done it, which was a ridiculous thought.

'I bet they manage to prove we were there,' Harry said. His voice was even. 'It's what the police and lawyers manage to argue that counts. Then that's another job done from their point of view. The police are pleased they've kept the Chief Constable happy. The prosecutor justifies his job. And we hang.'

'And if we go to Ireland we might get blown up.'

'It won't make much difference what we do then. It just depends where you fancy your chances more. And I'm for Ireland.'

Bob looked out to sea. It puzzled him that Harry was prepared to join up over this and he thought Harry must be in quite a panic. It was a pity, Bob thought. He liked it here, particularly when the sea was calm. It spoke to him of something in himself he dimly remembered. But he stood up, put on his coat, adjusted his cap and followed Harry.

CHAPTER TEN

The track up the hill to the barracks at Blackforth was desolate with nothing around except moorland and a cliff edge. As Harry and Bob trekked up, they felt the sharpness of the wind.

Bob glared ahead. The sense of injustice that had been growing in him over the last few years seemed to be threatening to consume him, and every step towards the army camp added to it.

'We can't be as anxious to get away as this,' he moaned.

'Most definitely,' Harry replied. He looked at Bob hard. 'We were there,' Harry said. 'We look as guilty as you can, if that's the way they choose to look at it. Maybe our names won't crop up if we aren't around to remind anybody of our ugly mugs.' His tone was one that might be adopted when talking to a simpleton.

Bob shut up. He'd learned when it was a bad idea to disagree with Harry.

They approached the gate to the camp, Harry with a steady stride, Bob a step behind. When he saw the gate, his impression was of steel and spikes, and it was anything but welcoming. The metal, barred gate was held erect by concrete posts, rolls of barbed-wire strewn over the top of it; on either side of it stretched out barbed-wire fences. A concrete guard post was just behind, to the right of the gate, and a soldier stood behind the gate in combat uniform, under a steel helmet, and holding a rifle. He was a sharp-looking lance corporal with a lean face, who looked as if he made the most of any authority he had.

'Business?' he snapped.

Harry spoke for them. 'We want to speak to Sergeant Hainsworth.'

'Business?' the guard replied.

Bob wondered if he could say anything else.

'Recruitment,' Harry replied. 'We want to join up to go to Ireland. We know they're looking for people.'

'I'll find out for you.' The soldier walked to his post, entered it, and Harry and Bob could see him picking up a telephone. He spoke for a moment or two before returning. 'Sergeant Hainsworth's away,' he said. 'He's recruiting in Linfrith and won't be back for a week.'

'Is there anyone else we can talk to?'

The guard glanced at Harry. 'Are you in a hurry?'

'There might be someone who could stand in for him.'

'There isn't,' the soldier replied, then grinned, 'so you'll have to wait till a week on Monday for the chance to get away from the seaside and be shot at by the Irish.'

Harry gave him a sardonic look in return. 'Thanks for the help.'

'No problem.' The soldier grinned again, and Harry and Bob turned to go back down the hill.

'Bastard,' Harry said when they were out of earshot.

'He didn't have to enjoy it,' Bob agreed, 'but it's not his fault the sergeant major's not here. Are we coming back a week on Monday?'

Harry gave him a look. 'We'll probably have been arrested before then. Maybe we could go over to Linfrith. There's a thought.'

'If we can get there,' Bob replied. 'Have you got the fare left? I haven't.'

'Nor me,' Harry said. 'I wonder if there's someone I can borrow it from.'

'You're always borrowing and never paying back. Is there anyone left you could ask?'

'It'll take thought,' Harry said. 'Have you anyone you could tap?'

'They'd want to know why. I'll have to think.'

'If we stay here we'll have to stay low,' Harry said.

'We can't afford to do anything else,' Bob said.

They continued trudging back down the hill. Bob kicked a stone. Harry muttered. Then he spoke clearly to Bob. 'We weren't on that beach with Anne Talbot. Have you got that?' he said.

'Got it,' Bob said, though he wasn't sure he'd got anything. 'About those two soldiers selling the lavender—' he said.

'What about them?'

'Would it be useful if we could find out their names? Maybe Hilda knows them.'

'She might – if they gave her their real ones.'

Bob was beginning to despair of Harry. 'Why wouldn't they? In any case, she'd recognize them, I'd recognize them, and you would. One was a private and one a lance corporal. We could find out who they are.'

'Do you even know their regiment? Because I don't.'

'I didn't go close enough to make out their badges, but Hilda probably knows. Anyway, one was very tall. He must have been getting on for six feet and he had a tash. The other was slightly shorter and had a squashed nose like a boxer's.'

'That's good. They might be able to find them from that, though you do make them sound a bit like us,' Harry replied, then said in a clear voice, 'but we can't go to the police.'

'Don't you want them to be caught? They might do it again.'

'We've got to look out for ourselves. It's like in the trenches. You've got to make sure you survive. If the police want to talk, they come to us.'

'Got it,' Bob said, lying again.

They trudged on, heads down, shoulders hunched. Bob kicked another stone. Bob supposed he could understand why Harry was so scared. Harry had been with a girl just before she was murdered and the police would want to speak to him when they found that out. And Bob was forced to admit he was scared too. As Harry had pointed out, they would have him in too.

CHAPTER ELEVEN

Bob and Harry were bent down, foraging in blackberry bushes by a stream, in the company of another young lady, a broad-framed girl with fair hair and a cheerful expression. Blackberry-picking was a useful occupation as it didn't cost anything, and, if you gathered enough, you could sell them. Bob would have been glad to pick blackberries with Nancy Harland any time. She had an easy-going manner, and Bob enjoyed her company, but she was plump and not the type Harry spent a lot of time with. They were here because she was their alibi.

'Dreadful about the girl,' Nancy said.

This was a topic that couldn't be avoided around Birtleby.

'What girl?' Harry said, continuing to pick a blackberry.

'The body they found in the dunes on the East Sands.'

'Did someone find a body there?' Bob said, forcing surprise into his tone.

'You must have read about it,' Nancy said. 'It was found on Friday and the paper said she would've been killed on Thursday.'

'When we were at Blackforth Castle?' Harry said in a voice that sounded too innocent to Bob.

'Yeah.' She frowned and thought about this. 'Short black hair it said. Green coat. You didn't see anyone about like that?'

'No,' both Harry and Bob said quickly.

'You two are always hanging around and talking to girls. I thought you might have noticed her.'

'When?' Bob asked.

'Whenever.'

'You see quite a few girls with short black hair,' Harry said.

Conversation dried up and they concentrated on picking blackberries, with Harry eating as many as he put in his basket.

'You're not going to make much money,' Nancy said.

'We had a good time with you that day,' Harry said.

'It was all right,' Nancy replied.

'How did she die?' Bob asked, with what he hoped was a look of ignorance on his face.

'Blows to the head. Blood everywhere. All over the sand.' Nancy's hand shook as she picked a blackberry. 'A good gory murder story.'

'Too gory for me,' Bob said.

'Why would anyone do that to the girl?' Harry said.

'Money,' Nancy said. 'Her purse is missing. And there were pounds in it.'

'Couldn't have been us,' Harry said with a laugh. 'We never have any money.'

Bob laughed too, but wondered if it sounded more like a snort of anger. He picked another blackberry and tried to keep his thoughts on that, but they strayed.

Hadn't Harry been spending a lot that evening? Bob thought of the drinks and the expensive cigarettes he'd been buying. Of course, it was the day Harry was usually given his unemployment money and Bob supposed that accounted for it, but had Harry been spending more than usual? Bob shook his head and thought back to Harry's face after they had left Anne Talbot. He'd looked unconcerned, and he'd been so jokey with Nancy not much later. But had that cheerfulness been forced? Bob tried to remind himself this was Harry he was contemplating. They returned to their blackberry-picking but Bob found it more and more difficult to concentrate on it.

CHAPTER TWELVE

Inspector Blades was seated in the interview room at the police station opposite an anxious-looking, middle-aged man in a dark-blue, fine-wool suit, who looked as if he had dressed to make an impression; and a very serious woman with carefully groomed hair in a neat bun, with thin, pursed lips, who was around the same age, and whose fingers kept playing with a pearl necklace Blades was sure she had made a point of wearing to help her make an impression.

Hodgkins was seated to Blades' left and had a pencil poised above a black notebook. His face looked slightly flummoxed. Blades supposed he was more used to writing down information about stolen bikes and lost purses. The room was bare, with a wooden floor, a wooden desk, and wooden chairs.

The couple opposite Blades were Robert and Muriel Robinson who ran a boarding house in town, and who had come forward with information about the dead girl. At least they said this might be one of their lodgers, as a girl of that age and appearance who'd been staying with them had disappeared.

'What was the name of the young lady who was staying with you?' Blades asked.

'Anne Talbot,' the woman replied. 'I know the spelling because she wrote it down in the book.' As she said this, she pointed out to Hodgkins he'd missed out the 'e' in Anne.

'Do you know her home address?' Blades asked.

'16 Abbey Street, Leeds.'

'Had she stayed with you before?'

'No. She just turned up. On spec without booking. Young ones these days. They don't plan. They do things when they enter their heads. She saw my sign outside the door after she arrived, not that I had a room for her that night. I had to ask a neighbour to take her the first night.' Muriel's face showed astonishment, and her fingers twirled the pearls with greater speed. 'But I could fit her in after that. So it worked out. She didn't have her bag when she was going about looking for rooms so I wasn't sure of her, but I suppose it was heavy. It turned out she'd left it at the station. She sent for it afterwards.'

As words flowed from Muriel, Blades studied her. He took in the mid-calf length of the dress, with the fashionable hint of a scoop in the top, and the thin gold bracelet on her left wrist. She held herself erect as if this were the self-righteous angle she addressed life from, and though the steadiness of her eye made her formidable, the lines of the mouth suggested kindness as well.

'What makes you think your lodger was the young lady found dead on the beach?' Blades asked.

Muriel tugged at the sleeve of her dress.

'She didn't… she didn't come back.'

Robert spoke. 'I heard someone coming in at the door. I thought it was Anne, but it was a friend of Beatrice, our daughter, not that I knew at the time. She left later. I didn't hear her going.' He stopped as if aware how muddled this sounded.

'This was when?' Blades asked.

'The Thursday night. I don't – I didn't look at the time.'

Blades reflected on Robert, who was a slight, thin man, with an ineffectual set to the chin.

'You saw the article in the paper?' Blades asked him.

Robert replied as if answering a different question. 'We thought she'd slept in. We didn't know her habits. We don't know her. She was a guest. A paying guest.'

'But when you checked her room, it hadn't been slept in?'

'The maid went to do the room,' Muriel said. 'It was one less room for her to do as far as she was concerned. She didn't even mention it till she'd finished at the end of the morning.'

'But you've checked since and there's no sign she's been back?'

'She'd not returned before we came to you,' Muriel said, and Robert shook his head to agree.

'And she was like the girl in the paper?'

'Yes,' Muriel said.

'In what way?'

'She had black hair cut in a bob. I don't like that fashion. It's not like my day. But that's how she wore her hair. And she had a green coat on. I remember especially because she came back for it.'

'That was when?'

'About mid-day on the Thursday.'

Inspector Blades put the photograph of Anne on the table in front of them. Muriel reached for Robert's hand and he held hers, as both pairs of eyes fixed on the photograph.

'Oh, God,' Muriel said.

'The bastard,' Robert said, 'doing that.'

Muriel looked away, but Robert couldn't take his eyes from the photograph.

Inspector Blades pushed it closer to them. 'It's a shock,' he said, 'but please, look at it carefully.'

Muriel forced her gaze back to it.

'It does look like her,' she said.

Robert said, 'That's a girl who's dead and who's had her face damaged. How can we tell? The girl we knew was alive and well.' Blades waited as they continued to study the photograph. 'But,' Robert continued, 'it could be her.'

'It might,' Muriel agreed.

'But it's hard to tell.'

'I'm sure it was her,' Muriel said.

'Definitely,' Robert agreed.

Blades looked at them for a moment, before he said, 'It's definitely hard to tell, you mean?'

'It does look like–'

'It is her, Robert.'

'I think it is. Yes.'

'We need to have the body identified. Would you look at it?' Blades asked.

'God,' Muriel said, and wrung her hands.

'Do we have to?' Robert said.

'It would help.'

CHAPTER THIRTEEN

Anne Talbot's room at the lodging house had been simply kitted out. There was a single bed, a dressing table, a wardrobe, and not much else. Muriel Robinson hadn't been able to face showing them the room after she'd been to help identify the body, which had been achieved mostly by the girl's clothes, so Robert Robinson now hung about near the door of Anne's room, shifting from foot to foot while Blades walked over to the wardrobe and opened the door. In it he saw skirts and blouses, all fashionable but tasteful. Hodgkins hovered near the door too, his eyes flicking around the room. Blades moved over to the dressing table and pulled out a drawer. He glanced at the lingerie, not without a shudder. Looking at someone's personal things seemed to bring them back to life. In another drawer, he found a romantic novel with a bookmark half-way through. He grimaced. He glanced around and noticed Anne's bag on top of the wardrobe. It was an anonymous suitcase made of a green fibre, with no helpful labels. He opened it but found it empty. He told Hodgkins to put Anne's clothes in it.

'We'll give you a receipt for these things,' Blades told Robert.

'Thanks.'

Blades looked out through a tall, sash window at the seafront; the Links spread itself out green before him, with the choppy sea behind. This was a room with a view of an innocent enough landscape, but Anne had walked into it and not returned.

He looked around at Hodgkins who was already in the process of packing Anne's clothes. Then he turned to Robert and said, 'I'll need to ask more questions – of your wife as well.'

'Perhaps we could go down to the sitting room,' Robert said.

'All right,' Blades said. 'I'll need you to take notes,' he said to Hodgkins, who shoved in the last of Anne's things and shut the case.

The sitting room was a rather grander affair with photographs of different parts of Birtleby in dark-wood frames; a chaise longue; and both a grandfather and grandmother Victorian high-backed chair. There was a piano by the window. Muriel was perched on the chaise longue where she was attempting to recover poise. She looked questioningly but grandly at Blades. Robert stood beside her. He shifted from one foot to the other.

'I realise how awful this has all been,' he said, 'and I'm sorry I have to disturb you with more questions.'

'By all means,' Muriel replied.

'Can you tell me anything about Anne's movements that day?'

'She had breakfast about ten – with me,' Muriel said. 'Then she went out. She came back about one or two.'

Hodgkins scribbled in his notebook.

'Did she have a meal with you then?'

'No. She said she had come back for a change of jacket.'

'There were workmen at the house, painting the windows and fence,' her husband interjected. 'They might be able to tell you something.'

Blades was pleased at the information. 'Did they speak with the girl?'

'Only to pass the time of day,' Muriel said.

'One of them said she went off with two young men when she left in the afternoon,' Robert said.

Blades turned his head towards him. 'Did she know the two men?'

'I don't know. I didn't speak with them much. We were busy.'

'Who were the workmen?'

'They worked for Roper the builders,' Muriel said. 'We make a point of using them. They're so efficient, always polite and they clean up ever so well where they've been working.'

Blades knew the name of the firm, which was a well-established local one.

'We'll give them a visit,' he said. 'What time did she go out again?'

'About two or three. Yes. About then,' Muriel said.

'Did she come back later?'

'If she did, we didn't see her.'

Blades gave this thought. The railwaymen had said they'd seen Anne with the two young men and the kitten at about three o'clock, which fitted in with what he'd just been told.

Another question occurred. 'She wore a green coat you say, and blue skirt. Can you tell me anything she might have been carrying with her?'

Muriel thought for a moment. 'She always carried a blue silk handbag.'

'And we haven't seen one in her room. I wonder where it went. It would have contained her purse.'

Muriel was speaking rapidly now. 'There would've been money in that, no more than a few pounds though from what Anne said. Oh, and she always wore a gold ring with a small garnet – on the middle finger of her right hand. I don't remember from viewing the body whether it was on it or not.'

'It wasn't,' Blades said. 'So, we have a missing bag, purse, and gold ring.'

'That's sad,' Muriel said.

Robert squeezed her hand to comfort her, and she squeezed back.

'You've been ever so helpful,' Blades said to Muriel and Robert. 'I am sorry about the ordeal but we need to catch whoever did this.'

'Definitely,' Muriel said, and Robert agreed, with a vigorous nod.

'And we have to ask for more patience from you. Would you be able to come down to the police station so we can take a formal statement, have it typed up, and you can sign it?'

'Of course,' Muriel said, and Robert nodded.

Blades knew he could have told them to do this but he wanted them to feel helpful. There might be something they'd forgotten.

CHAPTER FOURTEEN

Anne Talbot's autopsy was held on Wednesday, 25 August. To Blades, it was a blur of impressions: steel cutting through skin; the smell of intestines; blood; the mess of organs – heart, liver, lungs; grunts of surgeons; the glare of theatre lights; the bareness of worn lino floors and whitewashed walls; the grind of a saw through the skull; the sight of a brain being brought out by hand from the bone; more blood; and the to-and-fro of surgeons' voices in disagreement. Blades felt a churn in his stomach, and a stab of pity for this girl, who'd been defenceless on that beach, and now lay on a body block. He felt an urgent desire to be elsewhere and an equally compelling need to ignore that. Throughout the procedure, Blades had stood uncomfortably close to the surgeons to watch them, and when they'd finished and walked to the sink to clean their hands, relief surged through him.

When the two doctors had first met, Dr Parker looked reluctant to hold out his hand in greeting to Dr Langford as, Blades supposed, he was used to being the authority. Dr Langford proffered his readily, though there was a trace of condescension in his face. But they were both practical people and had co-operated well.

'Predictably she wasn't a virgin,' Langford said, reaching for a towel. 'Women who find themselves in that position aren't.'

'Though she hadn't met up with anyone for sex,' Parker replied, starting on washing his own hands. 'As you said, she was menstruating.'

'And, as you said, there was no sign of a sexual assault.'

'Which might be surprising,' Parker replied.

'How was rigor mortis when you first saw the body?' Blades noted the scrutiny in Langford's face as he said this.

'Complete.'

'Body temperature?'

'Absolutely cold, both indicating death about between 12 and 36 hours previously.'

'Apparently. How was the weather in this neck of the woods?'

Parker thought for a moment. 'Warmish,' he said.

'Hmm,' Langford said. 'And the body was covered by sand. I've no doubt our inspector friend will want us to try to be accurate.' He looked across at Blades. 'But it's difficult to come up with something that will stand up in court.'

'The body was found at about five o'clock in the afternoon,' Blades put in.

'But not examined by me till about nine o'clock at night,' Parker said.

'Night-time. It would be cooler then. Death 12 to 48 hours previous?' Langford said.

'So, she was killed before nine o'clock that morning, or at any time 36 hours before that?' Blades asked.

'We think,' Langford stressed. 'Which is as definite as we can be, though we could try to be more specific as you will insist but I don't guarantee what we say.'

'Though there is one other point with this case,' Dr Parker said. 'When the body was moved round, blood flowed out of the left nostril.'

'I'm not sure why it would have done that,' Dr Langford said.

'In my opinion, if she had been dead longer than 24 hours, the blood would have coagulated.'

Dr Langford raised an eyebrow but said nothing at first. Then he said, 'I can't think of any studies to have shown that.' He paused, then said with a note of humour, 'But we can manage to agree she's dead.'

Blades' heart was in his boots.

'That's helpful,' Blades replied, 'though everybody already knew that.' Blades sighed. 'So, we're looking for someone who could have been in the vicinity between 12 and 48 hours before the first examination of the body, or perhaps even further back than that? That might narrow it down to a few hundred suspects.' The disappointment of this hit home, but then he brightened up as he realised that, even if the timescale was vague, at least it didn't disagree with what his witnesses had told him.

'Can you be definite about the cause of death?' Blades asked.

Dr Langford spoke first. 'Blows to the head.'

Blades muttered. He hoped it was indecipherable. Again, what Langford said had been obvious.

'There's a small lacerated wound on the right temple and another by the right ear, as we said during the examination,' Langford continued.

'When you used a huge variety of medical terminology. Could you give a summary of conclusions?'

'Certainly.'

'And those wounds were caused by what again?'

'The damage to the jaw area looked as if it had been done by something blunt,' Langford said.

'I would have said the wound by the right ear was caused by something sharp,' Dr Parker said, 'as the one by the temple, and the wounds round the mouth could have been caused by a sharp edge too.'

'Which was the one that caused death?' Blades asked.

'The one to the temple,' Langford said, 'though there were also wounds on the lower lip. Punctures. Right through the lip.'

'Any chance any of it was caused by a knobbed stick?' Blades asked.

'Could have been,' Langford said. 'Some of the injuries might suggest that, some of those wounds around the mouth, others a blow from a pointed stick, or even the marlin spike from a soldier's bayonet. I don't see how the injuries to the lip could have been caused by the stone beside the body.'

'Or not,' Parker said, 'or she could have been walloped with the stick, and someone raised the stone and dropped it on the head.'

'Possibly,' Langford replied. 'The damage to the temple couldn't have been caused by a fall after an initial blow to the jaw. She'd have had to twist right round on the way down.'

'Spun round by a blow?' Blades said.

The look on Langford's face suggested patience but was spoiled by the sardonic smile.

But Blades continued, 'She wouldn't have stood and watched while someone lifted that enormous stone.'

'She would have been lying there stunned after the first blow,' Langford said.

'Possibly one blow did all the damage,' Parker said, 'but she'd have had to be drugged if she lay and waited for it. We could test stomach contents.'

'No way was it one blow,' Langford said.

'I'm not getting anything precise and concise here,' Blades said.

Langford looked at him. 'It wasn't a precise death,' he replied, 'but we'll write up our reports.'

Reports that would not help much, Blades thought. 'If you would,' he said, looking from one man to the other.

'Thank you for your help,' Langford said to Parker.

'A pleasure. Where are you staying?'

'The Metropole,' Langford replied.

'At least it's not the same place the girl stayed at,' Parker said.

'She was here on holiday?'

'Yes.'

'And here she rests.' Langford's voice was contemplative.

'Till she's taken back to wherever she came from to be buried,' Parker said.

Blades noticed how calm the two were now the stress of the examination was over, although his own mood hadn't changed. As Blades gazed across at the body bag containing Anne's remains, his mind remained on the horror of the violence.

CHAPTER FIFTEEN

Blades was sitting in his office at the police station, looking at Chief Inspector David Walker, the large-limbed man with heavy features, and large, sweeping moustache who'd entered and introduced himself. As Walker looked around, his stare seemed threatening, though Walker was probably only taking in the worn lino, the need for fresh paint on doors and walls, and assessing him. Being a local inspector, Blades had always known this wouldn't remain his case, but he was still irked at the arrival of the Yard as he would have liked more chance to make progress by himself.

Blades noticed the conventionality of Walker's clothing: the dapper suit, and the tie neatly knotted and straight. He remembered what he'd heard about him, that he'd been a Chief Inspector at the Yard for a brief time, and his previous murder case hadn't led to a result. But Walker would be examining Blades' work; Blades had put much effort into it and he hated being criticised.

Walker seated himself opposite Blades. There was a self-righteousness in the way he held himself, and a hardness in the look he aimed at Blades. He didn't have the look of a person who wasted time, and didn't.

'I read the articles,' he said, then paused.

Blades looked back at him. He shifted in his seat.

'We need to work more on relationships with the press.'

'Why?' Blades asked.

'Police statements should reach national newspapers too, and shouldn't be general. According to your release, the body could have been discovered anywhere around Birtleby, and at any time during that day. We need the co-operation of the public, so we need to give them enough information to have them queuing up to help us.'

Blades knew his Chief Constable disapproved of that approach. He said he wanted his police to have space to pursue inquiries properly. Blades became aware he was scowling and stopped himself. 'We didn't have a lot of information initially,' he said.

Walker replied as if he hadn't heard this. 'Did anyone come forward at all after the newspaper story?'

Blades had been pleased about the leads he'd established, but perhaps he'd have the chance to talk about those later. 'A hysterical woman who's been reporting suspicions about male neighbours for years. Others that were unpromising. And a sailor. Today.' Blades had been pleased about him. 'The article did help. He was back at Larmouth when he saw the newspaper. A lot of them at that base are from this area and they have the local rag sent over.'

'Larmouth?' Walker's eyebrows arched.

'It's on the other side of the bay. The sailor's name is Pulteney. He went to his officer after he read about the murder, and the officer got in touch with us.'

'And?'

'Pulteney saw the girl and she was with two men.'

'Good.' Walker sat back in a more relaxed manner. 'Did he see them clearly? Could he describe them? He didn't know them, did he?'

'I haven't questioned him yet, sir. He's being sent across.'

Blades told Walker about his interviews with the workmen and the owners of the boarding house; he was relieved the chance had arrived to tell what he'd managed to discover, and, as he did so, he was pleased to see Walker's face no longer tense.

As they waited for Pulteney to arrive, Blades tried to build a relationship with Walker, and he started to chat about football and the chances of pay rises, though his mind kept puzzling over the case; and the smells and sounds of the autopsy were never far from his thoughts.

'Is this area new to you?' he asked Walker.

'I've passed through it. You're from here yourself?'

'Yes.'

'In the service all through the war, or were you out at the Front at all?'

Blades wondered why Walker had asked that, even though it was a question often put by people; he assumed Walker was wondering about the continuity of his police work.

'I didn't go out,' he said, but didn't elaborate.

'Did many from this force fight?'

'A few. Like everywhere, volunteering was encouraged, which disrupted everything. Temporary constables were taken on, who weren't as good. If they'd been fit they'd have been conscripted into the army, but they did a shift for us. Then we had to let them go when men returned. It was much the same where you are, I suppose.'

'It was,' Walker said. 'I decided not to volunteer either. Some people were jealous of the police being exempted from conscription but I always disagreed. Everybody in normal police complement is able-bodied, and of fighting age. If they'd conscripted the lot of us, there'd have been nobody left to police the country, and what would that have led to?'

Blades frowned. He'd wanted to do his bit, but his wife, Jean, had persuaded him. They had a son, she said, and she didn't want him to lose a father. And, when she'd lost her brother on the Somme, she'd gone on about not wanting to lose her husband. But it had been difficult for Blades.

'Of course,' Walker said, 'we often had to take on extra responsibilities because of those who were away, but you rose to it.'

Blades remembered the way Walker had strutted into his office. There were people like him to whom, with the thinning in police ranks, the war had presented career opportunities that might not otherwise have been there.

Then Pulteney arrived, and the two of them were seated opposite him in the interview room. Perhaps they ought to put police posters on these walls, intimidating ones, Blades thought, or perhaps the fact there was nothing to distract from the process of question and answer was a good thing. Anyway, there they were at the empty wooden desk, seated on hard wooden seats. Blades was particularly aware of the scrape of Walker's chair and the creak of his own, then the breathing of Pulteney, which was quick and nervous. Looking at Pulteney, the first thing Blades noticed about him was his uniform didn't fit, which made Pulteney's arms look unusually long, though perhaps they were. Pulteney was tall.

'So, what's the information you have?' Walker asked.

Blades supposed it must be difficult for a rating to be faced with two police inspectors, and Pulteney did look subdued. Blades contemplated the long, lean face with its protruding eyes, as he and Walker waited for him to begin.

'I did see the girl. I'm sure it was the girl. She was with two men. They were walking along the East Sands at the time and I was going in the same direction. They were having a good time when I saw them. The girl was laughing and a cat was following them, a ginger kitten, and they were joking about that.'

Blades tried to stop a smirk. The ginger kitten, he thought. Witnesses were linking up. He and Walker glanced at each other.

'She was giving it something to eat from a bag, so it followed them. One of the men grew annoyed with the kitten, the taller one. So the girl took it over to the railway hut and handed to the workmen there. She said, "Here's a right one for you. Have fun." She went back to the men and they walked on along the path.'

'What happened after that?' Walker asked.

'They went on walking. They looked happy. Relaxed. The girl was giggling. Then one of the men put his arm around her and that started her giggling even louder. She wasn't discouraging him.'

'And?' Walker said.

'That's when I turned back.'

'What makes you think this was the girl whose body was discovered?'

'The description in the paper. That's what the girl looked like. Short black hair. A green coat. I'd seen her before, the day before. Down the beach at the Central Sands. She was on her own then, looking at the water. A biplane flew over and she turned to watch it.'

'You must have got a good look at her face?' Walker said.

'Yes.' Pulteney's face held a self-satisfied expression.

He'd seen her the day before? Blades thought. If he'd then seen her the next day, was that because he was watching out for her? Following through on the line of questioning, Blades took out the photograph he had of Anne, and laid it on the desk. Pulteney blanched as he stared at it. 'Is that what he did to her?'

'It's shocking. I'm sorry,' Walker said. 'But is it her?'

Pulteney hesitated, 'I... it's... yes. That's her.'

'You're sure?' Walker said.

'Yes.'

'Can you describe the men?' Walker continued.

'I could have a go. One of them was like a boxer with a burly build and a squashed nose. He didn't look like a man you'd want to argue with.'

'How was he dressed?' Walker asked.

'Grey suit. Cloth cap, light grey. Oh, and he had a limp.'

Blades looked across at Walker. The description of the suspect Pulteney was giving was helpful.

'And he carried a stick,' Pulteney said. 'A heavy walking stick with a brass knob.'

'Did you see the shape of the knob?' Walker asked.

'No. They were too far away. I'd recognize him again though.'

'And the other fellow?' Walker asked.

'He was sort of nondescript. I noticed the girl more. He wasn't the sort of person you'd look at twice.'

'What height was he?' Walker said.

'He was about the same height as the other one, no, slightly shorter. They must both have been just under six feet, or thereabouts. He'd a darker sort of suit. But it was grey too, I think. And he was thin.'

'Anything else?'

'He wore a hat.'

'Would you recognize him again?'

'I don't know. Perhaps if I saw them together. I saw them as a pair. Maybe I'd recognize them as that.'

Blades wasn't sure how useful that would be. Pulteney might identify one suspect with accuracy, then guess at the other one.

'Were their suits smart?' Walker continued.

'They were shapeless, cheap.'

Blades thought it time he joined in. 'What were you doing there?' he asked Pulteney.

'Walking,' replied Pulteney, then added, 'I often walk along there. It's something to do, and you can watch people strolling about. I was with my friend Chris. We had a laugh and joke about them.'

'These were young men going with a young lady into the dunes and you say you were watching them?' Blades asked.

'There were three of them. Not because I thought I might get a look at anything.'

'A look at what?' Blades asked.

'Nothing.'

'Nothing?'

Blades looked at Pulteney's appearance and demeanour again. There was clumsiness in his movements, and a halting nature to his speech that was curious. He wondered if Pulteney was simple. 'Were you watching them to see if they might do anything they shouldn't?' Blades asked him. Pulteney didn't answer, just stared back. 'People do here,' Blades said. 'See what couples are getting up to and then try to blackmail them. That's what the Foxes do. You know about them, don't you? Not that there's anything foxy about it. Do you go in for that?'

Pulteney had a frightened look in his eyes. 'No,' he said.

Walker resumed his own questioning. 'Are these local men? Had you seen them before?' he asked.

'I don't remember it.'

'So, you've no reason to have any sort of grudge against them?' Walker said.

Pulteney looked annoyed. 'No,' he said.

'Who's your friend Chris?' Walker asked.

'He's from Birtleby. He's a friend I meet up with. He was invalided out of the army. Shellshock. Though he's all right now. We meet down the seafront and go about together.'

'We'll need to have you give us his address. In the meantime, thank you for your help, Mr Pulteney. We'll have a constable take your statement and you can sign it.'

Pulteney sat up straighter in his seat as relief showed itself in his face.

'If we succeed in getting suspects,' Walker continued, 'we'll ask you to attend an identity parade and see if you can pick them out.'

'I'd know the big one, I'm sure. I'll be glad to help.'

Walker took Pulteney through to Hodgkins for his statement, then returned, at which point he and Blades shared reactions.

'What d'you think, Blades?'

'He won't come across well on a witness stand.'

'No. But there are corroborating witnesses, and we might turn up more. What he says does fit in with the statements of the workmen you interviewed.'

'It does,' Blades agreed.

'I wonder if there's any chance those two men they saw are still around.'

'If they're local they will be,' Blades replied.

'We should put descriptions of them in the press,' Walker said. 'Particularly a description of that big one. They might have been doing this sort of thing here before, giving girls the chat, and making nuisances of themselves. Another witness might come forward.'

'And we need to get the men going around the dance halls and theatres, asking the girls,' Blades said.

'The women will be scared,' Walker said. 'It might reassure them, make them feel we're doing something.'

When Blades and Walker returned to Blades' office, Blades walked over to his desk, and started sorting out the paperwork on it. He picked up files and started putting them in a briefcase.

'You'll need an office,' he said to Walker. 'You might as well have this one. I'll share with the constables.'

'I'm sorry,' Walker said, though why he should care Blades didn't know, and didn't suppose he did.

Blades opened a drawer and emptied it.

'I don't want to put you out,' Walker said.

'You're not doing that,' Blades said. 'You have to work somewhere.' Then he paused and turned towards Walker. 'But can I stay on the case?' he asked.

Blades hoped Walker would ask to keep him on it. It was Blades' patch but he supposed Walker usually worked with his own men.

'Why?'

'I've never worked on a murder investigation, but I'd like to.'

Blades knew his Superintendent had called in Walker as he wanted Blades for more local matters, but Walker would benefit from local knowledge. And Blades knew this could be useful experience for him.

'You're from here,' Walker said. Indeed, Blades thought. He knew the scoundrels, and would have instincts about what sounded right and wrong in this area. 'But you're used to being in charge,' Walker told him. 'Would you adjust to my authority?'

Blades thought for a moment before replying. 'I want to learn from you, sir.'

'You're punctilious in your instructions to your men, I've been told. And they have to be carried out to the letter.'

'That's not a bad thing, surely, sir?'

'I don't want my thinking muddled by someone else trying to take over.'

'I definitely wouldn't do that, sir.'

'I have a colleague to work with. Sergeant Page. But he has no experience of this sort of thing. The sergeant I usually work with has had to take sick leave.'

'I'm keen, sir,' Blades said. Walker said nothing for a moment but Blades could see he was swithering. 'Being acquainted with the area does matter,' Blades said.

'I suppose. It would be good to get this solved.' Blades noticed a spark of self-interest in Walker's eyes. He might be expressing reluctance, but Blades sensed Walker couldn't believe his luck. 'Hopefully it's a one-off, but killers can get a taste for it. And you do have more experience than Page.'

'Eighteen years in the force, sir.'

'We could put Page in charge of door-to-door inquiries, train him up.'

But Walker still hadn't said yes. There was silence, and Blades wondered what else he could say to convince him.

Then Walker made up his mind. 'All right,' he said. 'Your Chief Constable will have to agree but, as far as I'm concerned, you have your wish. You're in at the sharp end on a murder hunt and I hope you sleep at night afterwards.'

CHAPTER SIXTEEN

The bar parlour at the Victoria was smoky, and there was only a low, guttering gas light, enough to give a shine to the brass fittings at the bar, but not enough to show the extent of the wear on the rugs and furnishings. It was comfortable and warm though; a place where people huddled away from the world, and Bob and Harry were seated there now.

Elspeth Summers was pouring a half of stout. 'I'm surprised you can come in here after being fresh like that with me,' she told Harry who scowled, then gave her a beaming smile.

When she finished, she drew across the foam with a flat stick there for the purpose, wiped the glass, and handed it to Harry, who grinned at her and carried it over to their table. Bob looked at the drink Harry put in front of him. He was only half-way down his previous one, and he wished Harry wouldn't be so greedy with beer, which ought to be savoured.

Harry sat beside Bob, picked up his own glass and sipped. He smiled, then looked across the room at Elspeth who had picked up a newspaper and started reading it, elbows on the bar.

'Nice,' Harry said. 'You ignore customers and have a good read instead.'

'At least I can,' Elspeth said.

'Hoity-toity,' Harry replied.

Elspeth pulled a face and continued studying the newspaper. As she did so, she frowned.

Harry studied her. 'Is something up?' he said. 'They're not putting the price of beer up?' He laughed.

Elspeth glared at him. 'Some things aren't funny. You know that?'

'Like machine gun bullets,' Harry said.

'They were hilarious,' Bob said.

'Quick-fire but definitely not gags,' Harry added.

'You know that body,' Elspeth said.

'You mean yours?' Harry said. 'I've been studying that one.'

Elspeth pouted. 'The one on the beach,' she said.

'Don't depress us,' Bob said.

'It says here they're making progress with their inquiries. Maybe they'll get the bastard.'

'What progress do they say?' Harry said. His voice was quieter and there was a tightness in his lips.

'A witness has turned up who says he can identify the men, the two tall men the police said they were looking for. It's a sailor. He says he was walking behind them and saw them walking and laughing with the girl, the same girl, he's sure of it. I hope they get them.'

'Does it say who they are?' Harry asked.

'It describes one of them. Sounds like you, Bob.' And she laughed. 'The sailor's billeted over at Larmouth which is why he hasn't come forward before. He was over here on furlough. But he saw the reports in the paper.'

Harry walked over to the bar and pulled the paper over towards him.

'Manners,' Elspeth said, trying to pull the paper back but not managing to do so.

Harry's eyes raced over the page till he found the story.

'It's my paper,' Elspeth said.

'You can have it back in a minute,' Harry said as he stared at the article.

'What does it say?' Bob asked.

Harry's fist tightened. 'What Elspeth told us.'

'Let's see.'

Bob joined Harry at the bar and pulled the paper towards himself.

'Is that it?' he said, stabbing his finger at an article.

'That's it,' Harry said. 'Witness Steps Forward. That's the headline. Progress in the Body under the Sands Case.'

Harry peered around the room as if expecting to see policemen everywhere, then walked over to the door and opened it.

'Where are you going?' Bob asked.

'There's something–' He stopped, as if not knowing how to complete the sentence, then continued, 'There's something I've got to do.' He walked through the doorway and slammed the door behind him.

'What did he do that for?' Bob asked. 'Look. He's left his beer.'

'I'll read it to you,' Elspeth said, and she did, in a sombre if steady voice. 'Did you meet that girl?' she asked.

'No,' Bob said, and returned to his table where he picked up his glass and studied it.

Other customers came in and Elspeth started pulling pints for them. Bob sipped beer and considered Harry. If he was that worried, there was something for him to be anxious about, and not only Harry, him as well. If this sailor had seen them in the area where the murder happened and on the same afternoon, he might have seen enough to incriminate them, not that Bob remembered seeing a sailor there. He racked his brains but couldn't think of any sailor he knew, so there was a chance it wasn't someone who'd noticed him about before, and, if the man had only seen them from a distance maybe he couldn't identify them. Bob saw Elspeth looking over at him and he didn't like her wariness. Why had Harry been so stupid as to march out like that? Bob sipped and attempted to look casual. There were lots of young men of their age about this area. Why should anyone suspect them? But that look on Elspeth's face worried him.

CHAPTER SEVENTEEN

As Harry was pacing along the beach down past the Victoria, smoking and looking at the waves, Blades and Hodgkins came up on him.

Constables had been punctilious in their questioning of young ladies about young men in the habit of pestering women, and Harry's name had cropped up. A couple of young women had mentioned Harry's exploratory hands and short temper, and another had said she'd been sure she'd seen him around the beach with his friend Bob on the day of the murder.

'Sorry to interrupt you,' Blades said, making no effort to keep irony out of his voice, 'but the Chief Inspector wants to question you.'

'Fuck,' Harry said, before crushing his cigarette underfoot. 'Is it about that bloody murder?' he said. 'Why on earth would you want to question me?'

'You were seen on the beach around that time,' Blades explained.

'Was I?' Harry said.

'Yes,' Blades replied. 'We just want to ask questions.'

'Or arrest me and hang me,' Harry replied.

'Why would you think that?' Blades asked. He looked at Harry's malevolent face, which was an impression of Harry that was to remain with him, but Blades put patience into his voice. 'We're questioning a lot of people. It doesn't mean anything but you might be able to tell us something that will help. Then we can talk to other people.'

'Fuck,' Harry said, but followed them quietly to the car.

They picked up Bob too as Harry, though reluctant at first, had been helpful and told them where Bob was when they'd asked about his perennial sidekick. Blades had left Harry in the car in Hodgkins' custody while he went into the Victoria. He found Bob seated, still with his beer. Fear. That was the expression Blades saw on Bob's face when showing him the police card, and Blades noticed how well Bob's appearance fitted Pulteney's description: the build, the nose, and the stick that lay beside him. Blades couldn't stop a smile. 'We're following up witness reports,' he said. Bob said nothing, just stared back, continuing to look afraid, which confirmed Blades' suspicions of the man. 'And we heard you were on the beach on the day Anne Talbot died. Our Chief Inspector wants to ask the questions, so if you could come along to the station to see him?'

Blades attempted to restrain another smile as Bob muttered while he picked up his jacket from the back of the chair and put on his cap. When Bob stood up, the solidity of his physique was even more noticeable, and Blades thought Bob did look as if he could do violence. But Blades noticed there was something querulous in the chin for all that.

'See you soon,' Bob said to Elspeth.

'You hope,' Elspeth replied with a grin. Bob scowled back at her.

Bob found himself slumped in the back of the police car beside Harry with Blades and Hodgkins in front. Bob acknowledged Harry and said, 'Our boys in blue have fucked up again.'

'That's what fuckers do,' Harry replied.

Blades turned around and gave them a stare. 'Shut it. Answer the questions nicely and you can go home.'

'Yes, Officer,' Harry said, though he bit back a different reply. He stared out of the window, Bob glared ahead, and neither said anything else during the journey.

They processed the men one at a time. Once in the interview room, Harry slouched forward on his chair, and stared at his feet. Blades and Walker sat on seats across the table from Harry and inspected him in silence. Blades would have enjoyed interviewing Harry by himself but would follow Walker's line of questioning with interest. Harry felt in his pocket, took out a cigarette packet, saw it was empty, and put it back. He grimaced.

Blades thought Harry an unremarkable-looking young man. Though tall, he was thin and, though his features were regular enough to be good-looking they weren't, mostly because of a dissatisfied expression that looked habitual. Blades lit up a cigarette and handed it over to Harry, who took it and drew in smoke although it didn't make him look more relaxed.

Walker coughed, then asked in a steady voice with more than a note of authority, 'Can you tell us where you were on Thursday afternoon?' The tone seemed to Blades to hold barely concealed contempt but, as Harry turned his head to look at Walker, Blades couldn't tell whether this had annoyed him.

'Yes,' Harry said, but didn't continue.

Blades broke the silence that followed. 'So, where were you?' he asked.

'Blackforth Castle – and I've two witnesses, Bob Nuttall and Nancy Harland.'

'Do you know why we're asking you?' Walker asked.

'Someone said they'd seen us on the beach. And I've just told you we weren't there.'

'You and your friend Bob often go around giving the girls the chat,' Blades said, 'and some of them don't like you very much.'

'Some young ladies are too choosy.'

'You saw the description of Anne Talbot in the papers,' Walker said. 'About five feet seven, short black hair, a green coat and blue skirt. You didn't happen to come across her when you were chasing skirt?'

Harry drew in smoke and leaned back in his chair. 'No,' he said.

Walker scrutinized him, and, in return, Harry looked as if he were trying to start a staring match.

'You were seen running away from the beach with your friend,' Blades said, which wasn't quite true. A couple of young men had been seen running from there and the descriptions might match, though they had been dressed as soldiers, which didn't. 'Then, when you saw our witness, you turned and ran off in the opposite direction. Why were you doing that?'

'I didn't,' Harry replied. 'Who's your witness?'

Blades considered the witness, a middle-aged visitor from Linfrith, a gentleman, who'd been walking along the beach with his son. He'd been helpful, but Blades wasn't sure how useful the testimony was. Blades didn't reply.

'It's enough he recognizes you,' Walker said.

'He's wrong,' Harry said. Blades studied Harry and saw the lack of worry at the accusation.

'You did try to sign up to go away to Ireland,' Walker said. 'We've been told about that.' Blades noticed the genuineness of the surprise on Harry's face, but Harry didn't deny the statement.

'Soldiering's the only trade I know,' he said. 'It's difficult to turn up jobs just now.'

'You've been hanging around for months,' Walker said. 'Why try to enlist the day after a murder?'

'Perhaps I didn't know there'd been one.'

'Did you?'

Harry paused, then said, 'No.'

'And we have a witness who says you were on the Ridges.'

'Not me,' Harry said. 'I was in Blackforth.'

'So, who's this Nancy Harland?' Blades asked.

'She's a maid at End House on the Shore Road.' Then a grin appeared on Harry's face. 'See. She exists.'

A frown appeared on Walker's face, but Harry's eyes were clear. Blades gave Harry more thought. There was an arrogance about this young man.

'What were you doing over at Blackforth?' Walker asked.

'Out for a walk. It was Nancy's half day and she often goes over there so we did. We had a good laugh, ate ice cream and came home. Where's the harm in that?'

'None. If that's what you did.'

'I'm not lying. Ask Nancy.'

Blades took out the photograph of Anne Talbot and laid it on the desk. Harry gazed at it as Blades and Walker watched his expression.

'Who's this?' Harry asked.

'Anne Talbot. Did you see her?' Walker asked.

'It would be difficult to recognize anyone from that,' Harry replied. 'I don't think so.'

'Did you see anyone with her?' Walker asked.

'No.'

'Did you kill her?' he asked.

Harry turned a look of self-righteousness in his direction. 'You've a nerve,' he said.

'Did you?'

'Did I hell.' His voice was raised with anger, or a convincing impression of it. 'Why don't you catch the real killer?'

Harry's cocksureness was even more apparent, but Blades did his best to avoid the reaction of dislike.

'We're trying to,' Walker said.

As they'd no more questions to ask, Harry was dismissed and Hodgkins brought Bob from the room next door. Though Bob was less defiant, the interview followed the same pattern. He denied being on the beach, and gave Nancy Harland's name for an alibi.

'I don't believe you,' Walker said to Bob.

'I'm not bloody lying.'

'You've persuaded this Nancy to lie too?' Blades said.

'Have we hell,' Bob said.

'Did you hit Anne Talbot?' Walker asked.

'No.'

'We have your stick,' he continued, 'and we'll test it for blood.'

'And you won't find any,' Bob said.

'Was it Harry who hit her?'

'I don't know anything about anybody hitting anybody.' Bob's voice came out in a squawk, then a look of grievousness appeared. 'Are you desperate for a conviction? Because we didn't do it.'

That tenseness about Walker's mouth was hardly noticeable but Blades could see he was beginning to get frustrated. 'If it was Barker, tell us.' Walker's eyes looked as if they were trying to bore through Bob. Blades wondered about the sanctimony in Bob's voice. Was it put on?

'We didn't do it,' Bob said.

'Do you want more women to die?' Walker said. 'If your friend did it, tell us.'

'I didn't see Harry kill anybody,' Bob said.

Walker laid the photograph of Anne Talbot's corpse on the desk while both he and Blades looked at Bob's reaction. Bob's eyes fixed themselves on the picture.

'Did you do that?' Blades asked.

'No.'

'Did Barker?' Walker asked. 'If he did and gets away with it, he could do that to someone else.'

Bob looked at the picture. 'I don't know anything about it.' There was fear in his expression, and anger in his voice. If Bob was lying he was doing so well, Blades thought.

'Whoever did that to her, it's disgusting, and it definitely wasn't me,' Bob protested.

'So, we finish here and question Nancy Harland?' Walker said.

'That's up to you,' Bob said, 'but if I knew anything I would've told you.'

Walker and Blades returned to the room Harry was in. Walker contrived a deliberate triumph in his step and Blades attempted not to let his dejection show. 'Your friend admits to it and says it was both of you,' Walker said.

Harry didn't say anything at first. Blades tried to read his face but not much showed. Then Harry said, 'You're lying. We weren't with Anne Talbot on the Ridges. We don't know her.'

Walker brought his fist onto the table. 'Don't lie to me.'

Harry's expression remained blank but his voice showed irritation. 'Why don't you go after those two soldiers everybody's on about? Don't you want to catch the people who did the killing?'

'We've witnesses who say you were there.'

'Who?'

'You passed workmen in a railway hut when you were walking by the train line. They identify you.'

Harry looked surprised at that. Blades thought he even glimpsed fear. 'I don't know how they can,' Harry said. 'I wasn't there.'

Blades tried a kinder tone. 'A confession does help with the sentence.'

'I didn't bloody do it,' Harry said. 'You're looking for someone to pin this on. You should catch the real killer.'

Blades considered returning the annoyance but decided it would be unproductive. He expected they would be closing the interviews and releasing these men, while they tried to assemble more evidence, and he and Walker would no doubt pay a visit to Nancy, and see what she said. One thing was sure, Harry was less convincing than Bob, even though Bob was the one with the incriminating stick. Why would that be?

CHAPTER EIGHTEEN

'They let you out,' Elspeth said with a sardonic smile, as Harry and Bob trudged back into the saloon bar. 'That's a surprise. I didn't expect to see you two again.'

'Two halves of stout,' was all Harry said before he sat in a seat, stretched his legs out, leaned back, and sighed.

Elspeth showed annoyance in her eyes, but not her voice. 'Sir.' She picked out a glass and held it under the pump.

Bob seated himself. He sat forward in the chair, unable to even attempt to relax. He looked at Elspeth with wonder. They were back in the Victoria, still free men, which he'd taken for granted before, but which he'd begun to appreciate more now. How pretty Elspeth looked with her auburn bob and ample bosom. Even the sullen chin didn't detract from her looks. He looked at Harry, and saw the weariness and annoyance in the stretched-out form. 'D'you think they'll have us back in?' he asked him.

Harry pointed jaded eyes in his direction. 'If they can't find any other suspects, they'll want to arrest somebody to look good. Though if we were toffs they wouldn't treat us like that. Complete bastards that pair. They showed no respect.'

'A pair of nutters,' Bob said.

'Just because they don't know who did it,' Harry said. 'But why pick on us? If I could get Walker in a dark alley he'd find out what a blow from a stick is like.'

'You could borrow mine if I still had it. They want it for analysis. How am I supposed to get about?' Bob's voice was accusing. Meanwhile, Harry was mumbling to himself.

'What?' Bob asked.

'As if I'd do that to a girl.'

'Did you?' Bob said before realising what he was saying, and then wished he hadn't, but the words were out and couldn't be taken back.

'What?' Harry said. His hand tightened on the handle of his glass. 'You've known me for how many years and you ask me that? You could get this glass in your face.'

'Not the violent type at all then? OK. I'm sorry.'

And they both looked away from each other. Harry swore.

Then Bob asked again. 'Did you?'

'What?'

Bob raised his arm in anger but only pointed at Harry with it. 'Why don't you answer the question? It's a simple one, and I'm in this as much as you. I have the right to know. But you don't reply.'

'Of course I bloody didn't.'

'All right then.'

Harry clenched his fist, slowly relaxed it, then clenched it again. He stared at Bob, then looked away at the picture of Gloria Swanson on the wall.

'Another tart,' he muttered. 'Why can't we get away from them?'

Bob found himself gawping at his foot. Then he looked up again. 'Didn't answer the question or didn't do it?' he said.

'Didn't bloody do it, you cretin.'

'Don't cretin me.'

'Don't be one.'

Bob's right hand was in a fist. 'I left you with her and she turns up dead. That's all I know.'

'Shite. You were with me all day. Was I relaxed and happy or what?'

'Yeah, but–'

'What?'

Then the question blurted out of Bob. 'Where do you get all the money from?'

Harry glared at him. 'What money? I get a little bit more than you. You know that. They give out more to someone on the dole than someone on the sick which is what you get.'

'I suppose.'

Then they sat in silence.

Then Bob found the courage to say, 'They said her purse was missing.'

'And her ring,' Harry said. 'Do you see me wearing it?'

'You could've sold it.'

'I'm not so stupid as to be hawking a dead woman's ring around where she died.'

'You've still got it?'

'I didn't take it.' Harry sighed. 'Look. We were kissing away. My hand–'

'What?'

'It accidentally touched her breast.'

'As it happened?'

'She called me everything, tart that she obviously was, though it was an accident.' As Bob looked at Harry, he wondered why Harry was bothering trying to make an obvious lie sound convincing. 'I was furious. The kind of man she said I was. And her in that short skirt and with that make-up on. And we've seen her giving the chat to more than one guy over the last few days. I was livid.'

'Why do you hate women so much?' Bob asked. 'Is it because they didn't have to go to the Front?'

That shut Harry up. He sipped beer as if he'd just remembered it was there. 'Yes,' he said in the end. He shifted in his chair.

'Is that why you killed her?'

'You can't really think that. Be reasonable. Of course I didn't. I just left in a bit of a temper. She was a self-righteous bitch, and her with all that money to spend while we tramp around after work that isn't there. But there's nothing you can do about it. And I didn't.'

Bob studied him. He sipped his own beer, then pulled a face. He'd lost the taste for it. 'We could be hanged for this even if we didn't do it. You know that, don't you? Why do you have to take out your bad temper on women?'

Harry moaned, then silence fell for a moment before Harry said clearly, 'I walked off and left her. She shouted after me and called me a few names. I just walked off.'

'You didn't attempt to apologise, explain?'

'Oh, yeah, to the likes of her?'

'The police will try to do us for this.'

Bob took out his last two cigarettes. They shared them. As Harry noticed the now empty packet, he sat further back in his seat and thoughtfulness entered his eyes. Bob crumpled the packet and flicked it into a wastebasket.

'I could forget about that shell-hole you pulled me into,' Bob said.

'I saved your life that time. That was a non-stop barrage.'

'But you could kill me off this time.'

'Oh, yeah?' Harry said, but closed his mouth and said nothing more. He stared ahead and smoked his cigarette.

As they smoked, Bob calmed down enough to even ponder the taste and the feel of his cigarette in his lungs. He noticed Elspeth had been washing glasses at the end of the bar nearest them and Bob wondered what she'd heard.

CHAPTER NINETEEN

Other suspects had been suggested to the police, and the two soldiers selling lavender on the seafront had been suggested by more than one woman. Now one of them, George Wilkinson, sat upright in the interview room at Birtleby Police Station, looking across at Walker and Blades.

George was taking in Walker's moustachioed smugness, and the tense scrutiny of Blades, and he was regretting being separated from his friend, Andy Hanson, who was sitting in a cell awaiting his turn to be questioned.

George was a burly private though he didn't feel imposing as he looked across at the two police inspectors studying him from the other side of the desk. George couldn't help thinking of the giant rats he'd seen in the trenches, rats that had grown huge devouring the corpses of soldiers. Wherever George went, whatever he did and whatever happened to him, his mind stayed firmly in the trenches.

He would have been in a sour mood anyway but the two MPs who had brought him here had a streak of cruelty in the humour they'd exercised on the way, when they had mocked him about the fate awaiting him.

George remembered having a sense of humour once, though his had been lighter, and stemmed from a sense of fun. Something divided him from that more spirited, unbelievably young person; something huge that pushed down on him. A grocer's boy. That was what he had been, nobody special, but he'd had hopes. Then they called you up, sucked your youth out of you, and now accused you of murder. When the MPs brought him here, they'd made it clear this was about the death of that girl on the beach, and George felt as if he could do with his soldier's rifle now.

Blades offered George a cigarette, and George looked at it warily but accepted it. Blades reached across with his lighter, and George drew at the cigarette.

'What were you doing on the Ridges on Thursday night?' Walker asked.

George looked at him and took in the accusation in the question. George drew in smoke, and thought for a few moments before putting an appeasing smile on his face.

'Walking,' he replied. 'Lots of people walk along the Ridges. We were off-duty for a few hours and went down to Birtleby. We often do. It's the nearest place to camp. And you can meet girls there and have a chat. What guy doesn't do that?'

Then he stopped and looked at the pair opposite him to try to gauge the reaction.

'We had a report of two soldiers on the seafront pretending to sell lavender so they could chat up women. They were being annoying.'

George became aware of how fixed Walker's glare was. 'I wouldn't annoy women,' George replied. 'I like them.'

He'd thought it a good ruse to sell posies so he could joke about with girls. They'd found his humour appealing once, but George supposed he'd changed. He made such efforts to look smart, parting his black hair in the middle in tune with fashion and sleeking it back, but nothing helped.

'It was reported to us you and your friend were seen running away from the Ridges at about eight o'clock at night.'

George's chest had gone tight. He sucked in a breath.

'I didn't run anywhere.'

'Then when you saw our witness, you stopped and ran off in another direction. Was there something for you to feel guilty about?'

Something was going wrong with George's breathing. It was quick and shallow. 'No,' he said. His hands gripped at the arms of his chair.

Walker leaned further forward. 'What were you in a panic about?'

George looked away and up at the window. Little light came through its narrow opening, but behind it you could see a view of a brick wall, about ten feet away. No vista of hope there.

'I wasn't running,' he persisted.

Walker glanced across at Blades. 'All right. You weren't running.'

George couldn't help thinking of these two as officer types. To him, officers were part-time trenchers who went back to their billets in farmhouses, and jaunted about on trips to French villages; this pair had probably never seen a trench at all.

'What did you do in Birtleby that day?' Blades asked him.

George thought him slightly the less pompous, but didn't trust the gimlet eyes. 'We got there about eleven and hung about the seafront.'

'Did you meet anyone?'

'No one special.'

'You just hung about?'

'Yeah.'

'For about nine hours?'

'Yeah.'

The scrape of Walker's chair was abrupt. George looked at him and took in the mood of impatience.

'Why were you selling the lavender?' Walker asked.

'Money for fags. Booze.'

'Did you see Anne Talbot?' Blades asked.

George turned to look at him. He'd been trying to work out how to answer this question, and he hadn't.

'You know who Anne Talbot is?' Walker asked.

George tried to stop himself gaping at the two policemen. 'Everyone knows that. That's the girl who was killed.'

The policemen took turns to launch questions at him. 'Did you see her?' Blades asked.

'I don't know. I don't know what she looks like.'

'She was short and kept her hair in a bob. Black hair. She was pretty they say,' Walker said.

'That description fits a lot of girls. I might have done and I might not. I don't know.'

Blades added detail to the description. 'She was wearing a green coat and a blue skirt.'

'Doesn't ring a bell. Look, we talked to a few girls. Not that any of them wanted to know that day. And we left it at that. Maybe she was one of them and maybe she wasn't.'

'Somebody killed her,' Walker said. 'Somebody who saw her that day.'

'It wasn't me.' George scowled at Walker, then glared at the wall instead.

'Why did you go up to the Ridges?' Walker asked.

You were supposed to fight your corner. They taught you to do that in the army, but all George could do was blurt, 'Something to do. Like I said, we didn't get anywhere with anyone so we thought we'd stretch our legs.'

'We've a witness who says she saw a soldier quarrelling with a girl on the Ridges at two o'clock,' Blades said.

George turned to the sharp voice and moaned, 'It wasn't me. We were just stretching our legs.'

'We've got your knife,' Walker said.

'Was Anne Talbot killed with a knife?'

'The marks on her could have come from a marlin spike on a soldier's bayonet,' Blades said.

'Then it was someone else's.'

'We'll have yours examined for traces of blood.' Walker's eyes seemed to bore right through George, but all he could do was stare back.

'You won't find any,' he said.

George tried to put fight into his voice, but he knew this pair would have him if they decided on it. At the Front you had known it had to be your turn sometime. It wasn't always the soldier beside you who fell. George remembered a prayer he had said then. But perhaps it would be better if they did hang him. He was tired of smelling the rot of bodies at night, and of hearing the spit of bullets in the wind.

He thought back to his first day at the Front. They put him in Signals, which sounded less dangerous than many postings, but he found out differently. His first job was to go with Sergeant Leggatt to the Signal Dump in Piccadilly Tunnels to fetch two drums of cable, and somebody must have thought they'd given out a simple job.

It was Ypres, which was like nowhere he'd seen or imagined on Earth. Where you expected grass, there was mud; where there had been trees were stumps; where there should have been birdsong was the blast of shells, and all the time the ground shifted with the thud of them.

Minenwerfer, whizzbangs, HEs, HVs, shrapnel: the Bosches must have been trying to wipe out every trench there, and Leggatt ordered him to scramble out from the precarious safety of the trench they were crouched in and make his way with him towards another one.

'Don't be mad,' George had shouted. 'We'll be killed.'

That was when the sergeant grabbed hold of him by the collar, half-choking him, and hauling him up onto the parapet, before pulling him away from the trench. A shell burst to their right, and out of smoke staggered two soldiers, one of whom was badly hurt –
the other soldier was attempting to help him towards the trench Leggatt had lugged George out of. Another shell burst and George threw himself to the ground, only to find himself being dragged up again. Then there was another explosion almost on top of them. George screamed at Leggatt and attempted to pull him into a shell-hole, only to be yanked out again by Leggatt. Leggatt dragged George, and cursed at him like a banshee all the way across the mud and holes between there and Piccadilly Tunnels. Tears gushed down George's face, and urine poured down his leg.

Leggatt led them to the cable drums, which had to weigh half a hundredweight each. They were impossible to move quickly with, but George found himself being cursed and bullied and bashed into half-carrying and half-dragging one back. When they reached their own trench, George pushed the drum in, and jumped in beside it, only to land on top of a corpse with just half a head. George screamed as he stared at brains. He rolled off it and lay in a huddle. And shook. And shook. He couldn't speak to anyone for hours after that, just lay at the bottom of the trench, away from the body, and they couldn't make him do anything else for a long time.

George stared back at the two policemen. He had been reduced to a gibbering wreck before. He knew what that was like, and he'd resist it.

'You must have been running for a reason,' Walker said.

'I didn't run anywhere,' George said.

'You weren't walking quickly?'

'We'd forgotten the time. We didn't go slowly. If you're not back prompt, you find yourself in the Guard House.'

'Were you back in time?'

'Just.'

It had been the helplessness he'd hated most. A bullet would find you or it wouldn't. Walker drummed his fingers. Blades coughed and looked impatient. George fidgeted. He shifted in his seat. He looked at the window, then across at the door, then at the brick walls. He felt helpless now.

CHAPTER TWENTY

Whether George Wilkinson's nervousness signified guilt or innocence Blades didn't know, but it did show the effect of the thought of the rope. George was taken to his cell, leaving Blades and Walker on their own in the interview room. Walker stood up, strode across it, stopped, turned and faced Blades.

'I'm not surprised women don't take to him. He's a shifty looking scoundrel.'

'They like those – often enough.'

Walker ignored the reply. 'He does look capable of anything.'

'All we can prove is he was in the area when the murder was committed, which might or not mean a thing.'

Walker's look was thoughtful. 'We'll see what tests show about that blade of his. Now we'd better see what this bloke Andy Hanson is like.'

And that was that. Walker resumed his seat as the door opened, and Hodgkins led in the other soldier, who sat across from them in the chair designated, his eyes flicking about from one police officer to the other. He shifted about in an effort to find a comfortable position despite what looked like a spasm in his back. Blades and Walker examined him.

Andy Hanson's face held a transparency Blades thought should be helpful and, despite the broadness to his frame and what looked like a hardness in his muscles, there was a cringe in his chin. There was also mistrust in his eyes, and an irritation. Andy bit the nail on his right thumb, noticed what he was doing, then put his hand firmly on the arm of his chair.

'Did you sell much lavender that day?' Walker asked.

'I've been telling George I don't want to do that anymore.'

'Really? Why?'

'I don't like the way he is with women.'

'What way's that?'

'His chat's no good. They take offence.'

'In what way is it so bad?'

'In every way. That's not how I was brought up.'

Walker paused. Blades pondered Andy's relationship with George, and supposed George was the leader.

'So why have you been going around with him?' Walker asked.

'It was supposed to be a lark and the chance to get extra money for gaspers, but it's not much of a laugh when you annoy the girls the way he does.'

'He gets aggressive with women?'

'They get aggressive with him. He has a knack of being insulting, sort of accidental like. And they don't go for that.'

Walker waited a few moments before asking, 'Did he murder Anne Talbot?'

'He didn't murder anyone, not when he was with me, and he didn't go off by himself, except long enough for a slash. I don't like him much because he's got no manners but I've never seen him violent.'

'Why were you running away from the Ridges?' Blades asked.

Andy stared at him. 'We didn't run anywhere. But you see, or don't see, I'll try to be clear, we'd hung about the seafront most of the day so we walked along the Ridges for the sake of it, to stretch our legs. But it takes longer than you think, and we didn't want to be late back to camp, so we weren't walking slowly, but we weren't running away from anything either.'

Walker spoke. 'The injuries on the woman would be consistent with those from a marlin spike on a soldier's blade and your MPs have taken yours for examination by us.'

Hanson's jaw held a self-righteous jut as he spoke. 'You won't find blood on it.'

Walker and Andy Hanson stared at each other. Blades did find Andy's look of innocence convincing but that might not mean anything.

After the interviews had finished, Blades was interested to hear Walker's thoughts because of what they would tell him about his new colleague, as well as for the light they might shed on the case.

'They could have done it,' Walker said, 'talked over their stories beforehand, even exchanged knives with other soldiers without their knowing. All these knives are the same and soldiers don't watch their kit all the time in barracks. There might not even be traces of blood on their own if these two have been careful.'

'That sounds too clever for this crime,' Blades said. 'This is a spur-of-the-moment job, a stupid crime done for stupid reasons. Someone annoyed with a girl because she wouldn't put out and he thought she'd been leading him on.'

Walker's smile was tolerant. 'You might be right but there would still be plenty of time afterwards to think, and work out how to cover up.'

Blades frowned. 'I suppose.'

'But you're right. Most murders are done for muddled reasons, and when they cover up afterwards they're too rattled to think that through properly. You never know your luck. There might be evidence on those knives. But there might not. And we can't charge them with leaving a beach in a hurry, which, as you said, is the only thing we can prove.'

'I agree.'

'But I'm not dismissing this pair from my thoughts.'

CHAPTER TWENTY-ONE

It was an overcast day, and the choppy waves were a mixture of dark greens. A fishing boat bobbed offshore. Gulls wheeled about the sky, and screeched. There was a breeze, which Blades hoped might clear the mind. Blades was trudging beside Walker along the track by the railway line as Walker had decided to return to where the murder had occurred. Blades supposed it was Walker's method, that it would allow him to think through the murder, and Blades thought it a reasonable idea.

'According to the railway workers, Anne walked along here with two men, capering, giggling, and playing with a ginger kitten,' Walker said.

'What do we know about Anne?' Blades asked.

'A good question. We don't know much, but let's see.' Walker scratched the side of his nose as he thought. 'She was a bit foolish. She was a single young lady who came to an isolated spot with two rough men she didn't know well. She worked as a secretary and went on holiday by herself, again, surprising. An independent young lady too bold for her own good. We might know more when we can get in touch with the mother. She's on holiday up in Scotland and travelling around.'

'Bob and Harry deny being with Anne, but then they would.'

Blades followed Walker's gaze at the expanse of sand and dunes they were walking through. 'She came here with them?' Walker said. 'She was the kind of young woman who would get herself murdered.'

Blades' eyebrows drew together. 'An area with a reputation, where couples come to have it away.'

Walker looked at him. 'She wouldn't know that. She was a stranger.'

'You could work it out.'

Blades mulled over Anne. He imagined her skipping along here, in her gaudy green coat worn for its brightness not its taste. She'd been laughing, her face alive with her youth, and her silliness no doubt, but wasn't that an innocence?

Walker's eyes swept around and over the dunes. Apart from the sand and grass, there was nothing there. 'She could see for herself it's a lonely place,' Walker said. 'She ought to have had more sense. Did she just enjoy teasing men? A dangerous occupation, but she can't have come with them for sex, according to Langford's examination.'

'Worldly, but not as worldly as she thought.'

'Pulteney's description of Bob is clear,' Walker said. 'And there's the kitten. That tallies.'

Walker stopped and gestured. 'Over here.' Blades looked at sand and shells and pebbles and grass; a spot much like any other around there. 'This is where they must have stood while she went over to that hut to get rid of the cat. It's a pity they didn't go over with her. Then the workmen would've got a better look at them.'

Blades nodded his head. 'She was relaxed. A young lady with two handsome young men.'

'I wonder how it played out if it was the two soldiers she was with.'

'The lab did report blood on one of their knives. George Wilkinson's. And he's intense. She wouldn't give out – she couldn't – he got annoyed.'

Walker frowned. 'So, it follows you kill her with your friend close by?'

'If they were a pair of predators, why didn't they rape her?'

'Who knows?'

'We'll never know why they killed her unless they tell us.'

Walker's face screwed up with concentration. 'George is the violent type, but then so's Harry. Either could have done it. But you'd think those workers would have recognized army uniforms even at that distance, and there were three of those railwaymen. They can't all have been short-sighted. Harry and Bob are our strongest leads even if they come up with an alibi.'

'It was a crime done for spur-of-the-moment reasons, that probably wouldn't make sense if we knew what they were. So there isn't any point in guessing at them.' Blades paused and reviewed the thought.

'It's stupid to kill someone because you fancy them,' Walker said.

'It's stupid to kill for any reason. Are Bob and Harry stupid?'

Walker thought for a moment. 'Harry is.'

By this time, the policemen had finished walking through the dunes and they were standing looking at the area where the murder had taken place. The stone had been taken away, as had the body, and the place was full of even more scuffed-up footprints, but Blades remembered clearly what it had looked like when he'd first seen it.

'A private spot,' Walker said. 'He must have been worked up about getting it.'

'Harry's obsessed with women. And he gives them a slap when they annoy him.'

'He could have done it.'

'And Bob's a follower.'
'I think he'd follow Harry anywhere. I think he has.'
'We need better identifications. Pulteney isn't enough.'
'And we need to check that alibi.'

CHAPTER TWENTY-TWO

Anne's mother was a plump woman with a taste for the Edwardian length of dress and coat that swept nearly to the ground, and she had her hair long and swept up on her head, also in the Edwardian fashion. If there had ever been anything of the modern in Irene Talbot's appearance or manner, it was a memory, but she was upright in her comportment and came across as self-respecting. Her face may still have been handsome, but was crumpled with grief. She had walked into the police station on the arm of a woman friend, after being located at last. The lady she was with was her sister-in-law, Eda Fleming, a thin lady with wispy hair and faded eyes who looked as if she was finding every step into this official place tortuous. Constable Hodgkins ushered them into Walker's office, then found Blades who joined them.

Walker had a pile of papers on the desk in front of him which he must have been working through. He greeted Irene and Eda with concern on his face, before despatching Hodgkins to find tea and biscuits for them. He indicated seats to them.

'You've had quite a journey,' Walker said.

'I'm so sorry I wasn't here sooner,' Irene replied. 'They couldn't find me to tell me the news and it's a long way from Scotland. It's dreadful about Anne. I can't take it in. How did this happen?' Then the words stopped flowing, the face puckered up, she reached for her handkerchief and tried to recover control of her features.

'I wanted Anne to come with me,' she said, then burst into tears. Then she had another go at speaking. 'I wish she had but she wouldn't.' Irene had to bring the handkerchief up and wipe her cheeks. After that, she'd recovered enough to speak. 'She wanted to go off by herself. "And what do you want to get up to?" I asked her, but young girls these days, they're so independent and she'd been to Brighton last year and there had been no problems, though I'd managed to find her a respectable place to stay there. The lady I worked for recommended it as she knew the landlady, and it was lovely. She looked after her from the beginning of the stay to the end. And Mrs Winters recommended another lady this time, so I thought it would be the same. But it wasn't possible to book far ahead because I wanted Anne to come with me on my trip to Scotland instead, so when that had been sorted out she couldn't get into that lady's house, but we were told of another reliable lady, and then Anne wrote and said that didn't work out when she got here, so I don't know anything about this other person she stayed with, and look what's happened.'

Then Irene ran out of words and breath, and Eda Fleming took over. 'Anne was ever so strong-willed,' Eda said. 'She was an independent young lady. But she was capable, getting on well in her job. She'd risen to be the manager's personal assistant.'

'She was a good girl,' Irene said. 'I never expected her to end up like this.'

'She was,' Eda said. 'Respectful, polite, neat, hardworking.'

'And she wasn't one for the boys, she wasn't.'

'She'd had one or two boyfriends, of course. She was a pretty thing.'

'But she didn't misbehave. She didn't.'

'Did she know anyone here?' Walker asked Irene.

'No.'

'So why did she come here?'

'It's a well-known place,' Irene said, 'a popular resort and it's on the same coast she went to last year. It's the same kind of place she went to, and she'd enjoyed that and it worked out all right, so we never thought.'

'I see,' Walker said.

'Irene and Anne had ever such a row about it,' Eda said.

'They did?'

Eda turned to Irene. 'You said you were worried about Anne growing up too fast, and young ladies didn't travel about by themselves in your day.'

'I did,' Irene said. 'Oh, I did.'

'She said she felt the responsibility,' Eda said to Walker, then turned back to Irene. 'There was only you to look out for Anne, after Alan died.'

'Alan was your husband?' Walker said.

'Yes,' Irene replied. 'And it wasn't easy bringing up Anne by myself. There was no stopping her when she put her foot down,' Irene said.

'They exchanged ever such sharp words about it,' Eda said to Walker.

'If Alan had still been here, he'd never have allowed it, but she wouldn't listen to me,' Irene said. 'She was so sure she knew what she was doing. And look what's happened.' Irene wrung her hands.

Blades considered her. She was not only upset about the death of her daughter, she was worried about whether she'd behaved as she should as a parent, both of which were as you would expect.

'Did she have any special friends?' Walker asked.

'Boys, you mean?'

'Or men.'

'She wasn't the flighty sort,' Eda said, and Blades wondered if it was being emphasised too much.

'There was that boy who worked in that French restaurant. But she soon saw through him and sent him packing. And there was that soldier. But he drifted off after a woman who looked as if she had money. No. There wasn't anyone.'

'No particular girlfriends?'

'Friends from work, of course. No one around Birtleby.'

'Perhaps we could talk to them and find out more about Anne from them.'

'Well, there was Ina and Harriet. Anne worked at Goldberg's off Main Street. I don't know their addresses. I'm sorry. Anne was a private girl. Perhaps if she hadn't been…' Irene's voice tailed off.

'She normally stayed at home with you?' Walker said.

'No. I'm in service. I'm housekeeper to Mrs Winters. Have been since Alan died two years back. I'm lucky to have that. I could have ended up in the workhouse. But if you're willing to work and you're respectable… that's what I always told Anne. There was no room at Mrs Winters' so Anne lived in lodgings nearby. With ever such a nice lady. She's in our church. I often chat to her about Anne. And she was taken with her. Anne was respectable.'

'We don't doubt it,' Walker said.

However, Blades did; as he assumed did Walker. Blades doubted Irene Talbot knew her daughter wasn't a virgin, though she may have suspected it. And if Anne ended up dead on a beach after going there with two young men she barely knew, it showed a definite lack of judgement. But Anne had been bright by all accounts. You'd think she'd have avoided ending up like this. It would be interesting to know what her female friends could tell them about her, if they would.

'And I'm sorry,' Walker said, 'there doesn't seem to be doubt about the identity of the body, but to complete the formal identification, could we ask you to come to the mortuary and look at it?'

Irene burst into tears again; Eda put her arm around her to comfort her, and then burst into tears as well.

CHAPTER TWENTY-THREE

Blades and Walker sat opposite each other on the badly sprung seats of their third-class train carriage, with other passengers pressed hard against them and no opportunity to discuss anything about the case. Expenses had to be justified and were minimal. The smell of smoke from the engine permeated, the noise of the pistons and a rattle harassed the ears. They watched coastline, villages and towns judder past, and they smoked and exchanged the odd remark about train travel, the weather and the football. Walker and Blades were travelling to Leeds, a journey that had to be undertaken because Leeds was where Anne had worked, where her lodgings were, and where they would find out more about her.

The first place they visited after arrival was Anne's place of work. It was a factory that manufactured women's clothes; a tall, brick building with narrow windows that didn't let in enough light. As Blades and Walker walked along the corridor past the workroom, they felt overwhelmed by the sound of machines. When they reached the office, Blades glanced at the woman who must have replaced Anne as secretary. She was seated where Anne would have been. She was tall, older than Anne and her face turned pale as they stated their business. She buzzed Mr Mullen, who could see them straightaway, and showed them into his room.

Mr Mullen's office was designed to be the impressive space in the factory. It was a large room with a wide window which, in contrast to those on the factory floor, did let in plenty of light. Mr Mullen was seated behind an expansive oak desk with, on the wall behind him, framed fashion shots of stock.

He was a man in his forties with thinning hair and a paunch. Blades imagined he enjoyed having Anne work with him.

'It's a dreadful tragedy,' Mr Mullen said. 'What can I say? And what can I do to help?'

The words flowed quickly. The self-important look in his face was designed to give gravitas, Blades supposed.

'If you could tell us one or two things about Anne,' Walker said.

'What is it you want to know?' Mullen said. He sat back in his seat and stared at them, trying to work them out.

'What was Anne like as an employee?'

'Excellent.' A look of what may have been forced enthusiasm appeared on his face. 'She'd been here two years and had started off as a clerical assistant who did typing now and again, but she was my secretary and personal assistant of late. She was bright, well-organized, and conscientious; a good timekeeper, and never off ill.'

'The ideal employee,' Walker said, and there seemed a note of doubt in his voice.

A critical look appeared on Mullen's face. 'It's possible to do the job of secretary well. It just takes a certain type of mind and efficiency. And she had both.'

Blades decided that was said with genuineness. 'She wasn't flighty with customers?' he asked.

'Certainly not. She was a respectable girl. I don't know anything about her social life but she never caused any gossip here. I would have heard about it. I don't know anything about friends outside work but everyone who works here was where they were supposed to be that Thursday – at work here. I assume she met her killer in Birtleby.'

Blades wondered if Mullen would willingly say anything that might incriminate his factory.

'She must have had pals here?' Walker asked.

'The girls do meet up to socialise. Hettie and Ina. She went about with them. I'll send for them.'

This he did, departing with alacrity, and leaving Blades and Walker his office to use as an interview room.

Hettie and Ina were in their work dress, high-collared blouses above skirts well below the knee. As they were ushered into seats, they looked with suspicion at Walker and Blades.

'She was a nice girl,' Hettie said, 'and a respectable one. We were ever so upset when we heard.' Hettie was the older of the two, had a severe cut to her jaw and anxiety in her voice.

'Who'd have thought it? It's what every girl dreads. She wasn't raped, was she?' Ina asked. Blades supposed Ina would have been the same age as Anne. He noted the curvaceousness under the high collar, and the lines around the mouth that suggested it was more used to laughter than grief.

'No,' Walker said, at which the ladies sat a bit further back in their seats as if more relaxed by this, although Blades noticed Hettie still rubbed her hands against each other as if washing them, before realising it and forcing them to stop.

'Did you go out and about with her much?' Blades asked.

'Outside of work, no,' Ina said, 'but we often went out at lunchtimes. It was a sort of weekly thing, out to the local café for a natter and a treat. She was a bubbly girl, bright, interested in everybody, and chatted nineteen to the dozen. She was fun.'

'Too much of a sense of fun at times,' Hettie said, 'but she had no airs and graces. She was a down-to-earth person. She'd have made a nice wife. It's a crying shame.'

'Do you know anything about men friends?'

'Nobody lasted long. She kept seeing through them,' said Ina, 'but there were a few.'

'A few too many,' Hettie said, her face settling into primness. 'I told her off for that more than once. Men are no better than they ought to be – present company excepted. But she was out for her fun, always boasting about how easy she found it to attract a man, and about the fancy places they took her to and what they treated her to.'

Ina's face showed wonderment at Anne. 'I think she made half of it up myself,' Ina said. 'She wasn't as bold as that.'

'Do you know if she knew anyone at Birtleby? Was she going to meet anybody there?'

'We thought she must have been if she was going by herself, but she denied it,' Harriet said, 'though I suppose she might not say. According to her she would manage to meet up with a fellow there all right. We wondered why at Birtleby for a holiday. It's an expensive place, but she said she'd soon get a man to treat her to things.'

Ina's face showed sisterly concern for Anne. 'Dinners and shows and such like. That's all she meant,' Ina explained. 'If you can believe even that.'

'She was confident about herself with men?' Walker said.

'Yes,' Ina replied. Harriet nodded.

The pattern with which people talked about Anne was the same, Blades thought. They started off by saying she was a bright, respectable girl. They weren't going to speak ill of the dead. But then other aspects of Anne came out. This was a girl who was fascinated by men, and who had to be with them, and a girl who didn't always take her mother's or her friends' advice. There was something odd about this efficient office girl who was so inefficient with men. Blades wondered about Anne. Was this a potential murder victim looking unknowingly for her murderer? A dreadful way to think of her, but it might the best way to describe her, because, if she hadn't behaved the way she had, she wouldn't be dead. The murderer would need even more thought, but if they could understand Anne, they might have a chance of finding him.

CHAPTER TWENTY-FOUR

The house Anne lodged in was in a working-class area, in a row of terraced houses inhabited by tradesmen and steelworkers, but the small gardens out front were tidy and the doors and windows recently painted. Anne's lodgings were on a corner and possessed a garden larger than the others, in which flourished red and yellow dahlias. A large lady welcomed them, introduced herself as Martha Albright. She showed the detectives Anne's room without fuss or delay. Blades thought her a straightforward sort.

This was the second of Anne's rooms Blades had explored and he hoped she'd left more of herself here.

'It's not a big room,' Martha was saying. 'And there's my husband and my two girls in the house as well. The girls are eight and ten and they can share a room easily enough at that age. They go on about wanting their own, of course, but we need some extra money. My husband's a painter and decorator, and trade can be uncertain at times.'

Between them – Blades, Walker and Martha – they easily filled the room.

'I'll leave you to it,' Martha said. She glanced around with nervousness, as if death might be catching.

Blades looked around. The room had been painted and papered not long ago, but in dull colours and patterns. There was a single bed, a dressing table and mirror, a wardrobe and a couple of shelves of books. The furniture looked old but presentable. Blades read the titles on the books: *Snow on the Desert's Breast; The Orient Came to Eastgate; The Lovelorn Lord*. They were romantic novels such as a young woman might fill her time with, and, looking at them, they would feature the kind of dashing aristocratic man Anne was unlikely to meet.

Underneath the bed was an array of shoes. Blades counted a dozen, ranging from sensible to fashionable to fanciful and uncomfortable looking, but all would show off an ankle. In the wardrobe was a collection of inexpensive but cheerfully chosen clothes, designed to make a young lady feel attractive. On the dresser, there was a writing slope containing letters, which Walker picked up to take with him. There was no other personal writing. There were pictures on the wall of scenes from the countryside around Leeds, which no doubt belonged to the landlady. A picture frame with a photograph of Charlie Chaplin looking forlorn, but loveable, appeared to be the only piece of Anne that might be present.

'She was clutching at life, but optimistically,' Walker said.

'What?'

'Her father dead, and her mother just surviving, Anne works dutifully, finds herself a reasonable job, but it doesn't take her far from where she comes from. She wanted to go to the seaside to see what else there might be in the world, and have fun.'

'I suppose,' Blades said.

'And she didn't manage to look past the young men she met. I wonder what these letters will tell us.'

'A diary might be useful.'

'If she was the kind of young lady who kept one.'

'And there was none in her room in Birtleby.'

Blades opened the drawer in the cabinet beside Anne's bed. It held handkerchiefs, a compact, and a restaurant menu, but no diary. Walker and Blades looked at the menu.

'Why would she keep that as if it were precious?' Walker asked.

'Perhaps it was a place someone took her. I wonder who it was.'

'The Lavigne Restaurant. That's where that waiter she dated worked.'

'The waiter she dumped.'

'I wonder how he felt about it.'

'According to all accounts she was only one of the young women who'd caught his eye.'

'Worth a thought though.'

When they left Anne's room, they encountered Martha again in the hallway. She looked as if she'd been listening and watching for them.

'Do you know anything about her friends?' Walker asked.

'She wasn't allowed to bring anyone back here,' she replied. 'I've children. I want the place respectable and, if I'd thought she wasn't, she wouldn't be rooming with me.'

'No doubt, but she must have had friends?'

'There were always boys after her, if that's what you mean. She was pretty.'

'There was a young man, a waiter, French I think he was,' Walker said.

'He was no more French than I am. The restaurant he worked in had a fancy French name, though I've never tried the food there. That might be French but he was born and brought up in Leeds. Pretended to be foreign if he thought it would impress a girl. But it was obvious. You'd think it would have put them off.'

'Did she still see him?'

'Not after I'd found out all about him. I soon told her what was what with that one.'

'Do you know his name?'

'Alphonse, he said, but it turned out to be Arthur Platt.'

'Was there anyone else?'

'No one special I know of, though a few others tried. I warned her off most of them.'

Blades thought it no wonder Anne went mad after men when she was away from home if Martha guarded her as if she were her own.

'I've never had a daughter that age,' Martha said, 'but I will. Eileen's ten now. Time passes quickly.'

'Do you know about any of Anne's girlfriends?' Walker asked.

'She knew other girls at work I dare say. I don't think she was close to anyone.'

The more Blades got to know about Anne, the more he felt for her. She was strong in her way but there was a suggestion of vulnerability there, and it had found her out.

After they left, Blades suggested a meal at the Lavigne Restaurant.

'Expenses won't run to that,' Walker said.

'We could have a look at that waiter before we question him.'

'It can't have been him she went to Birtleby to meet up with. He lives in Leeds. And they weren't seeing each other anymore.'

'She dumped him. Might he have followed her to sort her out?'

Walker looked at Blades for a few moments as he considered. 'He might have done.' He reached in his pocket for his wallet and made a show of how little he had. 'No meal in a French restaurant there. Which is just as well. I hate French food. But you're right. He might be worth questioning.'

CHAPTER TWENTY-FIVE

There were white lace curtains across the wide front windows of the Lavigne Restaurant, with gold lettering announcing 'Restaurant Français' on the glass in a grandiose script. Above it was a sign with the name, La Lavigne, in even more florid lettering, red on white, with a gold trim.

Walker and Blades strode in and swept interrogative looks about them, to the discomfiture of a couple at a corner table, a middle-aged man with a younger woman, who may have been on an assignation. The white lace theme continued onto the tablecloths. On the walls were mirrors with ornate gold frames. A brass gasolier provided an intimate atmosphere with its subdued lighting.

A man whom Blades assumed to be the restaurant manager advanced towards them; he was middle-aged, with a waistcoat tight across a paunch, a neat moustache, and greasy, black, thinning swept-back hair streaked with grey.

'Good evening,' Walker boomed. 'My name is Inspector Walker of Scotland Yard.' At this, Walker produced his card. 'We'd like to speak to Arthur Platt.'

Blades looked at the manager.

'Well, it's not me,' the man replied. Blades noticed his accent suggested not French origins but Leeds.

At that moment, a young man appeared from the kitchens bearing a tray laden with plates. He was thin, with dark curly hair and an insincerely subservient expression on his face.

The manager turned to him. 'Arthur,' he said. 'What have you been up to? There's a policeman here who wants to talk to you. You'd better give your customers that lot and go through the back with them for this.'

'I haven't done nothing,' Arthur spluttered as he stopped to take this in, then resumed his task with a mutter before returning and leading Walker and Blades into the kitchen area.

Blades noted it was clean. There was a woman over the stove, stirring at a pot, of which there was a large number more on shelves behind her, with stacks of plates on others. She was about the same age as the manager and Blades supposed they might be husband and wife. She was stout and had the lined face of the habitually busy.

'It's the police,' Arthur said. 'They want to talk to me. I was told to bring them in here.'

The woman gave him a questioning look.

'I dunno what it's about,' Arthur said. 'I expect they'll tell me.'

'Never mind me,' she said to Walker and Blades. 'I have to get on with this.' Her accent wasn't French either.

'Of course,' Walker said.

'So, what am I supposed to have done?' Arthur asked.

'You tell us,' Walker said.

Arthur looked back at him but said nothing.

'Do you know a young woman called Anne Talbot?' Blades asked.

Arthur's reply was instant. 'That bint. Yes, I do.'

'You're dating her,' Walker said.

'I was. She chucked me.'

'Why?' Walker asked.

'Ask her,' Arthur said. 'But she didn't think I was good enough for her. Her with her hoity-toity airs, but common as muck herself.'

'You resented that, then?' Blades asked.

'A bit. Why are you asking?'

'She's dead,' Walker asked. 'Found murdered on Birtleby beach.'

'I read about that,' the woman over the stove said.

'That was Anne?' Arthur said. 'And you think I–' Arthur said. 'What a sick thing to think. I dated her for a while, for God's sake, then she threw me over. So I started dating another girl.'

'He often does,' the woman said. 'They come and go. Why not? Young folk having fun. Finding out about life. It's normal.'

'It could be,' Blades said.

'But some young men can take things the wrong way,' Walker said. 'Where were you on Thursday, 19 August?'

'That's when she was killed?' the woman asked.

'Yes.'

'It couldn't have been him,' the woman said. 'He was here working all week, including that day. He'd never have managed to get there and back, do that and his work.'

'You can swear to that?' Walker asked.

'Yes. So can Jack. That's the man you met on the way in. So can anyone Arthur served that day. And Arthur wouldn't have the gumption to murder anybody, never mind manage to escape afterwards. He can't wait at table without being reminded of this and that.'

Arthur gave her an annoyed look, but bit back a reply, probably out of relief he had his alibi.

'So, what was this Anne Talbot like?' Blades asked.

'She was pretty, and fun,' Arthur said. 'I liked her. But she was a tease. It was a job getting a kiss out of her. I'm sorry for her ending up like that. But I can see she could annoy someone.'

'Did she say to you she was going to Birtleby?' Walker asked.

'No.'

'She didn't talk about anyone she might have been going to meet there?'

'She didn't talk about it when she was dating me, though that's a while back.' Arthur screwed up his face in thought. 'And I can't think of anyone she might have been meeting either.'

'Did she talk about other boys, other men she knew?'

'Not to me. It would've annoyed me.'

'I suppose it would.'

As they had reached the end of that line of questioning, Walker and Blades turned and left. Outside the restaurant, Blades asked Walker, 'D'you like him for it?'

'Wish I did. But no. The alibi's solid. And he's wet.'

'His chef friend was quick in giving him the alibi.'

Walker looked at Blades. 'You think there's something going on between that pair?'

'She might have a soft spot for him. Like a son to her.'

'The local force will check the alibi. If it's good there ought to be plenty of witnesses to it.'

They trudged down the street. They had found out all they were going to in Leeds.

CHAPTER TWENTY-SIX

It was a sunlit afternoon and, as light streamed through branches, it caused a dappled effect. Harry and Bob were walking along a woodland path, under plane and sycamore trees resplendent with summer leaves. The afternoon was warm, and there was a light breeze. Their alibi was what had given the police pause for thought when interviewing Harry and Bob, and the two men were mindful of the need to make sure of Nancy, which was why they found themselves on the other path out of Birtleby, the one that led to the berry-picking areas where they'd arranged to meet up with her.

'The score's this,' Harry was saying. 'Someone did it, they need to make an arrest and, if they can make a case against us, they will.'

Bob kicked a stone which shot off into undergrowth. 'It wasn't us. Why can't they arrest the ones who did it?'

Harry pulled a face. 'I agree. And I don't think their witnesses are enough by themselves, not if this alibi holds up.'

'We didn't admit we were there.'

Harry shot him a meaningful look. 'If they take it further, we keep on denying it. We go on about being at

Blackforth with Nancy. They can't know exactly when the crime was done. Not to the minute, or even the hour.'

'How do you know?'

'Because I read it in the paper. All there is to go on with these things is rigor mortis and body temperature. In the murder trials you read about, doctors usually disagree about when the murder happened.'

Bob gave him a wondering stare. 'You read it in the paper?'

'A pity you can't. You might learn a thing or two.'

'I know no one gets a medical degree from studying a newspaper. You don't know as much as you think.'

Harry frowned back. 'Maybe enough. Look, we spent the afternoon with Nancy, and we laughed and joked all over the place with her. That's behaving in an innocent way. You'd think that would help.'

'I don't know how they think murderers behave.'

'On the Front, everyone I knew was totally screwed up after killing someone. They weren't in the mood to buy ice creams.'

They turned into a glade by a stream and saw Nancy, bent down over a bush, picking berries. She spotted them at the same time, waved, and smiled. They waved back.

Bob was thinking of a time when he had killed someone. He had raised the rifle, fired, and a German soldier had fallen, writhed, then gone still. It had felt unreal that a life had been ended by pulling a trigger, and hard to comprehend the relationship between the movement of a finger and the fact of death, as if it ought to take more than that. When next Bob ought to have been aiming and firing, his whole body had shaken. The soldier beside him had to do the shooting for both, and Bob had been too ashamed to look him in the face for days after that. Not that, when he saw Nancy, Bob had any idea why he was thinking about this. The war intruded, wherever you were.

'Want a berry?' Nancy said, offering him one. She started to put it in his mouth as if feeding a pet, then took it back. 'Smile, please,' she said. 'Sad face doesn't get.'

Bob stood there for a moment or two before he managed the appropriate smile, though he looked abashed, as if the whole thing was silly. Then she gave him the berry.

Nancy held out one for Harry too. He took it with a nonchalant look on his face, then smacked his lips. 'Lovely,' he said, but his eyes held coldness. There was no disguising the fact that Harry and Bob were on edge.

'You two feeling all right?' Nancy said. 'You look scary.'

'Scared,' Harry corrected. 'We've been the victims of police intimidation.'

'No, really?' She raised her eyebrows with exaggeration. 'They've caught up with you? About time.' And she gave them a mocking grin.

'It's no joking matter,' Bob said.

The grin left Nancy's face. 'What happened?'

'They think we did it,' Harry said. 'That girl, Anne Talbot, they think we killed her.'

'Why?'

'Because we were seen talking to her that afternoon.'

'It would be odd if no one did see you talking to a girl on her own, a pair like you.'

'You know we didn't do it.' Bob's stare at Nancy was intense.

She looked at him, puzzled.

'You will say we were with you that afternoon?' Harry said.

'You were, not all of it, but yes, you were.'

'We had a great time,' Bob said. 'We met you at about half two and walked about at Blackforth.'

Nancy thought about it. 'It would have been about then.'

'You will tell them that,' Harry said.

'If it comes to it and I'm asked, I can hardly deny it.' Nancy thought again. 'You were a right laugh. You didn't behave like two people who'd done a murder; and there was no blood on you.'

Harry and Bob looked at each other in a more relaxed way.

'We'll help you pick lots of berries,' Bob said.

'You'd better.' She picked a blackberry and held it out to Harry. 'Want one?'

He took it gladly. Bob had started thinking of a soldier he had known at the Front, who had been the same as any of the rest to begin with, till killing made him callous. He would pop his rifle over the top, first thing in the morning as per regulation, and, in his case, often hit someone because he was a good shot. After that, he would roll a cigarette and start talking about the movies or telling jokes – as if nothing had happened. In the end, he became weird, obsessed with the next opportunity for a shot, so much so they gave him special training to make him a sniper. Then, Bob lost track of him, but he had known him long enough to know it wasn't true that everyone was upset after a kill. But Harry didn't kill Anne Talbot, did he?

CHAPTER TWENTY-SEVEN

The house Nancy worked in as a maid was a Victorian stone villa set on a slope above the shore, with bay windows overlooking a small garden behind a well-trimmed privet hedge. Nancy had a feeling of security when she returned there. The family who owned it came from a prosperous background in wool, and they lived as gentlefolk, with a saloon car out front, a full household of servants, and children away at boarding school. The master and mistress kept the house well ordered, with household provisions of quality delivered with regularity, all bills timely paid, and servants who tended to stay.

Nancy slipped her jacket off and slung it on a hook behind the door in the servants' hall. The cook, a large woman with a ballooning apron, and hair pulled up under a cap, was kneading dough in the kitchen with large hands and straining elbows. Patricia Wentworth, for such was her name, glanced in Nancy's direction and grunted. Patricia was known to be grumpy when working, but there was a kindly turn to her lips, which suggested the different personality she showed in more leisurely moments.

The kitchen was a large working space, plain in décor, with grey floor tiles and a black kitchen range. The expansive dresser with its rows of shining plates gave decoration in a functional way, as did the cooking utensils with their copper gleam, stacked on the high wooden shelves on the walls. The most striking aspect of the kitchen was the cleanliness, which spoke of the industry of servants.

Elspeth was seated at the kitchen table with her sister, Amy. As Amy worked there, Elspeth often visited.

'Good to see you, Elspeth,' Nancy said to her before asking if there was anything left in the teapot.

'There will be,' Amy said.

'I always enjoy a visit,' Elspeth said. 'You've such a grand servants' hall. But then, anywhere's posh compared to the Victoria.'

'It's just the kitchen,' Amy replied.

The cup, saucer, and tea-plate Amy took from the dresser and offered to Nancy were fashioned in the same pink, floral bone-china as Elspeth and Amy's own. Amy poured tea and offered sugar, milk, and the customary biscuit. Nancy sat on a wooden bench beside the table and smiled with her politest expression.

'Thanks,' Nancy said, picking up the largest ginger nut. 'I need this.'

They exchanged demure smiles and raised teacups with the elegance of ladies as they sipped from them.

'I knew a man who stayed at the Victoria once,' Amy said. 'He liked it.'

'Wasn't a dipso, was he?' Elspeth sneered.

'You ought to try for a place here,' Amy said.

'It's too much like hard work,' Elspeth replied. 'I don't know how you lot manage. I had a job as a maid once and I know what you do.'

'At least we don't have men pestering us.'

'We should be so lucky in the Victoria.'

'Talking of which...' At this, heads turned towards Nancy. Amy's cup paused halfway to her mouth. 'I've just been berry-picking with Harry and Bob and a charming pair of young gentlemen they are.'

An alarmed look appeared on Elspeth's face. 'It's not long since they were in the Victoria,' she said, 'and that's what I was meaning to talk about with Amy.' Eyes swivelled in Elspeth's direction. Amy placed her cup in its saucer. 'They were in a foul mood.'

'They were?' Nancy asked.

'Why?' Amy wanted to know.

'I couldn't hear everything they said because they were trying to talk low, but they'd been questioned by the police,' Elspeth told them.

'They said that to me as well,' Nancy said.

'Bob was fairly going at that Harry,' Elspeth said. 'I hope they cheered up before they met up with you.'

'He was going at Harry?' Nancy said.

'Bob was telling Harry he knew Harry had done it.'

'What?' Patricia's attention was roused and she left her dough to take care of itself.

'He said so?' Amy was incredulous.

'Harry denied it but Bob wasn't convinced.'

As Nancy stared at Elspeth, she wrung her hands.

'So, they did see her that afternoon?' Nancy asked.

'Oh yeah, and Bob said he'd left her with Harry.'

'Bloody liars,' Nancy said. 'They told me they didn't know her.'

Patricia tried to return to kneading the dough but stopped and turned back to them. 'Have I met this pair?'

'I don't think so,' Amy said.

'I saw them later that afternoon. At Blackforth Castle,' Nancy told them.

'How did they look?'

'No different from usual, suspicious.'

'Young men around here always look shifty,' Elspeth said. 'That's because they're always after the same thing.'

'Those two haven't behaved bad with me,' Nancy said.

'I'd use that rolling pin on them if they tried to take liberties with me,' Patricia said, pointing at it with one hand, her broad face serious, the other hand on her ample hip.

'They've tried it on with me before,' Elspeth said. 'At the Hippodrome last Thursday – and you know how public it is. I had to walk away from them. A girl needs to be warned.'

Nancy looked doubtful.

'It's what everyone says about them,' Elspeth said. 'They can't keep their hands to themselves. And they don't half get annoyed when you don't give out.'

Amy became annoyed with her sister. 'You give all the men a bad name,' she said fiercely.

'It's surprising how many of them deserve it,' Elspeth replied.

'Yeah?'

'If you get murdered by Harry and Bob,' Elspeth continued, 'don't blame me. Oh, sorry. You won't be able to.'

Nancy wasn't listening as she was puzzling over something. 'How can they have been at Blackforth with me and on the beach with the girl at the same time?' she asked.

'They were with you at Blackforth?' Elspeth asked.

'Definitely.'

'They must have gone there later.'

'They said to make sure I said I was with them and that would give them a witness.'

'They did?'

'Yes.'

'If they're setting up an alibi, that sounds guilty,' Elspeth said.

'Does it?' Nancy said. 'What difference does it make if I say they were with me if it happened at a different time?'

'It depends on how accurate they can be about the time of the murder,' Elspeth suggested.

'It could confuse the jury?' Amy said.

'And if I say they were with me it helps them get away with it?' Nancy said.

'Only if they did it,' Amy replied.

'I don't want to help anyone get away with murder.'

'You know what people round here would think of you,' Elspeth said, her voice low, her eyes intent, 'if they thought you were covering up for a murderer.'

'I don't fancy that,' Nancy said. She looked round the trio but could see no reassurance there. 'You say you heard Harry say he did it?' she said to Elspeth.

'They were talking ever so low, so you couldn't hear everything they said, but Bob told Harry he knew he'd done it, and he's Harry's best friend. They were both with her. What do you think happened?'

'Another girl could be done in if that murderer's not caught,' Amy said.

'Maybe one of us,' Elspeth said. 'Don't cover up for them. We've got to protect ourselves.'

'As I was at Blackforth, that's what I have to tell the police if I'm asked,' Nancy said.

'People could think you helped them do it,' Amy whispered.

Nancy looked askance. 'They couldn't think that!'

'Oh yes they could,' Elspeth said.

'And covering up for them's a crime,' Patricia said with her tone of authority. 'That would put you in the dock with them. You don't want that.'

'Did anyone else see you berry-picking?' Elspeth asked.

Nancy thought. 'I don't remember anyone.'

'They could accuse you of making up the whole thing,' Patricia said. 'You've got to be careful here, girl.'

'They could think I was lying and I could be hanged too?'

'It could happen,' Patricia said.

There was silence as Nancy sat with her brows drawn together in thought while the other three stared at her. Nancy's experience of life was limited not only because of age but circumstance and opportunity. She had never been further from Birtleby than Blackforth, and, once, Linfrith.

Amy poured her more tea but Nancy ignored it, and when Amy offered more to the others they refused, their minds occupied with weightier matters.

Nancy started to talk. 'You know—' Then she stopped, and the others waited, and she started talking again. 'Those guys had a dreadful time at the Front.'

'Yes?' Elspeth said. Her eyes sparked with annoyance.

'I know Harry did,' Nancy said. 'He told me about it.' Then she paused. Amy had a doubtful look on her face as her lips started to move before stopping, as she decided against making the remark she had thought of. Nancy continued, 'When he was in the trenches with all that mud and his friends falling beside him and the guns firing and the huge rats he says they shared trenches with—' She stopped talking, and her eyes glazed as she thought to herself. She nibbled a biscuit, and sipped tea, then said with a sudden firmness, 'If I were him, I'd hate anyone who didn't have to go to the trenches.'

'Did he say he hated anyone who wasn't out there?' Elspeth said.

'He said he did.'

'But everybody had a bad time,' Amy said. 'It doesn't mean they have to murder anyone.'

'I wish I hadn't handed out those white feathers,' Nancy said, 'when I think of the men who came back with arms and legs missing. Take Helen Dobbs who lived next door to us, her husband was dead, and she had only the one son. Alex was for coming out for a conchy and the time we gave him. We never let up till he'd volunteered. He was only out two weeks when he caught it. And now she's got no one.'

'I handed them out,' Elspeth said. 'I didn't know what I was doing either.'

'And if they hadn't fought for us,' Patricia said, 'the Germans would have been over here, murdering and raping us. There was a war going on. You were part of the war effort. You've nothing to be ashamed of.'

'You think?' Nancy said. 'Maybe. Maybe not. I thought it was the thing to do at the time, and they did go out, and they fought for us, and if we're not grateful to them, we've no sense.'

'What you don't see is what it did to them inside,' Amy said.

'What do you mean?' Nancy asked.

'It destroyed something in some, I reckon,' Amy said, 'like pity and normality. Some of them are still out there in their Armageddon. That's what some of them said it was; like the last bloody battle.'

Nancy sipped tea, her finger out in a lady-like manner as she held herself as straight as ever but with a hardened expression on her face that was new. She continued considering what she ought to do. She wondered if she'd just wandered into a battlefield of her own.

CHAPTER TWENTY-EIGHT

'I'm here to help with your murder inquiry,' the woman said to Constable Hodgkins in a stentorian voice. She was a large middle-aged lady with piercing eyes, dressed in a grey linen jacket, with a red fox fur round her shoulders. Hodgkins' response was to reach with alacrity for his sharpest pencil and turn to a fresh page in his notebook.

She continued, 'A dreadful thing, of course, to happen to a young woman. You work hard and go on holiday to relax and all that happens is you get attacked – and in a quiet place like this.'

Hodgkins waited for her to reach the point.

'Young people. They work so hard and try to make their way in the world and look what happens.'

'You said you had information for us,' Hodgkins said.

'I've more than that. I've your latest clue,' she said. 'I'm a butterfly collector; I'd forgotten to bring my box with me and I was fascinated by your common blue. Don't you think they're such a pretty colour? Jewels of the sky, wouldn't you say?'

'It hadn't occurred to me,' Hodgkins muttered, 'but I'm sure you're right.' He put the pencil and notebook down, not without disappointment.

'They're so fascinating you could eat them, which would be silly. I'd nothing to put one in, so I looked around and I was near your army camp. That's important, isn't it?'

Hodgkins replied, 'I suppose, but in relation to what?'

'And there it was, among the shrubbery, just the right size for my purposes: a Player's tin. Isn't that remarkable?'

'Is it?'

'If you've ever scratched around all over the place, looking for something to put a butterfly in, you'd think so. You usually can't find anything. So I opened it and that's when I saw it all. And it was extraordinary.'

'What?' Hodgkins said.

'Didn't I tell you? I thought I had. I'm sure I did. Oh, never mind. In the tin was a white, lady's handkerchief. And the handkerchief was embroidered in pink in one corner with the initials AT. What do you think of that?'

'AT?' Hodgkins said.

'Anne Talbot. It must be her handkerchief, and there was a whole collection of other things.'

'Do young ladies keep handkerchiefs in cigarette tins?' Hodgkins asked.

'Not in my experience. Anne Talbot seems to have done, or whoever took these things from her. And it was just outside the garrison boundary, so you should be looking for a soldier. You've got enough of them round here to question.'

'And do you have the tin with you?' Hodgins asked.

At this, the lady took the Player's tin from her bag and placed it in front of Hodgkins. She opened it for him and he gazed with puzzlement at the odd jumble inside before she took out the handkerchief and spread it in front of him, pointing at the letters AT in their pink thread, which had Hodgkins nodding. Then she displayed a fine gold chain, a scatter of russet and grey pebbles, and a silver, shiny fifty-centime coin.

'They're the kind of pebbles you find on the Ridges,' she said. 'I collected a few like this along there.'

Hodgkins picked up the coin and turned it in his fingers. 'She must have been fond of French things,' he said.

'You might know. I don't,' replied the lady.

Later, after Walker and Blades had been shown the evidence and turned it all this way and that, it was shown to Anne's mother. Walker and Blades had invited her over to the station and she had brought Eda with her again, presumably for moral support. When the tin, into which everything had been replaced, was put in front of her, Irene stared at it and pondered.

'I've never seen Anne with a cigarette tin like that,' Irene said.

'She didn't smoke, did she?' Eda said.

'She said she didn't,' Irene said. 'If she did, it was with friends when she was out and about. I never saw her with a cigarette. I didn't want her to smoke. I think it's a filthy habit for young ladies and I told her so over and over. And if she did, I don't think she would smoke Player's Navy Cut. That's a man's cigarette.'

'The tin may not be the significant find,' Walker said. 'What could be important is what's inside it.' And he lifted the lid and took out the handkerchief which he spread out on the table.

'May I inspect it?' Irene said.

'By all means,' Walker said.

Irene picked it up and turned it over and around, tutted, and handed it to Eda to inspect.

'Do you recognize it?' Walker said.

'No,' Irene replied. Then a thoughtful look came over her face as she took it back from Eda and looked at it. 'But I don't know. Maybe. It's a bit like one she had,' Irene replied, 'but I couldn't say for sure. Where was it found?'

'Just outside the army camp,' Walker said. 'A member of the public brought it in. We assume it was the souvenir of a soldier.'

'The tin must belong to him,' Irene said. 'Anne didn't have much to do with soldiers that I know of, although she could have met one here. There was one about a year ago but he hasn't been around for a long time. So, you think these could have been things a soldier took from Anne after he murdered her in order to keep them as souvenirs?'

'Possibly,' Walker replied.

'How ghastly,' she said. Irene fingered the bracelet but said nothing else.

'Is this Anne's bracelet?' Blades asked.

'If it was, I've never seen it before.'

'You don't recognize any of the rest?' Walker said.

'No.'

'A pity. Still, she might have owned that handkerchief?' Walker asked.

'Maybe. Or any of it, I suppose, if it comes to it, but I'm sorry I can't be definite. I'm not much help.'

'Still, we won't dismiss this tin. We have had a couple of soldiers suggested to us, and this lot was hidden just outside the camp. We'll have them in for questioning again,' Walker said. 'You never know. They might say something, admit it even. We'll continue to follow up everything. We will catch whoever did this. You can be sure of that. Someone will have seen something and someone will have seen something else and we'll find out who this was. They won't get away with it.'

CHAPTER TWENTY-NINE

The company of soldiers was struggling to maintain pace as they neared the end of their ten-mile forced-hike with full kitbag. Wind cut through clothes as boots tramped over moorland. Grey clouds bowled along, as if attempting to keep up with them, and the rough grass, bracken, and heather stretched out behind. As the men neared the camp on the cliff edge, the sea's greys and greens became clear. Satisfaction crept into the men's faces as they neared the barbed wire and steel gate at the entry.

'Halt.' There was nothing welcoming in the command of the sergeant major who waited for them.

They stopped and held themselves erect, staring ahead, but with relief on their faces, as the sergeant major strutted up and down the line to inspect them.

'Shoulders back,' he barked at one. 'What are you breathing heavy for?' he snapped at another. 'That was a Sunday afternoon stroll.' He glared at them one by one then roared, 'Dismissed.'

The men sighed as they unslung packs from shoulders and collapsed into a heap of limbs, before flipping out cigarettes and matches.

The sergeant major strode over to George Wilkinson, leaned close, and hissed, 'Not you,' before hauling himself upright again. 'Attention,' he bellowed. With disbelief, George pulled himself up and adopted the required stance. The sergeant major marched over to Andy Hanson and repeated the performance. As George and Andy glanced over, they could see two military policemen standing by the gate, their bony heads prominent as they glared at them. George had no idea why anyone would want to question them again but it didn't surprise him.

'We'll take over,' one of the MPs shouted to the sergeant major. 'Kit-bags,' he yelled at George and Andy. 'On your shoulders.' The two soldiers heaved them up. 'Marching on the spot quick-time. I said quick-time. This isn't a waltz.'

George and Andy suffered this for a full five minutes and felt it a miracle they managed it after the hike. George felt anger seething in his face.

'Halt.' The command did come in the end, but the soldiers knew it would be inappropriate to sink into the heap they longed for, and held themselves at attention even before the order came for them to do that. The MP glared at them for a minute before delivering the next order.

'And straight ahead to that truck,' he said.

They staggered over to it, unslung the packs, and threw them on board, before following them and allowing themselves the luxury of slumping onto the wooden seats. They muttered the word 'buggers' with feeling, though they hoped it didn't carry.

When their sergeant major strode over and leaned forward, they turned to stare at a gloating face, as he hissed, 'You've been found out. All that hanging about the seafront chasing after women. It's caught up with you. You're wanted in the police station about the murder of that young woman. And don't tell me you didn't do it. Everyone knows what you two are like.'

George and Andy spluttered and voiced frank expressions, but all the sergeant major did was stride away. The MPs climbed up into the cabin of the truck and relaxed onto upholstered seats that were sheltered behind glass and warmed by the heat of the engine, while George and Andy rode in the back where the wind could have a go at them.

'Bastards,' George said. 'They've knackered us to soften us up for those police inspectors.'

'They did it well.'

'Just because they can't pin that murder on anyone else. I know what I'd like to do to that MP and that sergeant major.'

'I'd like to rip his mouth off with shrapnel and see if he can still make sarcastic comments then.'

'Or a mine up his backside would be good.'

'He'd probably enjoy it.'

George laughed, Andy joined in and this turned into guffaws. One of the MPs turned his head towards them, then signalled with his hand to his colleague that the prisoners were barking mad. George started to pull a face in return before changing his mind, but he did laugh again in a manner that suggested anything but humour, and Andy joined in.

'Don't know why they'd accuse us of wanting to murder anyone,' George said.

'Mystery that,' Andy agreed. 'I'll strangle the one on the left if you take the one on the right.'

After a long ride, they arrived at the police station, an ugly brick building which the MPs marched them into. They stood in front of a desk while the sergeant studied them.

'Andrew Hanson and George Wilkinson?' he said, then, as they nodded, went on to say, 'I daresay we can find an uncomfortable cell for you.'

The sergeant gestured to a door and took them through it into the corridor leading to the cells. Their cell was brick with nothing in it but a couple of bunks and a barred window looking out onto the bare police station yard. He slammed the door behind them and locked it.

George and Andy heaved themselves onto the bunks, stretched themselves out and sighed. 'If they're going to hang us I wish they'd get on with it,' Andy said. 'I could see this crap far enough.'

'You could get your wish,' George said.

'I know,' Andy said. He stared at a brick, shut his eyes, then curled up to wait. As he had no alternative, George did the same.

CHAPTER THIRTY

Blades was looking at George Wilkinson with curiosity. Was this their man? George was back in the interview room, shifting on his seat and looking anywhere but in the direction of the inspectors. They'd given George half an hour in the cell before bringing him in here, in the hope of putting him on edge. Blades noted the dullness in George's eyes, and beneath that, resentment. But Blades wasn't hopeful. This felt like fishing.

'What've you brought me here again for?' George demanded. 'I haven't done anything.'

Walker led the questioning. 'You annoyed a lot of women when you were pretending to sell lavender.'

Questions were bursting into Blades' head but he schooled patience into himself.

'Good-quality posies,' George said. 'Sweet-smelling. Pretty. You can make extra money selling them. Women like flowers. And we like women. We chat them up for the same reason every guy does.'

'Do you follow a lot of girls?' Walker asked.

'Quite often, women want to be followed,' George replied.

Blades considered what his wife would have thought of this remark, then made himself think objectively.

Walker ignored George's response and continued, 'We've another witness saying she saw Anne Talbot quarrelling with a soldier on the beach.'

George scowled. 'I've told you,' he said. 'We were selling lavender on the seafront and we were nowhere near the beach.'

'But you walk back to camp that way?'

George started to say something, then closed his mouth.

'You admitted that the last time,' Walker stated.

'So ask something new?'

'And it's confirmed by about six different witnesses.'

'Why am I having to go through this again?'

'It's funny how evidence keeps turning up,' Walker continued. 'A tin's been found, near the camp, by the entrance used by soldiers to sneak out without permission or to sneak in when they're late back from furlough. So, we know it was a soldier Anne Talbot was involved with.'

George had turned his head in Walker's direction and Blades registered the surprise on George's face.

'She wasn't murdered with a tin, was she?' George asked.

'You know what was in that tin, don't you?' Walker said.

'No.'

'There was Anne Talbot's handkerchief, and her bracelet,' Blades said. 'They were stashed so a soldier could pick them up any time; in a hollow, under shrubbery, beside the spot where the fence has been partly torn down. You know the place, don't you?'

'No.' George looked from one to the other, then back. 'It sounds like a good clue,' he said, 'but it doesn't prove who the soldier was, and, like I said, it wasn't me.'

'He was from the camp,' Walker said. We have evidence from your commanding officer you were off-base at the time. And we've had complaints from young women about you being aggressive.'

'I don't get aggressive with anyone,' George said. 'When a woman's fed up with a guy, she makes that sort of thing up to get at him. She says this man raised his fist to her, or that one threatened her, but it's a lie.'

'We're policemen,' Blades said. 'We often have to deal with that sort of accusation, and, usually, it turns out to be true.'

George looked furious and he began blustering. 'You can't pin this on me,' he said. He pointed at Walker with anger. 'I don't know any Anne Talbot. I never met her. And I didn't murder her – or anybody else. You shouldn't be questioning me like this. Go out and catch the man who did it. That's what you ought to be doing.'

Walker said nothing as he watched George seethe.

Then George said, 'Andy, he's the one who annoys women. He's the one you should be questioning, not me. I've been telling Andy I don't want to go selling lavender with him anymore because of that. His chat's no good. It's offensive. And I wasn't brought up to behave like that.'

'You're saying Andy did the murder?' Walker asked.

George said nothing, just stared ahead of him, before blurting, 'I don't know anything about the murder. Like I told you, we didn't meet up with any Anne Talbot. I wouldn't even recognize her. Please believe me.'

Walker looked at George hard. 'The report on your marlin spike is in and there were traces of blood on it.'

'I should have cleaned it better after using it against the Bosches.'

'It is human blood,' Blades added.

'But you couldn't say it was Anne's.'

Walker paused. 'No.'

'So you've no reason to question me.'

'You haven't been skinning rabbits.'

George gaped back at them, looked as if he were about to reply, then changed his mind. Walker and Blades looked at him carefully, then Walker stood up, opened the door and called for Hodgkins, who came in and led George to a cell. Then Walker paced back and forward two or three times before he stopped to look at Blades. 'What do you think about him?' Walker said.

'He and Andy went across to the Ridges about four. It fits in with the time of death. And he has a guilty look about him,' Blades added.

'If you sat me in an interview room in front of two detectives, I might,' Walker said, which Blades doubted. 'But he might have done it. Anyway, we haven't got enough on him and he's going to keep quiet.'

'But we do have witnesses?'

'Who can mostly just place George and Andy on the seafront along with a lot of other people, so there's no reason why our friend shouldn't admit to being there.'

'You think we should drop it?'

'We'll interview Andy and see if we get anything from him,' Walker said.

Walker called Hodgkins back and sent for Andy. Walker tapped his fingers. When Andy arrived, he looked as if he had been disintegrating while waiting. There was a hesitancy in his step and a tic on his right cheek. He slumped into the seat, leaned forward and held out his hands as if pleading. 'We didn't do it,' he moaned. 'We talked to lots of girls on the seafront but I don't remember this Anne Talbot. There are a lot of girls who sort of fit the description but none of the ones we talked to were Anne Talbot to the best of my knowledge. I don't even like George. I'm fed up with him because of the way he annoys girls, perfectly nice girls whom he doesn't even know. But he didn't kill anybody while he was with me and we were together all afternoon, so he couldn't have.'

Then he ran out of things to say and his mouth closed in an expression of self-pity. He looked as if he might splutter something else, but changed his mind, as his eyes pleaded first at Walker, then at Blades.

Walker and Blades looked across at each other and there was doubt in Walker's eyes now, which didn't surprise Blades. From the tone in Andy's voice, Andy didn't expect to be believed, but that was what made what he said so believable.

'Do you know anything about a tin?' Blades asked.

Andy's mouth gaped. 'No,' he said.

Blades thought George could be a murderer because there was anger there, and stupidity and cussedness, but he doubted if Andy had it in him. Blades thought of other inquiries of Walker's he'd heard of, which had been promising but hadn't led to a conviction, and thought maybe this investigation would turn out like those. He looked across at his fellow policeman, his forehead furrowed in thought, and wondered what he planned to do next.

CHAPTER THIRTY-ONE

When the next clue turned up, it had nothing to do with soldiers. Midway through the morning, when Blades was working in the office, writing up a report, Muriel Robinson strode in, her majestic manner marred by a slight shake to her hand when she laid the object it held on Blades' desk. This was a red, leatherette-bound diary secured by a small brass padlock.

'I was sure you would already have this,' she said. 'I thought it would be with the things Anne carried about with her because she was so secretive about it. I only saw it once, when I had to go into her room, and she was writing in it then, and closed it when she saw me, so, knowing girls, I assumed it was about her love life and didn't ask her about it. But it has turned up.' Her look was triumphant, and there was a generosity in her face as if she had brought a priceless object. 'I feel so bad,' she went on, 'about not bringing it more quickly but I didn't know where she kept it.' And the lines round her mouth turned into a simper which was at odds with what Blades took to be her usual manner.

'Where was it?' Blades asked, thinking back to Anne's room, which he had searched.

'Would you believe it?' Muriel said. 'She kept it in the middle of the spare blankets and I don't mean under the one on the top, I mean right in the centre of the blanket in the middle. They're kept in the cupboard at the back with the other spare linen and pillows.'

Blades remembered looking through that cupboard; he had lifted everything up and looked underneath the pile of bedclothes. He muttered to himself. He had made a mistake.

As the door to his office was open, Walker had been able to hear this exchange. He walked in and picked up the book. 'Anne's diary?'

'Yes,' Muriel said, turning to him. 'But I don't know what's in it. It's locked.'

'And there's no sign of a key?' Walker said.

'No'

'Wonder what happened to that. Still, it's a cheap lock. It won't be difficult to open.'

He beamed at Muriel. 'We could hope this tells us the name of her killer, though it's not usually so easy.'

Muriel smiled back. 'Well, I'll leave it,' she said. 'I have things to do. We're busy.'

'People wanting to see where Anne stayed, I suppose?' Blades asked.

'Some of them, not that anyone will want to stay in Anne's room when it becomes free.'

'As we've said, it's technically still a crime scene, even if the murder didn't take place there. We'll tell you when you can let it again.'

'And I won't be able to.'

'You might be able to charge more for staying in it,' Blades said.

'D'you think so?' Muriel said, and turned her face towards him with a flash of eagerness that quickly disappeared. 'I'm inclined to think the opposite. But we've run out of eggs and I need to pick up milk, so I'd better be off.'

'If you find anything else, Mrs Robinson, please bring it in,' Walker said, 'and thank you again.'

She smiled back and left. Walker and Blades stood, looking at the diary. Blades turned it over to check if the back would tell them anything, which it didn't. Blades looked at Walker, then took a paper knife from a drawer and levered at the lock which was slight enough to yield to the thin brass blade. The two men found themselves looking at the first page of the diary which said: 'The Secret Thoughts and Loves of Anne Talbot.'

Blades and Walker both raised their eyebrows.

'A literary bent?' Blades said.

'Sounds like fantasy.'

'Hopefully not.'

Walker took the book from Blades and his fingers flicked through the pages. He said, 'Quite a few male names. Might suggest she was a goer.' Walker started reading, slowly, because he didn't want to miss anything, Blades assumed. Occasionally, he stopped and read a piece out. '"The office manager's called Ernest Mullen. He's middle-aged, with a paunch, sweaty skin and an enormous nose. His eyes follow you everywhere as if he's undressing you. He's said to have a wife but when he looks at me off-guard he looks as if he's suffering from dreadful temptation. His eyes linger forever over my chest. He's kept his hands to himself so far."' Walker looked across at Blades. 'Purple stuff, isn't it? I wonder if the poor man even glanced at her?'

'He could have done. She was pretty.'

'She enjoys the details. I'll bet you were in trouble if you didn't look her way.' Walker flicked over a page. 'There's a Frenchman here, Jean-Michel.'

'It's not that waiter who worked at that restaurant. He's not even French.'

'Arthur?' Walker replied. 'He called himself Alphonse, not Jean-Michel.' Then he read out from the diary. '"Out dancing at the Tivoli. Jean-Michel was so gallant. He knows the latest dances and leads you with such a dash." He doesn't sound like the lad we've heard of.' Walker turned another page. 'He sent her "a pound note, and cream powder for *your* pretty face"'. Walker turned another page. 'Some of this is fiction. "Jean-Michel is like the kind of French lord you read of in novels, who own a castle set high on a hill overlooking woodlands and a river sweeping down into a green valley."'

'He wasn't a servant?' Blades suggested.

'If he was as much as that. This is the writing of a schoolgirl, not a woman of the world.'

'Not a girl on the make?'

'Not at all.'

Walker turned over a few more pages. 'She broke up with the Frenchman when she discovered he was married. I don't suppose that would be motive for murdering her?'

'An extreme reaction, but it depends on how odd the Frenchman is. Where can we find him?'

'The Lavigne Restaurant in Leeds is mentioned here. We could go back there and ask, but he might not have anything to do with that place. Apart from the name and, presumably, the food, I didn't see anything French about the place.'

'There was a French centime in the tin.'

'That was odd.'

'Shouldn't we try to question him?'

'If we can find him. I'll get in touch with the Leeds police force and see if they can turn him up.'

'They might.'

'Or not. There is mention of a soldier here. I wonder if he fits in with the ones we know. And I see Harry and Bob's names here. If this tells us more about people we know were at or near the scene, that helps.'

'What does it say about Harry and Bob?'

'"Met two gallant young men on the beach. They are so scarred by the war. To think they fought for us and there are no opportunities for them when they come back.

It makes you feel guilty." She describes two young men in suits and one does sound like Bob. She even mentions their names.'

Blades grinned. 'And they're trying to say they didn't know her? Just that makes them look guilty.'

Walker riffled over more pages. 'I feel guilty reading things like this. Young girls and their fantasies. It's an intrusion reading them.'

Blades sighed as he took the diary from Walker and glanced through it. 'All girls like young men. It's dreadful to think she ended up being murdered because of that. Don't talk to strangers. It's what we tell young people, but it doesn't stop them.'

'Most people would say her mother was lax.'

'Letting her holiday by herself?' Blades said. 'Probably, though Anne sounds to have been a handful.'

'I wonder what Anne's feelings were for her mother? Perhaps she hated her. D'you think she was a rebel?'

'I don't know, but if she came here to meet a lover that diary might tell us.'

'It might,' Walker said as he took the diary back and flipped through more pages. 'I'll let you study this when I've finished with it. It's easy to miss something.'

CHAPTER THIRTY-TWO

With that glint in her eye and that jut to her jaw, this looked like a witness with things to say, Blades thought as he looked at Elspeth, though he also noted the shift from foot to foot and the tendency to pluck at the scarf round her shoulders.

Elspeth had just been ushered into the interview room at the police station, as she'd announced to Hodgkins she had come forward to give them information about their murder inquiry.

She was shown to the seat opposite Blades and Walker, and seated herself on the edge of it, though she held herself upright as she glanced from one face to another and back, unsure whom to address.

Blades noted the self-righteousness in the over-lipsticked mouth, and the vigorous use of powder. This was a young lady who looked as if she made an especial point of making herself appear glamorous, but who had a hardness in her face that suggested she wore that attractiveness as an armour. She had clear eyes, though, that suggested intelligence.

Walker introduced both himself and Blades, before continuing. 'You say you're a barmaid at the Victoria and you've information to give us about a couple of young men called Harry Barker and Bob Nuttall?'

Walker's look in Elspeth's direction was intense. Blades was conscious of hopeful anticipation and he supposed Walker felt much the same.

'Have you charged them yet?' Elspeth asked.

Blades looked at the quiver in her jaw and, as the question was a definite accusation, he was looking forward to finding out what lay behind it.

'Have you known them long?' Walker asked.

'A few months. They're always in the bar when they have the money, and there's a thing. They had far too much of that.'

'When?' Walker asked.

'Thursday. The day of the murder.'

There was a pause as Walker and Blades digested Elspeth's statement.

'What time on Thursday?' Walker asked.

'In the late afternoon, which was odd because they hadn't much when they were in at lunchtime, but when they came back they were treating everyone, and drinking whole pints of bass instead of halves, and smoking Turkish cigarettes.'

She looked at Walker and Blades with an expression of triumph. 'I remember it was Thursday because that's my afternoon off. Those two came into the bar about noon and lounged about smoking and drinking as usual. One of them asked me to go to the pictures with them.'

'Did you?' Walker asked.

Blades wondered if Elspeth was, despite her apparent intentions, about to provide Bob and Harry with an alibi for the time they had them down for Anne's murder.

'I didn't answer. I get fed up of telling the customers no, and that we only sell drink in the Victoria.'

'Quite right,' Walker said.

'They stayed till closing time, about two in the afternoon, then went out. Then Harry came back by himself and said, "Will you go to the Hippodrome tonight? I'll be back about seven." He doesn't give up that one. He has no sense.'

Seven in the evening? That was all right, Blades thought, as it meant they could still have been with Anne on the beach in the afternoon.

'Then, in the evening, I was sitting on the customers' side of the bar with a friend when Harry came in with that Bob Nuttall and sat with us. He treated me to a port wine, and my friend to a whisky and splash. The port wine was a shilling and the whisky and splash ten-pence halfpenny. As I say, he'd no money earlier on in the day, and was throwing about all this dosh in the evening.' Blades noticed there was a more relaxed look in the way she sat now, as if she was warming to her task, and there was the suggestion of a smile about the lips. 'And like I say, they were drinking the more expensive beer, not the cheapest, and they had more than one. They gave me a cigarette, and my friend and I couldn't help but notice they were Abdullahs. Nothing rough about them like the usual Woodbines they smoke, which I know because I've sold those to them at the Victoria. When they were in before, they were boasting they'd have money later, and there it was.'

Blades liked witnesses like this. You wound them up with a simple question and they talked until their clockwork brains had unwound. Elspeth had started leaning forward as if speaking to a close friend, and her voice was low as if she was trying not to be overheard, even though there was no reason for this.

'I didn't ask where they got the money from. It wasn't my business, but I wish I had now.'

'It would have been useful,' Walker said.

'How were they dressed?' Blades asked.

Elspeth considered. 'Harry was in a grey suit and felt hat, and Bob was... his suit was dark. He had brown shoes and a cap.'

'Did either of them carry a stick?' Walker asked.

'Bob always carries a stick. He limps. I don't know why. I haven't asked him. It's a wooden stick, quite heavy looking, with a brass knob.'

'How were they dressed in the evening?' Walker asked.

'The first part or the second? Bob changed for the Hippodrome. When I saw him in the Victoria, I told Bob the suit he was in looked filthy, and that he'd been a lot smarter at lunchtime. He'd got dirt all over one leg. What a way to turn yourself out to go out and about.'

'Did he say what had happened?'

'He said he'd been larking about with his friend, and Harry had pushed him right over, and he hadn't the time to change.'

'And you went with them to the Hippodrome?'

'Not with them, no, though we were there and we saw them. They were just behind us, Bob looking a lot smarter. We were in the two-shilling seats. I'm not quite certain of this but I think it was. They were in the same price seats. They went out in the interval but came back. I didn't look for them after that.'

That didn't matter, Blades thought, as the murder wasn't done in the evening, or they didn't have it down for then.

'And I've seen them since,' Elspeth said.

'When?' Walker asked.

'You lot had them in for questioning and I saw them after you let them out. I asked Bob about the suit he was wearing on the day of the murder but he clammed up.'

Different angles, different viewpoints, Blades thought. They told you a little and only a bit at a time, but you could hope these points would start to add up and give you the larger picture.

'And did I tell you they were in the bar the day the story of the murder came out in the newspaper?'

Walker started tapping his fingers and Blades frowned in his direction.

'You were there when they read that?' Walker said. 'How did they react?'

'Harry grabbed the paper from me so hard I thought it would rip. It didn't half annoy him when I told him the newspaper said a sailor had turned up who claimed he could identify the men. Has he identified Harry and Bob?'

Walker didn't answer this.

'And did I tell you Bob changed his hat that day as well? Isn't that odd?'

'I suppose,' replied Walker, who sounded surprised by the change of topic. Blades presumed Elspeth was feather-brained.

'Then after Harry had read the article, he stomped off out. He was in ever such a bad temper.'

'How did Bob react?' Blades asked.

'I had to help him read it, poor lamb, and the article did worry him. Then he said he'd better go after his friend, and he left.'

Her flow of words dried up, so she sat looking at the detectives, and they pondered what she'd said.

'Was any of that any help?' she asked.

'Yes,' Walker said. 'Thank you.'

She sat and looked at them for another moment, then, as if the key had been turned in her back again, Elspeth spoke quickly. 'They were in the bar yesterday,' she said, then stopped, looked around as if to check Bob and Harry weren't there, then continued, 'They were talking every so quietly at their table, and I was cleaning glasses at the end of the bar nearest to them because I wanted to hear what they were saying.' Then she stopped again.

'Yes?' Blades said.

'Bob was ever so angry with Harry. Harry was going on about Anne being no better than she ought to be and what did she mean turning him down, and it was no wonder he got annoyed with a tart like her. And I didn't hear everything he said because they were talking low, but that suggests they did it, doesn't it, or Harry did?'

'So, he admitted quarrelling with Anne and getting angry with her?'

'Yes.'

'Did he say he'd hit her?'

'Maybe. That could have been the bit I didn't hear, couldn't it? Anyway, he probably did, didn't he?'

'It sounds a possibility,' Walker said.

And Blades thought, yes, reasons for having Harry and Bob in again were mounting. In fact, with the number of corroborating witness statements they now had about the whereabouts of Bob and Harry on the afternoon, the proof they knew Anne Talbot, and the lies the pair had told about that, Blades wondered if Walker would think they had enough to do more than question them.

CHAPTER THIRTY-THREE

Bob and Harry strolled under the sycamore trees and by freshly mown grass as they meandered across the Links towards the shore. The walk then led them by awnings of varied hues, on the row of cafés and shops along the seafront. The usual crowds teemed: young men and women ambling along in holiday suits and dresses past nannies wheeling black prams, as white-haired gentlemen flourished canes, and children capered away from mothers. On the beach, pale limbs were stretched along the sands, or splashed about in the shallows.

Bob had dragged Harry there out of a need to stretch his legs and cheer himself up, but he couldn't help noticing Harry's mood was also anxious. Bob was glad to feel part of a throng. When they reached their favourite café, they ordered tea and sat over it. Bob attempted to savour it as he concentrated on the view of sea and sky. Harry pulled out a newspaper from his jacket pocket and studied it.

Then, as a couple of young women jaunted past, one of them jeered, 'It wasn't you two, was it?'

'What?' Harry and Bob replied almost together.

Hettie and Margaret were two young women who worked in shops in town, and had a taste for lurid lipstick and skirts too long and flouncy for current fashion; the young women looked slightly worn, not unlike their clothes, and had smiles that looked forced as if long hours of work had taken toll.

'That sounds practised,' her friend, Margaret, added.

'Are you the ones that killed the girl?' Hettie teased.

'What girl?' Bob asked.

'You'll have to do better than that,' Hettie cackled. 'Who doesn't know about "The Body Under The Sands?"'

'Great title that newspaper came up with,' Margaret said.

'Someone'll write a book about it,' Hettie said. 'Everyone's talking about that, and you say you've never heard about it.'

'You two bored?' Harry yelled back.

'You're perfect suspects. Who lies in wait on the seafront, chatting up every bit of skirt that visits Birtleby?' said the first.

'Who can't keep his hands to himself?' said the other.

Then they stopped joking as they reacted at last to the tenseness in the response from Harry and Bob. As Margaret pulled at Hettie's arm, she whispered, 'They're terrified. Why do you think that is? You don't think they're the ones, do you?'

'They can't be,' Hettie said. 'We know them.'

'Someone did it. It could have been them for all we know.' And she pulled at Hettie's arm to draw her away. 'Besides,' Margaret said to Harry and Bob, unable to desist from her habitual tormenting of young men, 'we don't want to get in the way of the arrest. The police are probably looking for you two right now.'

'I heard they've already got the men,' Harry told them.

'Don't believe it,' Margaret replied.

'It's a con…'

'…to put you off your guard…'

'…so the police can pounce.'

'Get out of it,' Bob shouted after them as they moved off.

'With pleasure,' Hettie said, 'and it's the only pleasure you're likely to get.'

Harry sat back in his chair and grunted to himself as he stared after them before he picked up his cup and sipped. 'Never mind them,' he said, but he seemed to Bob to be attempting to reassure himself.

'Surprised it hasn't happened before,' Bob said. 'It's too small a place. Everyone knows everything you do. And you know how quick people are to point a finger.'

Harry nodded. 'And look at the latest,' he said as he pushed his newspaper across the table towards Bob and pointed at an article which Bob peered at.

'It says they're looking for two men, and the description fits us too well. It asks for witnesses who saw them near the murder, and the police ask young women who've been approached by them to come forward. That two will.'

Bob perused the paper, then pushed it away. 'And I can think of more who'll do that,' he said.

'So can I. We've approached plenty of women.'

'Haven't we?' Bob said.

'The police will have us in for questioning again.' Harry scowled and looked out to sea. He swore. 'It's a pity we didn't manage to sign up for the army.'

'We could try again.'

'Never thought I'd hear you say that.'

'Or we could just scarper.'

That feeling of dread was there again, as if Bob could hear the whine of an artillery shell and waited to hear where it would fall. He glanced at the summer crowd as it drifted past, and took in the relaxation in the stroll of a couple whose hands touched as they shared glances. He felt a separateness from everyone he saw. He sat alone at a table with terrified thoughts and clammy hands. He looked across at Harry, sipped tea, replaced the cup in its saucer, looked at the waves again, then knocked his chair over in his hurry as he reached his decision. Harry crumpled up his newspaper and threw it on the ground as he also stood up, ready to go.

CHAPTER THIRTY-FOUR

They agreed to go back home and pack bags, before meeting up at the fairground. Everyone else was out when Bob reached his house, so it was easy for him, but Harry's brother was home. Usually, Ed worked, so Harry had not expected to see him, but today he was off sick. Ed wondered where Harry was going and how he got the money to do that, and Harry told him a pal had offered him a lift to Linfrith and a bunk for a couple of nights so he could look for work there.

'So we'd better go anywhere but Linfrith', Harry told Bob when they met outside the lettered-rock stall, where a boy was insisting to his father he ought to have a stick, and being told no.

They set off from there at a pace which contrasted with the leisureliness of those around them. The banter and laughter of people hanging around dodgem cars and bingo stalls was a bizarre backdrop. A father chuckled at his daughter, a curly-haired eight-year-old brunette, who was covering her face with as much bright pink candy floss as was entering her mouth. 'There's no need to hurry. It won't float off,' he was saying, as Bob and Harry strode past.

'We're not timing our run for it well. The next train isn't for two hours,' Bob said.

'We'll take a motorbus,' Harry said.

They hurried through the fairground and arrived at a cobbled street as an autobus approached. Since they were almost near a stand, Harry and Bob raced towards it, and Harry held out his hand as far as it would go. The bus stopped and they jumped on, hurried upstairs, and collapsed onto seats. They glanced at each other and around at the other passengers, of whom there were only two. As they were both young women, Bob couldn't help noticing them. One was a brunette and one a redhead. Both wore their hair short under cloche hats and wore straight dresses over slim bodies. Bob could have quite happily gone for either on a different day. He was sure one of them gave Harry the eye, which Harry was in no mood to acknowledge. As the two men looked out of the window, inside himself Bob screamed. Get moving, bus, why don't you? Then a stocky, bald man with a thin moustache appeared at the head of the stairs and pulled himself along by seat handles.

Page leaned down and whispered to them, 'I'm Sergeant Page from Scotland Yard, and you're under arrest. Come quietly and don't disturb the other passengers. My men are downstairs and we want to make this as low-key as we can.'

Harry and Bob sat motionless. Bob realised he and Harry should have split up or made a run for it the day before. As Bob glanced across, he saw the look of defeat in Harry's eye and realised he felt much the same.

CHAPTER THIRTY-FIVE

Prison was as demoralising and uncomfortable as Harry had imagined it would be, and he was unhappy at having to wear the convict uniform, which was fashioned out of thin grey cloth, even rougher than that used in army khaki and holding as little warmth. He was sharing a cell with another prisoner who was also on remand, a thin man with a weasel-like face and cunning eyes, who had a tash and a cough. He lay on his bunk, glaring with suspicion at Harry when he was brought into the cell.

As Harry peered about at the brick walls, two bare bunks, and one small barred window, he began to realise if he had thought life was bleak before his arrest, he had been kidding himself; he began to take a harder look at himself. If he'd behaved less like an idiot, he wouldn't have found himself in a pickle like this.

Harry introduced himself to the other man and asked him, 'Have you been in long?'

A grunt was the reply and Harry lay down on his bunk. After a while, he tired of lying still, stood up and strode about the room, which was three strides from one end of the cell to the other. He scowled at his cellmate, then thought better of that. With a friendly smile that surprised himself, he made another attempt to start a conversation with him, asking what the food was like, and what he was in for, but the man only grunted, so Harry started to resume his pacing. Then, the man spoke. 'I didn't do anything,' he said. 'They've got me in for breaking and entering but I wasn't anywhere near the place.'

'How long did you get?' Harry asked.

'I'm on remand. The trial comes up next week.'

'D'you have a good lawyer?'

'You need money for a good one, but there's somebody representing me.'

'They don't care. They want to get someone, whoever it is, and then their jobs are done,' Harry said.

'Their witness can't have seen me. Maybe someone who looked a bit like me.'

'They build their case on who saw you, then who else saw you, and where, and when, and what conclusions can be reached from that,' Harry said. 'I don't think they care much who the witness is. They've just the one, you say?'

'Two.'

'A pity you don't have anyone who saw you somewhere else about that time.'

'I was around and about where it happened. I just didn't do it.'

'Much like my case,' Harry said.

'Is it? What are you in for?'

'Murder.'

The man on the bunk stared at Harry, then turned his face towards the wall and said nothing.

'But I didn't do it,' Harry said. 'And nobody saw the murder itself. Tough cheese if you happen to be in the same area when it happens, wouldn't you say?'

But the man on the bunk didn't say anything. Harry couldn't see the expression on his face, but supposed he thought Harry must have done what he was in for.

'I'm like you,' Harry said. 'I didn't do anything. I was in the wrong place at the wrong time, and they've this witness, a sailor I've never even met before, who says he saw me with her.'

Harry felt like he was talking to himself, so he stopped. Then an idea occurred to him.

'If someone says they saw me somewhere else, that might prove I couldn't have done it.'

The silence from the man on the bunk continued and that depressed Harry, but then he started to wonder. 'I don't suppose,' he said, then paused, before continuing, 'you would say you saw me at the circus in Blackforth that afternoon, would you? It was the twentieth. You weren't in yet then, were you?'

But the man on the bunk said nothing, so Harry lay and stared at the brick wall. He started to count the bricks, he might manage to finish that. He suspected he would have plenty of time.

CHAPTER THIRTY-SIX

Bob had valued the ability to do whatever and go wherever he liked after leaving the army, so he hated the cell he found himself in. And they would hang him if they could. How had it come to this?

Life had been good once – before the war. He thought back to the boatyard he had worked in before joining up, the camaraderie of other workers, and the fatherliness of the foreman as he attempted to instruct others in his trade. There had been triumphs then, like when they finished a craft, and it slipped down the ramp and set sail with such a sense of purpose and triumph it had made him want to sail off in it, anywhere. But when he left Birtleby, he had found himself in the mud of the trenches, where your horizons consisted of mud and rats, and your rest-time was spent in a funk hole. And here he was in Linfrith Prison. He peered about the cell.

'It's a scunner when they first put you in, isn't it?' his cellmate said. Bob looked at him. He was a burly, bald-headed man with small eyes that stared at Bob from his bunk in a way that was friendly but which Bob didn't welcome. 'I got a bit drunk,' the man continued. 'And another man picked a fight with me. The trouble is, it's not exactly the first time it's happened. How about you?'

Bob didn't reply.

'You'll get used to it,' the other man said, 'and you'll get out in the end.'

This didn't cheer up Bob as he wasn't afraid of prison but of being hanged, but he still said nothing.

'At least it's warm and dry in here, and you know you'll be fed.'

Bob remained uncommunicative, so the other man turned away and left him alone. Bob was trying to work out how he and Harry had ended up here, as they hadn't committed the murder, or, at least, he knew he hadn't. As he lay on his bunk, shifting from one uncomfortable side to the other, he started to wonder why the police didn't suspect anyone else. He pondered Harry. He had left him with Anne, and Harry had quarrelled with her, after which she had turned up dead, but Bob, who had trusted Harry with his own life in the trenches, could not conceive that Harry had murdered her.

Bob had so many clear memories of Harry in the war, and Harry had always looked after him. Bob remembered one attack when the sergeant had issued a rum ration and Bob had knocked his back immediately, then taken another gander at the grey stone bottle, which still held plenty, and asked how much he could have. The sergeant said "as much as you like" so Bob held out his can and knocked back another one. Harry finished after one, and stopped Bob having the third he hankered after, which, thinking back, Bob thought could have saved his life. Bob was so afraid he would have been happy to go over the top senseless, but Harry had a calmer, and more sensible, head than him.

Then they pushed their ladder against the sandbags on the trench wall and stood and waited. They called it a ladder and it did the job, but it was only two bits of wood nailed together with three or four cross-pieces of other roughly cut wood. 'Five minutes to go' came the bellow. There was a sergeant standing next to them, a man held in high regard because of a medal he'd earned – a Distinguished Conduct Medal – but Bob couldn't help noticing he was rubbing a piece of earth between his feet, back and forward, back and forward, and he realised the man was just as scared.

As they stood, ready to go over, they carried a rifle, helmet, a full-size navvy's pick across the shoulders, the canvas pack on the back holding a blanket, two hundred rounds of ammunition, and twenty Mills bombs. Once they were over the top, they didn't travel fast.

When Bob had managed about forty yards, he found there was nobody else with him, except, for some reason, Harry, because everyone else had gone down under flailing bullets. Harry dropped into a shell-hole and pulled Bob with him, while the firing went on, and, when they peeped over the top to check, they saw the Germans were sniping at anything in sight, including the wounded, and even the corpses. Fortunately, the Germans didn't spot Bob and Harry in their shell-hole, and that was when Bob had decided he and Harry must be lucky together.

As time went on, more of their own soldiers crawled in, and together they felt they made more of a fighting unit. Bob and Harry had justified hiding by arguing they couldn't be expected to fight all the Germans by themselves. Now they did work their way towards the German lines, find a trench and take it over. Fortunately, it was mostly abandoned by the Bosches, with only one left in it, and he was hiding out, but he didn't surrender as they might have hoped. He had just lunged at Bob in a panic, pushing him over and pulling back a saw-back bayonet to slide it into Bob's ribs when a shot through the German's head from Harry's raised rifle sorted him out. Harry had quick reactions in battle and was ruthless, for which Bob was grateful. But Harry hadn't lost control of that part of himself, had he?

When they had tramped through the ground captured that day, which wasn't much, the sight was gruesome. Bodies lay around, thick as anything. Some fallen soldiers were still alive, and they were crying out, begging for water, and plucking at Bob and Harry's legs as they went past.

One man, a great hefty chap, held onto Bob's knees as he pleaded, but Bob was hurried past him by Harry. 'We'll be stuck in no man's land,' Harry said. 'We don't want to be here when it gets dark.' The others agreed and Bob had to leave the man. But he never forgot the head that had looked up at him, big, with a face that might have shown strength in other circumstances, beseeching him.

Bob wouldn't have made it through that day without Harry, and Harry had helped him through so many days Bob didn't want to believe anything bad about him.

But if Harry had murdered this girl, Bob had got him wrong. And he could find himself hanged alongside him. Why didn't the police follow up on other leads? Why did they have him and Harry down as the culprits?

The cell door opened, a guard entered and ordered them off their bunks. He led Bob and his cellmate, along with other prisoners from other cells, to a yard where they were supposed to exercise. Bob was supposed to walk round that? Were they trying to bore him to death? The stone walls were high with barbed wire strung across the top, and the open area for walking round was about twenty yards by twenty. The dirt was hard from the tread of feet and the prisoners trod it down more as they trudged under the eyes of the guards.

The prisoners tramped round in their sulky rhythm, exchanging brief comments. Then Bob felt a piece of paper being passed into his hand from behind but when he turned around the nearest fellow prisoner was looking at his own feet. Bob glanced up at a guard who at that moment was watching someone else, reached his hand into his pocket with a casualness as convincing as he could manage, and deposited the note there. He resumed his concentration on the lift and fall of his feet, though his hand itched to pull the scrap of paper out. An hour. That was how long they had to endure this 'exercise'. Then he would be able to look at the note in his cell.

Once he was back and the door had been closed, he threw himself on the bunk. He supposed he should try to hide what he was doing from his fellow cell-mate, but he peered at the note when he could. The note had been written on a piece of paper with rough edges that seemed to have been torn out of a notebook. It was from Harry and said: 'We stick to the same story and we're OK. We don't know the girl and we've never met her. We were at Blackforth that afternoon, right?'

Even though Bob had been at Blackforth, he was beginning to disbelieve it himself, and he was sure nothing would convince the police. But Harry was right about the need to concentrate on a defence and, as their story had always been they hadn't seen the girl that afternoon, they should stick to that, useless though it might feel.

From what they had been told, it wouldn't be long till the inquest, when they would find out how things stood against them. Anne's face flashed before Bob, fresh, pretty, too good for Harry or him. And she was dead. A shudder passed through Bob. Then he started thinking of himself again. How would he get out of this?

CHAPTER THIRTY-SEVEN

Bob and Harry saw each other the next morning in the back of a police car with an overgrown constable between them and were told they were forbidden to speak to each other. Because they were being driven to the inquest, the two prisoners had dressed in suits, which made Bob feel more like himself. As they exchanged glances, Bob noticed Harry's exaggerated air of confidence, and the nod and wink Harry gave him, as if he were attempting to suggest the same attitude to Bob. Bob thought, why not? If you're innocent, you can behave as if you are, and it might help in a courtroom.

When they arrived, they saw a crowd outside the courthouse: small boys with jeers on their faces; young women exuding horror and fascination; photographers from newspapers, holding cameras with popping flashlights; journalists with notepads and pencils; young, rough-looking men who might have been idlers on the lookout for a distraction; and, at the back, presumably less up to jostling with the milling crowd, older men and women with grey hair and faces and sad if wondering eyes. As Bob looked at the crowd, any bravado evaporated. Every holidaymaker with time to waste seemed to have gathered here. Bob remembered the stir the murder had caused in the town before their arrest and noted it had grown. It was the noise which disturbed Bob most, that aggressive cacophony of voices with its varied age, gender and timbre.

'Murderers,' one voice accused.

'You'll get what you deserve,' another yelled.

'Why did you do that to a young girl?' a female voice shrieked.

'Monsters,' shouted someone else.

The constable seated between Harry and Bob gave them each a handkerchief and said: 'That's to cover your faces with.'

'Is it clean?' Bob asked, checking, as he had doubts about the humour of policemen, and no doubt of their opinion of murderers.

'Of course,' the policeman replied. 'What do you take me for? Don't put it over your face then. Get your photograph all over the papers. What do I care?'

So Bob and Harry accepted the small squares of cloth.

The two policemen from the front of the car opened their doors and climbed out before opening the back-passenger door on the pavement side. The three policemen formed a burly guard round the two prisoners as they pushed a way through the crowd.

To Bob, the turrets on the castellated stone building of Linfrith's imposing courthouse suggested vats of boiling oil that would have been in keeping with the venom he felt around him.

The uniformed arms pushed and hauled Bob and Harry towards the open front door, as more jeers were shrieked at the pair and flashbulbs popped. A breeze lifted Bob's handkerchief up just before another flash and Bob jerked the cloth down. The group pushed and staggered into the building, the door was hauled shut behind them, and Bob luxuriated in the comparative quiet. The handkerchiefs were taken away and Harry and Bob found themselves able to straighten their jackets and ties. Harry pulled a comb through his hair and attempted to affect a nonchalant stroll, which Bob tried to copy as the policemen accompanied them into the courtroom.

Heads turned to face them and Bob was sure he heard a gasp, and he wondered if he and Harry were overdoing the carelessness, but felt committed to it. They attempted the unconcerned and self-righteous glare of the innocent and falsely accused as they gazed back at the earnest faces in the gallery, another varied group of humanity, mostly with expressions of condemnation. The faces that stood out to Bob were of people he took to be middle-aged burghers of a type whose self-righteousness he habitually dreaded; and severe matrons of the sort whose disapproval could be so eloquent. He also noticed young women and men who looked as if they were dressed for the beach and who may have just come from there, after hearing about the spectacle on offer. They even had sandwiches they were in the process of sharing round, though they managed to look up long enough to gawk at Bob and Harry as they were brought in. The jury, entirely male but composed of a variety of ages and class, all wore their most respectable suits, their most decent ties, and their smartest and most serious expressions.

As Bob and Harry sat apart from the rest of the court on a wooden bench, Bob felt as if he looked guilty already. Certainly, though the word murder had not yet been pronounced in this place, he felt on trial.

Mr Edmund Archibald, the coroner, thumped his gavel and silence fell. The onlookers in the audience gaped. As he addressed the gathered company, the gold glasses perched on the thin nose glinted under the white wig. 'We are here to conduct an inquest into the death of Anne Talbot on 19 August 1920. The purpose of the process is first, to establish the reason for death, secondly, to establish whether the death appears to have been natural, accidental, or deliberate due to murder or suicide. It is also necessary to establish whether there is a case for proceedings against anyone in relation to the death. I should say two men have been detained. They are here as I think it is their right to hear anything that is said and may be used in evidence against them if circumstances go that way and if the evidence is sufficiently strong to justify your giving a verdict against them. I have requested a jury coroner's court because of the need to give a preliminary weighing of such evidence.'

Bob wondered how real the apparent fairness of any of this was; did it give the jury the impression of a good case against them?

The coroner continued, 'Also, in their interests, I must insist no sketches be made of the prisoners and no written descriptions be published. Witness identification does play its part and should not be compromised.'

Bob agonised over this as he looked at the public gallery and thought there were a lot of people there who would happily describe them to anyone.

'Call the first witness,' the coroner said. 'Mrs Robinson.'

Mrs Robinson was a middle-aged woman with a hooked nose, pursed lips, and the most pious expression Bob could remember seeing. Bob had no idea who she was.

'State your name, please,' Archibald said.

'Mrs Muriel Robinson.'

'You were Anne Talbot's landlady?'

'Yes. She stayed with us from the Tuesday night.'

'The eighteenth?'

'That's right. And she was booked in for the fortnight.'

Bob frowned as he tried to remember what Anne had told them about her.

'She first came to me on the Monday.'

'The seventeenth?' the coroner asked.

'Yes. She'd seen my sign and she was going around looking for a room as she'd arrived for a brief holiday. It was odd a girl going about by herself like that, and worrying. As I didn't have a room that night, I suggested a lady who might, so I went over with Anne to try to make sure of things for her, and was able to. I could take Anne after that so she stayed with me on the Wednesday night and was booked in for the fortnight.'

'How did you find Anne when she stayed with you?'

'I found her quiet and respectful. She took breakfast with us, then went out. I'd known her to come back to change or stay in for a while. She liked to write letters.'

'Did she have men in?'

'She didn't have her own key so there was no opportunity for that. I never saw her with a man.'

'You didn't see her with anyone on the Thursday?'

'No. She left the house at about 10.30, saying she was going across to Wade Park, which is in the opposite direction to the Ridges. She came back at about 12.30 and went out again at about 1.30. I did notice she was writing in a book which I took to be a diary because she kept it close to her. She said she'd come back for her coat and I said it was such a warm day she probably didn't need it, but she said she'd be gone for a while and probably would later, which sounded sensible. I had a painter working on the outside of the building and he said he noticed Anne going in and out, and that he saw her with two men later, but I never saw anyone with her.'

'And did she take her coat with her?'

'Yes. It was her green one with the black fur trim.'

'The same that was found on her body?'

'Yes.'

Bob was glad they had never met Mrs Robinson as she sounded so precise he was sure she would have no difficulty in describing them or pointing them out, but there would be more witness statements to listen to, and Bob dreaded them.

The painter Mrs Robinson had mentioned was called next and Bob didn't recognize him. He wondered how clear a view the man had of him and Harry if they had passed him with Anne Talbot.

Alan Hawkins was a middle-aged man with thinning hair and a face whose skin was showing signs of tiredness, with some redness in the tone of it, particularly around the nose, which Bob usually associated with drink. He had a round tummy and folds of fat around the chin. He was nervous but not unduly so.

'State your name and occupation, please.'

'Alan Hawkins, painter and decorator.'

'You were at the house on Seabank Road on the afternoon of the 19th?'

'That's correct. I was employed to do house decorating on that day.'

'And did you happen to notice a young lady called Anne Talbot?'

'Yes. I saw her twice, when she came in at about 12.30 and when she left at about 1.30, going in the direction of Wade Park. She said good day pleasantly on both occasions but we didn't have any more conversation. And I saw her later on when she walked past, going in the opposite direction from formerly. On this occasion she was with two young men. They were laughing together and having a jolly time.'

'Did you have a clear view of the two men?'

'I'd a clear view of Anne, and I noticed the two men, who were on the other side of the street. They both had grey suits. One was carrying a cane.'

'Would you recognize them again?'

'I think I do. They looked a bit like, a bit like–' he hesitated before pointing at Bob and Harry, 'those two over there.'

'Are you sure it was them?'

'I think so.'

'You think?'

Alan Hawkins paused before replying, 'If it wasn't them it was a couple of men very like them.'

'Thank you.'

Bob felt relieved after Alan Hawkins' evidence as he was sure it suggested doubt about their identification. Dr Parker, the police surgeon, was next to walk to the stand, which he did with a calm stride, his face holding a neutral and professional expression.

'What is your name, Doctor?' the coroner asked.

'Dr Ernest Stanley Radford Parker,' he replied.

'And your qualifications are?'

'MD.'

'Do you remember the night of August the 20th?'

'Yes. I was called out at nine o'clock to the body of a woman found on the Ridges, and, when I arrived, proceeded to examine the body.'

'Tell the jury what you found.'

'The young lady had received injuries to the head and I am satisfied these were the cause of death. I felt there was no need of a post-mortem.'

'Which nevertheless was conducted by Dr Langford?'

'Yes.'

'How long would you say she had been dead?'

'The opinion I formed at the time was, as near as one could say, 24 hours.'

Bob and Harry exchanged looks at this statement, which they immediately attempted to hide. The words 'as near as one could say' were music to the ears, as also was the phrase '24 hours'. Dr Parker had said he had examined the body at nine o'clock the next evening, which put the death at nine on the Thursday when they were at the Hippodrome, and it might have been done later. Bob thought of how they had been nowhere near the beach then, so no one could place them there. Bob started humming a tune, though he stopped at Harry's warning look.

'And you were present at the post-mortem conducted by Dr Langford?' Archibald said to Parker.

'Yes.'

'We will hear more evidence from you when he has given his.'

'Thank you.'

Parker's professional manner held the suggestion of a stiffness as he left the stand, and Bob wondered at it. Dr Langford strode forward, giving an impression of arrogance. The glance he shot in Parker's direction was brief but condescending to Bob's eyes.

The coroner spoke. 'Would you give your name and qualifications, please.'

'Dr Stephen George Langford. MD, MRCP, DPH, BS, MRCS, MRCP. I am the Pathologist at the West London Hospital. I was requested to come down by the Home Office.'

'For certain reasons, it was decided to make a further examination in the presence of Dr Parker, was it not?'

'It was at a time as convenient and prompt as possible. It was conducted on the Wednesday following, the twenty-fifth.'

'Would you describe the body, please?'

'It was the body of a young, well-nourished, muscular female, who had suffered external injuries. Firstly, I noticed wounds on the lower and upper lip.'

'Describe those, please.'

'There were two puncture wounds, one of which penetrated through the lip, the lower one, and might have been caused by an instrument. The lower jaw was fractured and two teeth detached. It was broken inwards.'

'What was the wound on the upper lip?'

'It was a lacerated wound. The upper jaw was also fractured, and there were two teeth broken.'

'And were there other injuries?'

'A small, lacerated wound on the right temple and another by the right ear. The blow on the temple would have been caused by something blunt, and the wound on the right ear would have been caused by an instrument of a cutting nature or a sharp stone, as it was a wound of an incised character.'

Bob sighed as he didn't want to hear anything about these other injuries. This was a young woman he had met and whose prettiness he had admired. He glanced across at the group of trippers with sandwiches and noticed these had been put to the side, and there were expressions of distaste on the young people's faces.

Dr Langford continued, 'There was also a wound on the right cheek extending towards the temple as far as one and a half inches, which also occurred before death, I would have said. In addition, there was a small haemorrhage at the forehead. This implied a blow, done by an instrument or falling on something hard.'

Bob stared at the pathologist in wonder at the neutrality of his tone and expression, before he glanced at Harry who he assumed was feeling much the same as he was, yet whose expression still showed the detachment he had affected from the beginning.

'What was the condition of the brain?'

'There was concussion.'

'And these injuries were enough to cause death?'

'Yes. The brain and the nervous system would have been directly affected.'

'Could the injuries on the lips been caused by a blow from a fist with a ring on it?'

'I don't think they would have been, but I would not say it was impossible.'

'Could blows have been done with the stone, or by a stick with a knob?'

'Not all were done by the stone, which, in any case, would have been unwieldy and difficult to use quickly – when the body was tested for drugs that might have sedated the victim, there was no sign of any. Some of the injuries could have been caused by a stick with a knob though I would like to have the knob before me before passing an opinion.'

'Could you say when death took place?'

'I could not say definitely from the time of my examination. About six days I thought. I think Dr Parker might be able to shed light on that. Personally, going by Dr Parker's notes, I would say about 30 to 36 hours up to the time Dr Parker saw it. One must remember the body was buried and had clothes on, which would tend to keep a body warm.'

'Would 36 hours be the longest?'

'It would depend on external temperature. The fact it was outside at night-time would also have affected it.'

'Do you think death could have taken place during the afternoon preceding the finding of the body, Thursday?'

'Yes. That would make it between thirty and thirty-six hours before.'

Bob liked this witness much less and he noticed Harry's face held a frown. The time this doctor specified was when they had seen Anne.

'I think we will hear from Dr Parker again,' the coroner said.

Langford left the stand and Parker returned to it, not without nervousness in his face.

'Is it also your opinion the time of death could have been the Thursday afternoon?'

'It's hard to be exact,' Parker replied, 'but I would have said not. There was blood from the nose which was uncongealed, which indicates she couldn't have been dead that length of time.'

'Did you measure the internal temperature of the body at the time?'

'No.'

'Why not?'

'It didn't occur to me.'

'But surely that would have helped establish a more accurate estimate of the time of death and would be considered normal procedure?'

'I'm not sure body temperature is an infallible instrument by itself for the establishment of the time of death. In any case, I'm rarely called out to a murder case. My work is that of a GP first and Police Surgeon second. Normally, when working as a GP, there is no necessity for establishing a precise time of death, which is always difficult anyway, and I'm not sure it really is ever more than a guess. But yes, you're right, following normal procedure, I ought to have taken internal temperature. I made a mistake.'

'Death could have taken place on the Thursday afternoon?'

'I wouldn't have said so, though, as I've said, there is no exact science for the establishment of the time of death.'

Archibald examined him, the eyes behind the gleaming glasses giving an impression of aggression.

'And your opinion of the injuries as described by Dr Langford?'

'An accurate and helpful summary, though I don't think they establish the type of instrument used. Some might suggest a blunt implement and some a sharp instrument though all could have been inflicted in one blow by a very large stone with sharp edges in my opinion.'

'Such as the one found lying there?'

'Such as that one, yes.'

'Though this has been described as impractical for such a use?'

'It would depend on who was doing the lifting I suppose, and on their emotional state. A person at the extremes of anger does find extra strength.'

'But we are beginning to depart from the medical evidence. Thank you, Dr Parker. That is all.'

As he left the stand, Parker glared at Langford as if blaming him for his own professional discomfort as a witness, but the annoyance was soon replaced by a look of relief his ordeal was over.

Bob didn't think the medical men impressive. One suggested the murder was done with more than one blow, the other that it might have been a single blow, but with a stone that would have been difficult to lift. They disagreed about whether it could have occurred on Thursday afternoon, and Dr Parker had not even completed the basic procedure of taking the body temperature when he had examined it. Bob thought he and Harry might talk their way out of this.

Walker asked the coroner for a further remand for the prisoners till Thursday next at 12.15 as the Public Prosecutor had been communicated with and could be present then. Archibald turned to the prisoners and asked if they had anything to say. Bob kept his mouth firmly closed but Harry replied in a loud voice. 'I think it's time something was done. We've been hanging around for a fortnight for a crime we didn't commit. I'm fed up with it.' The coroner's eyes held a severe look to them, but there was an evenness in his tone as he said, 'You will be remanded till this day next week.'

Harry nodded at Bob, who winked back, and the police led them out, with Harry managing to put a saunter into his stride, which Bob attempted to copy. In the car, Harry ignored the constable placed between them and spoke to Bob.

'No case to answer, Bob,' Harry said. 'Public prosecutor? He'll be livid with the lot of them.'

Bob laughed and sat back in his seat, but it was not in the relaxed manner that might have suggested. In Bob's experience, when things looked easy, there was a shell barrage on the way.

CHAPTER THIRTY-EIGHT

When Harry lay on his bunk in his cell that night, he struggled for sleep. His mind was busy. He continued to try to tell himself he was confident about the outcome but, if the truth be told, his feelings were mixed. There was relief that the case against them was not being well made, but this was mingled with anger they had had to sit through the inquest at all, and anxiety at what the next day might bring. He wondered what the rest of the witness identification would be like, and could only hope all he and Bob had to do was sit tight. But he had found it difficult keeping his manner as confident as he had in the courthouse, and hoped he would manage as well when they next appeared. He thought it a pity he and Bob had been separated. If they had been able to talk together, this might have helped them keep up morale. But Harry did sleep eventually, if fitfully.

Next morning was overcast and drizzly but the warders seemed to take pleasure in the uncomfortable conditions for prisoner-exercise time. They shot sardonic looks in the direction of the men walking round the yard as they themselves stood in shelter under an awning. Harry found himself walking beside a short, sturdy man called

Simpkins who said he was on remand as well. He was in for assault which he denied, though Harry thought the aggressive thrust to the shoulders as the man swaggered about made the charge look believable. Harry had also noticed the guttural, menacing voice which the man had put to such good use in an argument with a warder the day before over the amount of stew he was allowed. So, Harry felt nervous when he found himself being addressed by him.

'You the murderer?' Simpkins' voice was hard and meaningful.

Harry stared back at him, but did not reply.

'People in here think badly about murdering women too,' he said.

'I didn't do it,' Harry told him.

'Nobody has in prison. Ask anybody. It was always somebody else. The police made a mistake, or the police have it in for me.'

'I didn't,' Harry repeated.

'But you stick to your story. Or someone in here might top you. A young girl like that. It doesn't bear thinking about.'

'It would be a mistake for them to try.'

And the way Harry said that shut Simpkins up for a moment.

'Would it?' he said.

'Yes.'

When Simpkins started speaking again, there was more care in his tone.

'Mind you, that Inspector Walker,' he said. 'I've heard about him. He does get it wrong.'

'He has. And it's all on witness identification. They've nothing else.'

'That goes wrong. I heard about one case…' Simpkins' voice tailed off as he thought. 'They took witnesses all the way from Dundee to the south of England to look at a suspect, who was supposed to have done murder in Scotland. Paid their fare. Took them round London. Put them up in a hotel. So, of course, the witnesses said the man had done it to justify going down there. And it turned out later he had a cast iron alibi because he was in Amsterdam at the time, and he'd never set foot in Scotland in his life.' Then Simpkins laughed. Harry couldn't see the funny side of it, but he was pleased to see a shift in sympathies in Simpkins.

'Are you from Birtleby?' Harry said.

'Yes,' the man replied.

'You weren't in here till yesterday?'

'No.'

'I wonder.'

The man gave him a hard look. 'What?'

'You could help,' Harry said. 'You might have been there or thereabouts, and you might have seen a sailor struggling with a girl.'

'But I didn't.'

'Their case is all what witnesses say,' Harry said. 'Witnesses never agree about what they saw. And I didn't do it.'

The man said nothing, just looked back at Harry.

'You could say what I want if maybe I helped you in return?' Harry said.

'And how would you do that?'

'I could maybe help out with your alibi?'

The man gave Harry a thoughtful look. 'I'm only in for assault. Why would I get mixed up in a murder?'

Harry stared back at him for a few moments, then said, 'Right enough. Why would you?' Then Harry shut up, and walked on in silence, scowling as he did so. He noticed a warder looked in his direction.

But Harry had started something, as he found out next morning when a prisoner sought him out to sit beside as they were working on mailbags. He was a tense figure, who looked as if he might be provoked to violence easily. The men Harry had mixed with in prison tended to look either dangerous or like runts for whom nothing had worked out so they'd ended up taking to crime. This fellow prisoner was muscular, dark-haired, and dark-skinned, almost foreign-looking, and he had a squint. He was in for grievous bodily harm and, like Harry, wanted someone to make a helpful witness statement. He asked Harry for more details of what he'd been saying to the other prisoner the day before, then said if Harry would say he was with him when the police said he was elsewhere causing physical mayhem, he would swear on the Bible about the sailor.

Harry had no opportunity to tell Bob about any of this before the inquest resumed.

CHAPTER THIRTY-NINE

First thing on Monday morning, Bob once again found himself sitting on the isolated bench beside Harry, as he waited for the inquest to be resumed. The first witness called was the sailor, Pulteney. Bob noticed that, as Pulteney stood on the witness stand, he ran a tongue along his lips, and his thumb seemed to be trying to dig a hole into the wooden rail. Pulteney was a tall, gangly man, with an oversize head and disproportionately long arms. Bob thought the poor fit of the sailor's uniform he wore made him look clownish.

Bob noticed on the public benches a similar mixture to the day before: trippers with mocking grins beside horrified women; disdainful young men; elderly, spinsterish women with accusing eyes; middle-aged, stout men with indignant faces; and journalists and photographers with cynicism written all over them. Bob glanced across at Harry and wondered how he could succeed in projecting such a cocky attitude, as Bob was sure his own attempt at self-assurance would convince nobody.

The coroner looked even more forbidding to Bob than he had on the previous day, his wig whiter, his cloak blacker, the gold of his spectacles brighter, and his hawk-like look even more menacing.

'Give your name and occupation, please,' Archibald told Pulteney.

'My name is William Pulteney, and I am a naval stoker.'

'You have stated you saw the deceased on the 18th, the day before the murder?'

'That's correct.'

'Is what you saw relevant to this inquiry?'

William's thumb attempted to press even harder into the railing as he stared at Archibald. Pulteney blurted out, 'She... she was on the beach near the waterplane sheds and she was wearing the green coat and black hat described by the police.' He stopped and flicked his tongue across his lips.

Archibald waited patiently, then frowned. 'That's nowhere near the Ridges,' he said, and wrote in a notebook as the jury looked with doubtful eyes at Pulteney, and whispers began to be exchanged on the public benches.

'But that's how I know it was definitely her I saw—' Pulteney looked round the gallery before he continued, 'Because I'd seen her on the 18th.' Then the words rushed out. 'I did see her the next day too, walking towards the Ridges, and she was with two men. They climbed over a fence at the beginning of the Ridges and they'd had to stop to do that, and you could see the faces clear as day. It was her they were with.'

'About what time was this?' Archibald asked.

'It must have been about two-thirty.'

'Why do you place that as the time?'

'I didn't look at a watch or anything but it would have been about then. It's just when it was.'

'So, you can't be sure of the time. Did you have a clear view of the two men?' Archibald said.

'I hadn't seen them before but, yes, I saw them that day, and saw them well enough.'

'You were able to identify them on the Parade and were in no doubt of your identification?'

'I was dead sure of one, that one over there,' he said, pointing at Bob. 'I think he was the other one.' He pointed at Harry. 'He must have been, I suppose, as they go about together, as people say.'

The coroner continued, 'And he has a stick?'

'The other one had a stick,' Pulteney said, and pointed at Bob.

'Constable, show Pulteney Bob Nuttall's stick,' Archibald commanded.

Pulteney looked at it for a while. 'I suppose it is,' he said. 'It was a bit like that.'

'Or not. Thank you,' the coroner told him. 'Take the stick away, Constable.'

'She offered the men something from a bag, fruit, I think,' Pulteney volunteered.

Archibald gave him a questioning look but merely said, 'And?'

'That's when I turned to Chris and said why don't we follow them?'

'Tell the jury who Chris is,' the coroner said.

'A friend. We go about together.'

'Why did you suggest you follow them?'

'I don't know.'

Laughter tittered round the public gallery.

'What did Chris say?'

'Yes.'

'He didn't ask why?'

'Why would he?'

Again, the public made no attempt to suppress amusement.

'Do you often watch people and follow them for something to do?'

'Yes.'

Pulteney sounded to Bob to be slow-witted, which led Bob to consider again Pulteney's expression and general demeanour, and he realised those would come across as simple to a jury. Bob sat further back into his chair and felt his limbs relax.

Pulteney went on to relate the story of the young lady and the ginger kitten, the fact it followed them, that she fed it and encouraged it, but then carried it over to the railway hut where she spoke to the men there before depositing the kitten.

'And what did you do after that?'

'We turned and came away.'

'I thought you'd agreed to follow them?'

'Chris didn't like the look of the stick and said if we annoyed him, a man like that might use it on us.'

'I suppose that's possible, and did you see the young lady after that day?'

'No.'

'And do you see those men in this room?'

Pulteney said yes, and pointed at Bob and Harry on their bench that, to Bob's mind, already identified them clearly enough to give lots of help to Pulteney if he had any doubts.

'Thank you,' the Coroner said.

Pulteney was dismissed.

Pulteney's friend, Chris, took the stand and, as Bob looked at Chris, Bob had no idea whether he had noticed him around before. There was something indeterminate about him, with his regular features, and height and weight, that looked on the face of it average. If you were to attempt to describe him, he could be anybody.

'Could you give your name and occupation, please?'

'Christopher Fleming. Labourer, at present unemployed.'

'Were you with William Pulteney on the afternoon of Thursday, the 19th?'

'Yes.'

'Tell me what transpired, please.'

'We noticed a young woman in the company of two men, and Pulteney suggested we might follow them.'

'You didn't see anything odd in this?'

'Pulteney is bit odd.' There was giggling on the public benches at this point. 'I thought it might not be odd for him. On the other hand…' he paused as he considered, 'I know the Foxes often do that around there.'

'The Foxes?'

'Foxy fellows, or so they see themselves. They follow couples to that stretch of beach to see what they get up to and if there's something they can blackmail them for. I thought Pulteney could've been up to that, though I wouldn't have gone along with it. I was just keeping Pulteney company and passing the time.'

Archibald appraised Chris.

'Are you sure the girl they were with was Anne Talbot?' he continued.

'From a photograph I was shown. I hadn't seen her before that day.'

'Did you have a clear view of the men?'

'I'm sure about one of them, but I dunno about the other one.'

'Which one can you positively identify?'

He pointed at Bob. 'I'd recognize that nose and build anywhere. And if he always went about with Harry Barker, I suppose he must have been the other one.'

'Thank you.'

Chris concurred over the time they had followed them, and everything Pulteney said he had seen, including the ginger kitten and the fact Anne Talbot went over to the railway hut with it and gave it to the men there.

The coroner seemed interested in establishing Chris' identification of the kitten, which, from the snickering, struck some members of the public as amusing, but the laughter stopped at a bang of Archibald's gavel. Harry leaned back and whispered to Bob, who smirked.

Bob wondered at the coroner. He hoped he was he suggesting it was possible the kitten had committed the murder, though he doubted it. And he thought Chris as unconvincing as Pulteney. Though Chris looked like a reasonable witness, that mention of the Foxes did not put him in a good light.

Questioned next were the workmen from the railway hut, of whom there were three. Bob peered at them as they gave their evidence. The foreman looked about thirty, the other two like teenagers. All looked overawed and spoke hesitantly as they related they had seen Anne Talbot, whom they were able to clearly identify, with two men.

One after the other, they repeated the story of the girl and the kitten, which they had had fun playing with, and which they had seen about before. The men they had seen with the girl were rough, and the workmen had felt sorry for her because she looked a better class. When the coroner asked them if they would recognize the men again, they agreed they would and pointed to the prisoners. As each did, Bob winced and, once more, felt indicated by their position in court.

The workmen all said one man wore a dark suit, while Pulteney had said both men wore grey suits. As stated by Pulteney, one had worn a light cap, though Chris had described it as dark, and all the railwaymen agreed the men wore no caps at all. They did agree it must have been about mid-afternoon, though they could not be any more specific. Bob thought the workmen's recognition of Anne Talbot from the photograph was suspect, as they were told it was the photograph of the dead girl, and they could have been led to their conclusions by this.

Though the coroner asked them all similar questions, one was the same. 'Would you describe the kitten to me, please?'

The courtroom was given a clear picture of a ginger kitten about six months old which was long-haired and had a white bib. It was keen on sandwiches, particularly any meat contained in them.

The coroner then turned to the jury who had begun to giggle along with the public gallery at the repeated description of a cat, and addressed them. 'I am sorry about the tedious elucidation of the description of a kitten, but the link does seem to establish the men identified by Pulteney and Chris were the same as those identified by the railway workmen.'

Harry tutted, as if annoyed with the flimsiness of the evidence, while Bob, who was inwardly blanching with fear, made a half-hearted attempt at a yawn.

A sturdy-looking man in his thirties was called next. 'Please give your name and occupation,' Archibald said.

'Charles Gordon Marshall,' the man replied. 'Builder's labourer.'

'You have stated you saw the two young men, Bob Nuttall and Harry Barker, on the day of the murder.'

'That's correct.'

'Please describe what you saw.'

'I remember which day it was clearly because it was the day before the body was found and that caused a stir everywhere. I saw Barker and Nuttall walking past St Andrews Church with a girl at about 2.30.'

'And which direction were they going in?'

'Towards the Ridges.'

'And you are sure that this was Harry Barker and Bob Nuttall?'

'I've known Harry Barker for about twelve months so there's no mistake. I didn't know the other man but he could have been the man sitting beside Harry.'

'He could have been or he definitely was?'

'He could have been. I was working on the housing estate scheme mixing concrete when I saw them on the right-hand side of the road with the girl walking between them.'

'And did you get a clear view of the girl they were with?'

'I didn't look at her closely and shouldn't know her again. Harry was dressed in a grey suit and felt hat, and the other man was about the same height as the man beside Harry. I can say that. And it definitely was the Thursday because it was the second day of the circus at Blackforth.'

'How far away from Barker were you when he passed you?'

'About twenty yards. I would have come forward before I did but I couldn't identify the girl and didn't think I should be of any use.'

Archibald considered whether to ask more questions, then said, 'That's all. You may sit down.'

Bob sat nonplussed through all of that, but he supposed if they questioned enough witnesses of this type an impression would mount up. Bob became aware of a shortness and shallowness in his breathing which he tried to control.

Archibald turned to the jury. 'We had already established two men walked with Anne Talbot along the Ridges, and the approximate time this occurred. This new witness establishes one of the men was Harry Barker.'

Another man was called, which worried Bob because he remembered him from Thursday afternoon. He was a small, sweaty man with a black bristle-brush of a moustache, a rotund stomach, and a habit of pulling his thinning hair across his head.

'Please give your name and occupation,' Archibald said to him.

'My name is George Blackwater and I am a bus conductor.'

'You have stated you saw Harry Barker and Bob Nuttall on the Thursday afternoon?'

'That's correct.'

'Could you describe this in detail, please?'

'I remember it was Thursday, 19 August and I saw them when I was on my way to work so I'm sure about the time, which was just after two. I'm also sure of the day because the shift I was going to was new to me, and I was given it because there was a rush. And two fellows got on the bus I was travelling on outside the Victoria.'

'Had you seen the two men before?'

'Yes. Occasionally, I went along the Parade with them, and we were demobbed together. It was Harry Barker and Bob Nuttall.'

'Would you point out the two men to us if you see them present, please?'

And George Blackwater pointed at them. 'We got off at the same stop, at the East end of the Parade, which leads directly to the Depot where I was going, and I noticed a young lady speak to them. She said, "Hello, Harry." I was about a hundred yards away at the time so I didn't hear the conversation between them.'

'Could you describe the young lady?'

'I should think she was about five foot seven. She wore a black hat and was about 18 or 19 years of age and of medium build. I don't remember how she was dressed. Then I turned and proceeded to the Depot and lost sight of them.'

'Do you think this girl was Anne Talbot?'

'The police showed me a photograph and it looked like her to me.'

'As you left them on the Parade, which direction were they walking in?'

'They'd just met up and weren't walking anywhere when I saw them, they were well placed for the Ridges.'

As George Blackwater left the stand, he avoided looking anywhere near Harry and Bob. Bob noticed Harry was glaring at Blackwater as if betrayed and felt much the same.

Archibald turned to the jury. 'And we have now established the man Harry was with that afternoon was Bob Nuttall, and I could call up many more witnesses like the last two, who will corroborate what you have been told, and confirm Harry Barker and Bob Nuttall were with Anne Talbot on the afternoon she died, and they walked along the Ridges with her. However, as the fact has been established reasonably well, and this is only an inquest, to save time, I will not call more.'

Bob's heart was in his boots, and he wondered at the process of proof here. One witness had seen such and such, and another had seen something like it, and when the pieces were put together, someone was hanged? Bob wondered how confident the coroner was about the identifications. If he was, why this business of establishing the identification of the kitten? On top of which, even though these witnesses had managed to suggest something that was true, as he and Harry had been there, did that prove they had killed anybody? Bob suspected there wasn't enough to convince a trial jury, and he hoped there wasn't enough to convince this one.

Chief Inspector Walker was called to the stand and Bob found himself studying him. Walker stood upright with hands relaxed on the rail in front of him.

'Give your name and occupation, please,' Archibald said.

'My name is David Douglas Walker and I am a Chief Inspector at Scotland Yard. I was called in and given charge of this case.'

'Have you interviewed the two men who have been established as being in Anne Talbot's company on the afternoon she died?'

'I have, and I have their statements here.' These he proceeded to read out. Walker stressed Bob and Harry's claim that, on the afternoon of the murder, they walked unaccompanied to Blackforth, and there met up with Nancy Harland with whom they spent the afternoon.

'This casts doubt on what previous witnesses have said about the accused's movements,' the Chief Inspector said, and stopped speaking as he waited for the coroner's reaction to this.

Archibald frowned and said, 'In that case it will be necessary to hear from Nancy Harland.'

Bob began to worry again.

When Nancy was called to the stand, she looked all around, until her eyes rested on Bob and Harry before they moved to the coroner, who addressed her. 'Give your name and occupation, please.'

'My name is Nancy Harland and I work as a maid at Roscoe House.'

Nancy's dress was long, which was unusual for her out of work hours, but it suited the formality of the occasion. Her fair hair shone as if it had been brushed over and over that morning, and what looked like her best jewellery sparkled from her neck and fingers though a strained look on her face suggested she would much rather be elsewhere.

Bob had noticed the hush in the court when she stepped forward, and shared their expectancy. He saw the eyes of the jury on Nancy, appraising, doubting, questioning, and working her out. Bob peered at her too. He knew Nancy and liked her; now Harry and he depended on her.

'You have been included in the testimony of Harry Barker and Bob Nuttall,' Archibald said to her.

'I've been told.'

'Would you describe your movements on that afternoon?'

Nancy looked across at Harry and Bob. Harry returned her look, a relaxed expression on his face, while Bob avoided her eyes altogether. Harry winked at her, and she hesitated for what Bob thought a long moment, then seemed to make up her mind.

'I didn't leave the house where I was employed all afternoon, as I had been given work to do, washing the laundry.'

There was an intake of breath in the courtroom, then silence, broken when the coroner spoke.

'The young men both say you were with them at Blackforth, that you walked about with them there, and visited the castle.'

Nancy spoke with a firmness in her voice and steadiness in her eye. 'I did not.' Nancy looked towards a woman on the public benches, who looked back with sympathetic eyes and a smile of reassurance.

Bob heard himself gasp and realised he was one of many doing the same in that courtroom. What was going on here? They had been at Blackforth Castle with Nancy. As he glared at her, she kept her eyes turned away from his and Bob noticed a tremor of nervousness in her hand as she played with the sleeve of her dress.

'Think carefully,' the coroner said. 'This is important for these young men. Are you stating they lie when they testify they spent the afternoon with you?'

'Yes. They asked me to say I did but I wasn't with them.'

'Did they say why they wanted you to do this?'

'They said it would help them out of a jam. I did see them that evening, but only from a distance. The house I work in lies across from the Hippodrome and I saw them coming out for a cigarette and then go back in – at about eight. They shouted across to me and I waved back. I've gone berry-picking with them before but I wasn't with them that afternoon.'

'There's no truth in what they say about being with you that day?'

'That's correct.'

'Thank you, Miss Harland.'

Nancy left the stand, and Amy Miller was called to give evidence, and then the mistress of the house. When they agreed Nancy's statement was truthful, each spoke with no trace of nervousness.

Something heavy settled on the back of Bob's shoulders as he realised it wasn't going to matter how good the identification of witnesses was. It was being demonstrated he and Harry were liars.

The next witness was a man Bob recognized from prison though he had never talked to him. A muscular, dark-haired man with a squint now stood at the stand. Bob noticed a confident look on Harry's face as he looked at the man, and wondered why.

'Please state your name and occupation,' Archibald said.

'My name is Dennis Alfred Simpkins, and I am a bus driver. I am at present in Linfrith Prison on remand.'

'Please tell of your dealings with Harry Barker in Linfrith Prison.'

'I'd been told he was looking for someone to say something to help him in court.'

Bob was surprised by this and looked across at Harry, who looked shaken by it.

'I don't like murder,' Simpkins went on, 'and I don't like men who murder girls. I asked him why he wanted help and he said what he was in for, and that it looked bad for him, so I asked him what he wished me to say. He said he wanted me to testify I was walking along the seaside road that afternoon, and I saw ahead of me a sailor walking with a girl. He told me to say I later saw the sailor returning by himself. I said I would if he'd give me an alibi in return. I then told him what lies to tell to support me.'

Bob's whole body was tensed up, and his breathing was short and sharp. He closed his eyes as he tried to resist the temptation to shriek at Harry. It was being proved they had attempted to concoct alibis. How could Harry be so stupid as to trust anyone he met in prison?

The coroner dismissed Simpkins, and Bob willed himself to look at the next witness, a thin, stooped man who looked as if he had spent a lot of time away from sunlight.

'My name is Alan Masterton,' he said. 'By trade I am a labourer but at present I am doing time in Linfrith Prison.'

'You have also had dealings with Harry Barker in prison,' Archibald said.

'That's correct. He asked me to say I saw a sailor quarrelling with a girl along the beach that afternoon, which I agreed to do to keep him quiet, but I didn't. I couldn't have, seeing that as I was in prison at the time.'

Laughter rippled round the courtroom, and Bob squirmed on his bench. He glared at Harry, who looked away with no trace of his arrogant act as Archibald closed the proceedings for the day.

CHAPTER FORTY

The police constable seated between Bob and Harry found the drive back to prison uncomfortable as the pair leaned across him, gesticulating and arguing with each other.

'You were going to talk us out of it!' Bob pointed at Harry as he said this.

Harry waved his own arm around as he said, 'I made the attempt. What more could I do?'

Bob shouted, 'You made their case against us.'

And Harry yelled back, 'No way.'

'Every way.'

'You two shut up.' The constable pushed them back from each other. Harry glowered, and the constable stared hard at him in return. 'We'll have no talk about your case,' the policeman said.

'Everybody else in that court has discussed it,' Bob said, his face screwing up. 'You don't think they just turned up and said all that?'

'You'll get your chance,' the constable said.

'After we've been convicted?' Bob moaned.

'You won't help yourselves by having a fight about it,' the constable replied.

'You said Nancy was sweet on you,' Bob said to Harry.

'She's a lying bitch.'

'We were with her that afternoon. What did you do to her?'

'I didn't do anything.'

'You annoy all the girls. You sweet talk them, then turn fresh and get a slap. They've got together to get revenge.'

Harry said nothing. Bob continued to scowl. The streets of Birtleby sped past as the car motored on, but he remained unaware of them.

'What've you got against girls?' Bob said.

'They should try fighting in the trenches. They wouldn't have such hoity-toity airs then.'

'And why did you ask every prisoner you met to lie for us?'

'They might've.'

'It's not like the army where we're all in it together against the officers, and anyone will cover for you. You're still out there, aren't you? You never came back from the trenches.'

'Aren't you?'

'You've brought the guns on us now. That lying about alibis made us look such a shifty pair, anyone would think we'd done her in. And they all thought we looked callous bastards with those stuck-up airs.'

'You've got to look innocent.'

'You've never looked innocent in your life. You don't know how.'

'If you had your way, we'd just sit there and let them get on with it.'

'They are getting on with it.'

Bob's face pinched with sourness as he looked at Harry, who turned away and stared out of the window. Bob attempted to look at the buildings going past but didn't take them in.

The constable looked pleased they had shut up. The car trundled on. When it halted at the prison gates, the driver gave the constable a nod, got out, and pulled Harry's door open. The constable leaned across and opened the other. Harry and Bob stepped out onto the tarmac on different sides of the car, but, when they came together to enter the prison gates, Bob took his chance and lashed out at Harry's face with his fist.

'Stupid fucker. You've got us in it this time,' he yelled as he struck out with his other fist, this time at Harry's stomach.

Taken by surprise, Harry retreated before more blows, which he blocked as well as he could with his arms, then lashed back with a foot at Bob's leg, at the spot where he knew the shrapnel was still buried in that knee. Bob crumpled onto the pavement.

'Bastard,' Bob said. 'I bet you bloody did the murder.' That was what was starting to make most sense to him; it was the only thing that explained the way Harry had been acting; and, as everybody appeared to think Harry had killed the girl, it dragged Bob into that. Prone on the paving but not finished, Bob lashed out with his other foot at Harry's leg as Harry moved back.

'I'll still talk us out of it,' Harry said.

Strong hands and arms pulled at the pair as the driver and the constable sorted them out.

'Stupid gits,' the driver said. 'The sooner we get you back in your cells the better.'

Bob and Harry were hauled in the direction of them. 'We're still mates,' Harry yelled after Bob. 'Remember how I talked us out of all those charges for being late after leave?'

Bob sighed. Was Harry thinking back to the war as if it were a good time? Perhaps he had never known any.

After he had been dragged into his cell and the door had been shut behind him, Bob lay on his bunk and swore. There was nothing to be done but lie supine on the rock-hard mattress, which became more uncomfortable by the minute. As he did so, he listened to the sound of a warder walking outside the cell; the faint hum of traffic in the distance; the snores of a fellow-prisoner in a nearby cell; and to the rhythm of his own breathing, shallow and short. He turned over and over as it was difficult to remain still.

CHAPTER FORTY-ONE

Bob was glad they were driven in separate cars to court as it meant he didn't have to share one with Harry. They had smartened up, with their hair slicked in place, wearing striped neckties in an attempt to give a contrast of colour to their dark suits. Bob was aware that Harry's face held none; that had drained away, as must the colour of his own, he supposed. Harry sported a bruise on his cheek, which added to his look of desperation.

Nancy was seated in the gallery, along with the chums who had lied with her; she did bear a guilty expression, but her chin had a pious set to it. Her friends held similar expressions.

The barmaid, Elspeth, looked as if she enjoyed her strut to the witness stand. She stood with hands on hips at first as if ready to do battle, then, as if remembering where she was, put them at her side and simpered towards the coroner. Edmund Archibald gave a half-smile in return.

'Would you give your name and occupation, please?'

'My name is Elspeth Summers and I work as a barmaid at the Victoria.'

'You have stated you saw Harry Barker and Bob Nuttall on Thursday, 19 August?'

Elspeth looked round the courtroom as if relishing the moment, then talked with rapidity in an officious tone. She said that when she saw Bob and Harry at the bar in the Victoria Hotel at lunchtime they had no money, but when she saw them again in the evening they had so much they were throwing it around so, where did they get that from? She also made sure she mentioned that Harry had somehow dirtied and rumpled his suit in the course of the day, and how did he manage that? Then she talked of the oddity of Harry's behaviour on another day when she had been reading about this murder in the newspaper, and why was he so jumpy about that? She gave the impression she would have talked endlessly of a number of other different things that had made her suspicious of Bob and Harry but, suddenly intimidated by the coroner's glinting glasses and the prying eyes from the gallery, she closed her mouth and, at the first opportunity, trudged back to her seat.

The coroner peered round the court before he made his pronouncement. 'I don't think we need to hear any more evidence. There are more witnesses. But I think we've heard enough to draw the preliminary conclusions that are the result of an inquest.'

The jury stared at him as he began to review the evidence. Some nodded as if in agreement with his pronouncements. Others shook their heads as if at the gravity of the act that had been done. Overall though, there was an impression of weariness, caused no doubt by the length of the proceedings, but also by the sins of men. The coroner told them there was no doubt about the murder, and no doubt about the connection between the girl and the men on the day and at the time just before the murder. There were enough witnesses whose statements linked, and the characters of the two men had been proven to be doubtful because of their attempts to provide a false alibi. The coroner pointed out that Anne Talbot's purse was missing and that her landlady had reported she kept several pounds in it; also that Harry and Bob had been spending more money than usual after the time of the murder. In addition, Bob had to change his suit later in the day as it had become dirty, possibly as the result of a scuffle. As the coroner's voice continued in its even manner, the jury continued to gaze at him.

'This case is one that should be considered as a whole,' Archibald said. 'It's one based on circumstantial evidence. The nature of such evidence suggests to some people less reliability. But circumstantial evidence is often more sound than direct evidence. Circumstances cannot lie, though people often do.'

Archibald sounded an erudite man, Bob thought, but it should have been enough they had left Anne alive. He shifted his right leg, as the knee joint was annoying him. He couldn't stop thinking about Nancy whom he hadn't expected to lie like that. He had even bought her an ice-cream when they had been at Blackforth Castle, and they had all had a good time together.

Archibald told the jury there was no need to hear from Barker and Nuttall on this occasion. If this moved onto a trial, the two men would have the chance to have their defence voiced then.

The jury retired, some clutching notes, others not. Some walked with pained expressions after all that sitting and listening, while others stretched with relish. Some showed dread, possibly at the thought of the decision they were going to have to make. But they only stayed out long enough for a relaxing cup of tea or coffee and a visit to the toilet, which suggested the decision was easy to make. Bob deplored their apparent lack of concern when they returned. It was not how he felt.

The jury foreman stood up facing the court, with a piece of paper held in front of him. His grey side whiskers gave him a distinguished look that fitted with a general impression of self-importance, which Bob thought may have been why the jury had chosen him as foreman; but he was giving thought to the paper in front of him as if he dreaded having to read it. When he did so, he spoke in a rush. 'The verdict of the jury is as follows: murder by Barker and Nuttall who led the girl to a lonely spot along the beach to do it.'

'Stupid bastards,' Bob screamed.

'Pillocks,' Harry roared.

The police led them out, struggling.

CHAPTER FORTY-TWO

The man opposite Bob was a relaxed, well-fed young man, whose suit in pale-grey, fine tweed Bob envied. Bob and Harry were in an interview room in the prison in consultation with their court-appointed lawyer, Alan Hoggard. Their counsel also exuded the smell of brandy as he glanced across at them over their case notes, and Bob supposed he had lingered over lunch in the kind of middle-class establishment he and Harry had never had the opportunity to frequent. Hoggard flipped over the finely-engraved lid of his gold watch, and Bob wondered how much time he would grant them.

'They've a promising case and you're in a pickle, after allowing them to run rings round you in those interview rooms. Now I'm supposed to work out a defence?'

'I didn't murder anyone,' Bob said.

'Nor me,' Harry said.

Hoggard gave them a quizzical look. 'I'm your lawyer and I will argue that, but it helps if I know the facts.'

'You mean you think we did it?' Bob said.

'I don't think about it one way or the other, but if you did commit the crime, it can help to tell me, because I'll know the pitfalls that await us at trial.'

'We're done for, Bob,' Harry said to him. 'Even our lawyer thinks we're a pair of murderers.'

'Did I say that?' Hoggard looked offended.

'More or less,' Harry said.

'Yes,' Bob said.

Hoggard took out a pen and notebook and wrote in it. 'In order to act as your defence, I need to know exactly what happened,' he continued.

'The girl was murdered all right,' Bob said. 'But not by us.'

'That's right,' Harry said.

The expression on Hoggard's face became grim. 'Why did you put Nancy Harland down as an alibi?'

'Because we were with her that afternoon,' Bob said.

'It's a pity she doesn't agree.'

'Someone's got at her,' Harry said.

'Difficult to prove,' Hoggard replied.

'We were at Blackforth Castle with her, and walked about, and had an ice cream. We had a great time, laughing and joking all afternoon, and now she says none of that happened?' The indignation in Bob's voice was clear.

'Are you sure it was that afternoon you were with her?' Hoggard asked. 'It would be unusual for a witness to lie so blatantly. Why would she do that?'

'She's afraid of something,' Harry said.

'Even if we could get her to retract, we need to have an exact timescale here. When were you with her?'

'From about two-thirty,' Bob said.

'No, it was definitely three,' Harry said.

'You don't even agree the time with each other. But let's argue you left the Victoria about two as Elspeth Summers said, and took a motorbus over to Blackforth, and got there about two thirty. That would work out, Elspeth Summer covering for you till two, and Nancy from half two, if she would do that, and if we agree with their time of death, and that's a minefield.'

'We did see Anne that afternoon,' Bob said. 'But the murder must have been done after we left her.'

'Bob, I told you not to tell–'

'He said he has to know the truth if he's to put up a defence.'

'If he thinks we've done it, he won't even agree to represent us.'

An exasperated expression had appeared on Hoggard's face. 'If any of what you've been telling me has been true, at what time could you possibly have seen Anne Talbot?'

'We left the Victoria earlier than Elspeth said, and got to Blackforth later,' Harry said.

'Their case is you were both with the girl, and it's apparent now you were, and it was always difficult to argue you weren't because they've got so many witnesses, even if they don't all agree with each other. And their argument is you colluded to kill the girl because circumstances point to that.'

'They can't hang us because we're likely to have committed a murder. They need proof,' Bob argued.

'Don't they?' Harry pleaded.

'They need enough to present a cogent case. Then the jury acts as judge and decides whether you did it or not.'

The statement hung in the air. Eventually, Bob said, 'I left Harry by himself with the girl because they were getting on well, and then he came back saying they'd had an argument and he'd left her.'

The lawyer looked at Harry.

'I didn't kill her,' Harry said.

'So, what did happen when you were with her?' Hoggard asked.

'We had a chat and a walk and we were getting on great so I made a pass at her.' Harry paused and the other two waited for him to continue. 'But she wasn't having any, so I left her by herself.'

'You just left her by herself?'

'Look, she was annoyed with me, right?'

'I see,' Hoggard said. 'Perhaps I'd better not ask what angered her. What was she doing when you left her?'

'I couldn't tell you. I just walked off.'

'Did you see any sign of anyone else?'

'No.'

'And no one else has turned up to say they saw her between the time you had your row with her and her body turning up.'

'When it's put like that it sounds awful, but I didn't do it. I don't know how she died. Honest.'

Hoggard contemplated him, then looked across to Bob. 'We could argue your innocence, Bob, if Harry were to admit he killed Anne by himself and agreed with any testimony you put forward.'

'But I didn't do it,' Harry said. There was a thoughtful silence as all three looked at each other. 'And I'll be hanged if I say I did.'

'Look,' Bob said. 'It's obvious even to me you killed her, you with your grudges about the war, and with that short temper of yours, but can you keep me out of it?'

'I didn't kill her. I didn't.'

The lawyer pronounced his words clearly. 'If we don't prove there was no collusion, you'll both swing. Do you want your friend to hang too?'

'There's no defence?' Harry said.

'There's always a defence. You're from round here and there must be people who can say things that'll help. We might even find a witness who saw you with Nancy Harland that afternoon, if you were. But don't ask any more of your fellow prisoners to speak for you.' He looked at Harry with sorrowful eyes. 'And I'll talk with Nancy Harland herself, and try to find out what's going on there, though I imagine she'll be unlikely to retract.'

Hoggard talked with them for an hour altogether about possible lines of defence, before looking at his watch again and leaving. He had spent longer with them than

Bob had expected of a gentleman of officer-class, particularly as Bob had the impression Hoggard thought they were both dead to rights.

CHAPTER FORTY-THREE

Back in prison, Bob lay flat-out on his bunk. He shut his eyes and tried to forget he was in a cell, but there were still the sounds of a gaol: prisoners called out to each other; a cell door slammed; and feet tramped along the corridor. He found it was just as impossible to turn a deaf ear to his thoughts. Bob had been overwhelmed by Hoggard's lack of confidence in their case; and he couldn't stop reflecting on the damning nature of the attempts of Harry to get them out of this jam, Harry, whom Bob had possessed such faith in. Bob started to pace from one wall to another, from the window with bars, to the door with no bars but a very large lock.

As he continued to pace, his breathing and heart rate accelerated. He willed his legs to stop, so he could lay himself on the bed and try to persuade his pulse to slow. Then, as he lay studying the windows, the thought occurred that if he tied sheets together and made a noose, those bars might be high enough.

He gave this serious thought. As a soldier, he was well versed in the mechanics and the pain of death. He had seen how long the man beside him could survive with part of his head shot away, and he knew what a stomach wound or one in the throat could reduce a man to. They had all come to envy the quickness of death by a bullet in the brain and had wished that had been the typical one. He worked out what hanging yourself by a sheet to those bars would do to him, and it would not break the neck. It would be a death by choking; he tried to work out how long that would be and what it would be like to suffer that helplessness and pain.

They would hang him anyway, with a proper rope from a proper height and by a practised hangman. And that would be quicker, less agonising, and more dignified, though he doubted there was such a thing as a dignified death. He turned his back to the window and attempted to sleep.

CHAPTER FORTY-FOUR

If there was one place where Blades didn't want to be, it was Birtleby beach. When the call came in, he had been settling down to an evening meal at home with Jean and Gordon, his son. Jean had poured him a beer, and there was a feeling that things were returning to normal after the inquest. Now he was staring at another body of a woman as it lay half-covered by sand in the half-light of evening, and he was wondering what was going on.

The body was not covered well, so it looked as if that had been done in a hurry. As it lay just off the track, Blades wondered at the sense in trying to cover it at all, as no one could have supposed it would have remained unobserved for long. He surmised the woman had met her killer as she had walked along that track, unless she'd walked along there with him. When he looked at the amount of blood that had seeped from the body, Blades was appalled.

The woman lay with her head back, arms and legs flung out. Her dress had ridden up her body, leaving the undergarments exposed, and Blades felt an urge to pull down the skirt to recover some dignity for her. Like the other woman found dead in Birtleby, she looked young even if, covered in blood and sand as she was, it was difficult to give anything like an accurate estimation of age.

Blades looked up at Walker who stood beside him. 'Who?' seemed to be the word that was forming on his lips though it wasn't given proper expression. Then, he looked towards Blades and did speak. 'But we've got them. They're in jail.' He looked back at the body. 'This shouldn't have happened.'

'No,' Blades agreed.

'And they're dead to rights. The jury agreed. We can't have got it wrong.'

'Perhaps someone else did this one,' Blades said.

'So, there are two different sets of murderers preying on young women on the same stretch of beach?'

It was the same patch of coastline, almost. Only a few hundred yards separated this crime scene from the last.

'It could happen,' Blades said.

'Is it likely?' Walker replied.

'Possibly not,' Blades said. 'That doesn't mean it didn't. A copycat killer?' he suggested.

'I suppose that's plausible,' Walker said. He stared at the body. 'Is it the same modus operandi?' Walker asked. Walker bent down and uncovered sand so that they could see the head more clearly.

'The bashes to the skull look similar,' Blades said.

'Perhaps this one was sexual,' Walker said.

Blades blinked at the non-sequitur. 'Parker will tell us,' he said. 'Will we be releasing Bob Nuttall and Harry Barker?'

'That's what we have to establish,' Walker replied. 'We'll gather our evidence and see.'

He looked up at the noise of someone approaching with quick steps. It was a flustered Parker. He would have been alerted at about the same time, Blades knew, but may have had further to travel.

'We should stop meeting like this,' Parker said.

'I'll agree with that,' Blades said.

'Please tell us it's not the same killer,' Walker said.

'They're not hanged yet,' Parker said.

'Consolation you think?' Walker said.

'Barker and Nuttall would think so – and we'll see what I think when I've had a chance to look,' Parker said.

He laid his bag beside the corpse, proceeded to take out instruments and notebook, then turned to the body. He muttered, lines clear on his forehead. He lifted the head to peer underneath, then touched the skin to gauge temperature, Blades assumed, and experimented with the movement of the hand and arm to gauge rigor mortis. He made notes, then set up his camera for photographs. He did all this in a silence which Walker and Blades respected, but Walker broke it eventually with an impatient cough.

'I don't suppose–' he started to say.

'Yes?'

'–you'd share preliminary conclusions?'

'You'd think it was the same murder as the last.'

Walker's face showed his dismay. 'In what way?' he asked.

'The obvious. A young woman of a similar age killed on a beach in Birtleby by blows to the head. But more than that. When you examine the wounds, they're very alike, as if done with the exact same implement or implements, though what it or they might be I can still only guess. Some of the blows seem to have been done with a sharp instrument, others with a blunt one, the initial blows being made to the lower portion of the head again, then the killing blow to the temple, and, looking at the blood under the head, this killing also took place where the body was found.'

'It's the same killer,' Walker said.

'It looks like it.'

'And murder again, not manslaughter?'

'It would be difficult to argue accidental death, and I'll do a thorough examination at the morgue to check for signs of sexual assault.'

'Time of death?'

Parker snorted. 'I don't know. I can tell you when it might have occurred. 12 to 36 hours previous.'

'No longer than that?'

'Probably not, though this time I'd better make sure I've taken an exact body temperature reading.' He opened his bag to take out his thermometer.

Walker looked across at Blades as he tutted, apparently to himself. Blades tried to put reassurance into his answering smile.

'The press is going to love this,' Walker said.

'Police Bungle Again?' Blades suggested.

'It's not how I'd put it,' Walker said, 'but it will help sell a newspaper or two.'

CHAPTER FORTY-FIVE

After the release of Harry and Bob – the Crown Prosecution had argued that no jury would convict them now – Walker and Blades had the job of sifting through other suspects. They decided to start by interviewing the two soldiers as they had been in the area on that day too, selling their lavender.

The morning they came for George Wilkinson, he hadn't had much sleep as he had been expecting to be hauled in for a chat ever since he'd heard about the second body, and dawn had found him glaring at the small rectangle of lightening sky visible through his dormitory window.

Daybreak had felt ominous to George since the trenches because that was when attacks started. He remembered what it had been like, standing at the fire-step by the improvised three-step ladder. There had been the sound of shells whirring and whining, and hundreds of artillery pieces had roared. The idea of the Allied bombardment of German lines was to soften up the enemy before the attack, but George felt he was the one being flattened.

In his mind, the whistle blew again and the men poured over the top, George amongst them. A glance behind was as terrifying as looking ahead. An officer was striding about, waving his pistol at anyone who hesitated, with a determined expression on his face. George recognized Lieutenant Anderson, the neatly shaven man who helped fellow soldiers write their letters home, and who gave encouraging words when they were being shelled. Now Anderson glared about with manic eyes out of one of the whitest faces George thought he had ever seen. The soldier to George's left faltered, and George thought he was going to throw himself down, or turn and run, because George could see the funk on his face, and George gestured in the direction of the officer behind them. The man – it was Doug, and George had shared bully beef and smokes with him and talked football and women – glanced back to see the lieutenant's pistol pointed straight at him, and Doug turned and stumbled further forward.

Then the ground in front of George erupted as a shell hit it, and knocked George back so he fell into mud. Dirt and more mud showered over him from another shell and buried him. He struggled for breath as his mouth and nose filled with dirt, and his hands and limbs scrabbled and pushed it away from him. This felt futile at first, but he was desperate; his legs and fingers found strength and will, and then there was a hole to breathe through, and he heard his breath rasp. Then he pushed more and more, until he felt a hand pulling at him, then another, and, between the hands and his own desperate limbs, the dirt was gradually pushed away, and he found himself struggling into the fresh air.

George had set off in this offensive line with so many other soldiers, but most of them now lay on the ground around him, either still, or twitching, prone, wounded, missing an arm here, holding at their own guts there. The sergeant major, Lampourt, had a shattered stump where his right leg had been, and he was lying looking at the remnant of his leg. When George gazed around, he could not see that lieutenant anywhere, and supposed he was under the mud, his pistol with him.

It was 1920 now and the guns had stopped firing long ago, but George still heard them before every dawn, which was when the police arrived now with their loud voices, large hands, and clumping boots, and he was as terrified as he had been at the sound of the shells, as he was handcuffed to one of the constables and hauled into a police car.

CHAPTER FORTY-SIX

'Jane Dawson.'

George stared back at Walker who sat opposite him in the police-station interview room. Walker had enunciated the words with deliberation, but who was Jane Dawson?

Walker added, 'You know her.' It was phrased as a statement, not a question, which irritated and puzzled George further.

'Do I?'

'Yes.'

George thought furiously. 'Andy and I did chat to a young woman.'

'Yes?'

'She was called Jane. Was her second name Dawson?'

'Tell me about the young woman you call Jane.'

'There's not much to tell, but I suppose–' He paused and collected his thoughts. 'She was a slim girl, of medium-height, with brunette hair cut in a bob. She had an attractive laugh, that one. I remember that.'

'Did she?' Blades said.

'She was cheerful as Christmas, and good company. Andy and I met her on the shore when we were selling lavender. She bought some and we chatted.' Blades and

Walker frowned at him as if pondering what he said, which George found disconcerting, so he started talking more quickly. 'Not that we were talking about anything much. It's great to talk about nothing, a movie, a song, don't you think?' But the policemen didn't reply, just waited. 'Then we went for a walk along the Ridges, and I thought I was getting places with her, so Andy dropped behind, and left me to it, but, to tell the truth, she was a bit of a tease. She didn't want to know and I ended up telling her what I thought about that, and then I went back to Andy, leaving her there, and that was that.' Then George stopped talking, and the silence felt disconcerting, but what else was there to say?

'You left her body there?' Walker said. His voice was solemn, his eyes piercing.

'She was alive when I last saw her,' George said, his voice rising. 'Look, I didn't kill anybody, and why would I kill Jane? She was a pretty girl. I like pretty girls.' Then he ran out of words and stared instead.

'That fits in with what witnesses have told us,' Walker said. 'We know you were there, with Jane Dawson, just before she died, and you've told us Andy left you alone with her, and you quarrelled with her. Later, she was found dead.'

George was terrified when he listened to this. Walker's voice sounded so reasonable, and it made him feel he had not a leg to stand on.

'I didn't kill her, honest,' George said. 'You've got to believe me. You've got to.'

Walker and Blades stared at George, and then Walker said, 'You can stay in a cell for now, and we'll question your friend Andy.'

CHAPTER FORTY-SEVEN

While they waited for Andy to be brought in, Walker and Blades had time to compare notes.

'It might be reasonable to suspect him, but when you listen to him, he's convincing,' Blades said.

'They always are,' Walker replied.

'So, what do you think? Guilty or not guilty?' Blades asked.

'At this moment, the case sounds promising.'

'Like the last one.' Blades studied Walker.

'Yes.' Walker returned the look. 'Again, we look for definitive evidence,' he said.

Then Hodgkins returned with Andy who slumped forward on the seat across the desk from them, his thumbs twisting each other round, and his eyes avoiding theirs.

'You know Jane Dawson?' Walker said.

'Who?' Andy replied, then stared at his thumbs.

'The girl you and George chatted up and walked with onto the Ridges.'

'We didn't–' he started to say, then stopped. 'Oh her. Was that her name? I wouldn't know. George did most of the talking.'

'Her body was found on the Ridges not long after you left her there.'

Andy sat upright in his chair and stared back at them. 'Was she? That's terrible. She was nice. How did she die?'

'You admit you were there?'

'Why would I kill a girl like that?'

'We have witnesses who place you there, and George has admitted you were both with her.'

Andy said nothing at first, then said, 'It wouldn't look good to deny it then. Yes. We were there with her but we left her alive.'

'You expect us to believe that?'

'Yes.' A look of anger passed over Andy's face. 'I wouldn't... how dare you? Of course, I'd never do such a thing as that. Naturally she was alive when we left her.'

'Then did you see anybody else around that afternoon?'

'We didn't–' Andy gave the question thought. 'I suppose... There was a sailor strolling in the same direction as us. He was following us. Big fellow. Long arms. Then I lost sight of him.'

'When did you last see him?'

'I don't know. He did come onto the Ridges with us, but we were talking to Jane and I didn't look behind me all the time, but he must have gone away at some point because when we walked back together, he wasn't there anymore.'

'Is this a man you'd ever seen before?'

They questioned him more about the sailor, and Andy was able to improve his description, which helped, because another witness, a man walking a dog, had described the same man, who was familiar to Walker and Blades. This was Pulteney, one of the witnesses in the investigation that had led to Harry Barker and Bob Nuttall being arrested, and now they knew he'd also been present at the second murder. One thing was sure, Pulteney wouldn't be able to blame Harry and Bob for this one, and Blades wondered how he would react when they questioned him.

CHAPTER FORTY-EIGHT

George stood on a grassy cliff edge and looked out at the waves. The cliffs were high here, sandstone, worn into runnels and ledges, and seagulls wheeled and cawed above him and below. When the police had released him, George had been surprised, but he was sure they would haul him back to the station at some point, so he had walked along here to think. He looked below him at a female gull on a nest, while the male strutted further off, glancing back with a look of ownership. George looked further down towards the waves as they crashed onto the rocks, and further out towards the horizon where a boat was fishing. Grey clouds puffed about the sky as a breeze chased flecks from the waves. On rocks close to shore a seal was stretched out, taking its ease.

It was a peaceful scene, though George felt uneasy here on the height with the wind clutching at him. He watched the waves running off to the horizon with envy, as if they possessed a freedom he had no concept of. He still felt trapped in that police cell, and in his memories of war: the mud, the trenches, the thud of shell, and the whine of bullet. He also felt the murders he had committed, not that he had killed either of the two women.

His kills had taken place in battle and had occurred far enough away for him not to smell fear in his victims, or watch their grasp at life as blood seeped out of them; but he felt his murders, though they had been done in the line of duty, were legal, defensible, and for which he had been given a medal that still lay, unopened, in the red, gilt-edged box it had been sent to him in.

George remembered seeing one German gorging on a smoke in the trenches opposite, and, lost in his contemplations, stepping forward to give George such a clear sight of him he could not fail to pop off a bullet. George didn't have any impression of the soldier himself beyond the angle of helmet and pose of arm and body, but he had paused longer than he should have before squeezing the trigger. For once, he had given thought to the life he was about to steal before the crack left his rifle as if by itself, the bullet found its mark, and the figure crumpled over. It was him or me, George had thought, but it had not been. The man had been enjoying his moment, as he drew in smoke from a cigarette, and George had reached out and taken it from him.

What right did George have to take any of the lives he had in battle? As little right as he would have done had he taken Jane Dawson's, George thought, and he pondered the looks in the eyes of the two inspectors as they had interrogated him. Yes, murder was dreadful. The police would spend a lot of man-hours investigating these deaths; they would make sure they caught the man, make him face trial, and be hanged by the neck till dead. George thought of Jane, of the lightness of her laugh, the softness of her skin, the way the light caught her hair, the cleanness of her smell, and of the quickness in her step. All snuffed out by a murderer. Jane would never laugh again, never love, never marry, never bear children, and never grow old.

George supposed it was just as true of the Germans he had murdered. George thought of the one he had killed in his quiet moment smoking a cigarette in his trench. It was a moment George himself had known so often, as he had revelled in the touch of breeze, the feel of earth underfoot, the sharpness of smoke in the lungs as he drew it in. That man would not know the relief George had felt in returning from war, and the pleasure of being reunited with family and friends. He would meet no Jane Dawson, or flirt or laugh with any other young woman, kiss no one, marry no one, and father no children. George had taken all of that from him with a squeeze on a trigger.

George was a murderer, and it was a heinous crime. He had not killed Jane Dawson or Anne Talbot, but what did it matter if they hanged him for that? What was the difference which murder they executed you for?

The sad thing was they might not. If they decided there was not enough proof, there would be no capital punishment for him. In that moment he knew he didn't want to get away with the killings he'd done, and he couldn't live with the thought of them.

George looked out to the horizon. What was it with distance? What promise did he always think he saw there? None he would ever reach, but he felt the urge to step out towards it all the same. It gave him such a sense of freedom when he did, as if he were leaving all sense of guilt on that grassy cliff edge – though that emotion only lasted a moment till the terror of the fall overwhelmed him.

CHAPTER FORTY-NINE

Pulteney bit his lower lip and screwed his hands into the arm of his chair before forcing himself to relax them. He stared at the two inspectors opposite him in the interview room, then looked away as the look in their eyes worried him. Then Walker spoke, and Pulteney took in the severity in the voice.

'We know you follow women because you've put that down in a statement and signed it. You do that a lot, do you?'

At previous meetings, Walker had been looking for co-operation from Pulteney as a witness, and Pulteney found the change in attitude difficult.

'Chris says you like following women,' Blades said.

'Did he?' Pulteney said. 'He can talk.'

'You do then?' Walker said.

Pulteney frowned and bit his lip.

'Do you have girlfriends?' Blades asked.

Pulteney stared back at him. Was it his fault women weren't interested in him? He did have a girlfriend once, called Maggie, though it had been years ago. He thought back to her. She was pretty, with blond though coarse hair, and there was a quickness about her that contrasted with his own slowness. She was outgoing and confident, and attracted many boys, so she had gained a reputation for being flighty, but Pulteney did not mind. She was fun, and she liked the attentions he gave her, for a while, but Pulteney had not liked it when she had grown bored. He worshipped her, and he didn't understand her when she spurned him. When he tried to kiss her that last time, she pushed him away, and when he made another attempt, pushed him even harder. He reacted and tried to insist on the kiss, but she slapped him and shouted at him he was forcing himself on her, and said she would call the police. He didn't know what to make of that, but he was more aware than ever of that body close beside him, the pert breasts, the strong limbs, the curving hips, the sweetness of her perfume, the quickness of her breathing, and that physicality caused something to lurch inside him, and he grasped at her, and pulled her back when she pulled away, before putting his hand up that dress as he had longed to for so long. Then his other hand opened his fly, and he found himself trying to force his way into her. But she was surprisingly strong and had a hefty kick, and he found himself floundering around on the ground trying to cope with the pain of her attack, while she straightened her dress and walked away.

And when he stared back at these two policemen, the guilt of that surged up in him, though there was no way they could know about it.

'No girlfriends but such an interest in women. That must be difficult. Is that why you follow women about?' Walker asked. 'You've this resentment you want to take out on one of them?'

Had he been accused of something? Pulteney wondered.

He did have that fascination for the sound of a woman's voice and the need to follow its music. He had done that ever since that first leave back in Britain. He happened to find himself behind two army nurses strolling in a park, and, as he hadn't heard a woman talking for months, he was fascinated by their chatter, the tone of it, and the lightness. He didn't know if the nurses noticed him, but he couldn't stop himself trailing after them and, after that, following the voices of women became a habit.

He supposed it was odd but, then, he knew he was. He had been slower than others at school, had learned to read and write and count, but with an effort, and always behind the rest. And he looked strange, with an oddly long, clumsy body, and he was slow in speech.

'D'you have to be such a gorm?' That was what his brother Geoff had said to him.

'I–' But before Pulteney had time to get words out, Geoff had always gone on to something else.

'Have you any idea how embarrassing it is being your brother?'

'I don't–'

'They call you Snail because you're so slow, so I have to be quick or they'll be on at me. I don't have any friends because of you.'

'I'm… I'm sorry.' But before he got those words out, Geoff was off, strutting away, sulking.

The village Pulteney had been brought up in was called Whitney and was a few miles up the coast from Birtleby. It was a fishing village with boats harboured at the mouth of a river. All the fishing houses had been huddled together near to it, with their muddle of roofs and dykes, and the drying nets spread out on the common green.

'Will ye buy my herring?' A fishwife was always at the cross on the green with her basket, in her long skirts, with a shawl over her head. The sharp smell of her herring wafted itself at passers-by daily.

And everyone worked together. They had to. As there was no properly built harbour, boats were pulled up on shore to berth them, and it took several of the fishermen to bounce and haul and push the boats into the water.

Then the women would haul up their skirts, put their men on their backs and transport them dry to the boat, as it would have been uncomfortable, if not unhealthy, for the men to go out to sea wet and with no way of drying clothes properly.

There was also the gutting of the fish, which was women's work, and you could hear their cackles as they knifed at fish in the open sheds. The smell of fish mingled with the tang of the sea and stench of seaweed left behind by the tides on the river bank.

At slack times, the men grouped together in the inns with their grog and their tales of nets full of flailing tails and fins; or stories of their arid hauling at rope, tacking, and the limb-wrenching manipulation of sails as the fishermen searched with nets through uncooperative waters; and their relief at being on solid ground. The same men, looking as if drink never passed a lip, stood in the chapel on a Sunday in their best suits with the tight collars and their hair spruced up, and sang out hymns in deep voices because belief was strong in that fishing village, and was what gave them the courage to struggle through trying lives.

Pulteney's father was a lay preacher. The miracle of the fishes was his favourite sermon, and he would wax lyrical about the hubbub of the crowd gathering to hear the oratory of Christ. He would stress the length of time that passed as they listened without feeling the hardness of the rocks or dirt they sat on. Then Christ became aware of the hunger of his followers and asked if anyone had food to share, and the five loaves and fishes were brought forward, and Christ broke the bread, and divided up the fish, and kept on doing this while baskets were taken round and, in the end, those several hundred people had eaten their fill. Pulteney always wondered at the bounty of Christ and imagined fish and bread spilling out into the crowd, and he thought it must have felt as it did when, out on a boat, a particularly full net of fish was hauled up, and the apparently endless silver thrashed about on the deck. It made Pulteney feel he wanted to know the bounty and love of Christ.

His father's other favourite sermon was the Ten Commandments, and Pulteney's father would draw himself up to his full height when preaching about this, and his grey eyes would flash out above that hooked prow of a nose under the untidy, grey, spiky hair, as he gestured with his long arms and talked of the pains of hellfire.

Pulteney knew well his attempted rape of Maggie was a sin and he felt the shame of it, and his father made even more certain he did, as he stood with a righteous look in his eyes and lectured.

Pulteney knew that as long as he lived anywhere near his father, he would not be allowed to forget his guilt, as his father would feel it his duty to make sure of that, as would his brothers. Then war had come, and, to Pulteney, it had arrived as a sort of peace. He had joined the navy and found his strange haven on board a ship on convoy duty on the Atlantic, which was hell enough to be a suitable sanctuary for him, he supposed. As a stoker, the bowels of the ship became his sphere, an uncomfortable one where the thrum of the boat's engine vibrated through the roof and walls of his world.

He looked at Walker warily. At least he was sure of one thing. The incident with Maggie had never been reported to the police. Maggie had just finished with him, and his father had dealt with him daily ever after. Fishers took care of their own problems. Which meant this had nothing to do with that.

'Tell me your movements on the afternoon of September the 10th.'

'I don't remember. When was that?'

'Last Friday. This is Tuesday. You ought to be able to remember what you were doing then.'

Pulteney stared back at him, fidgeted in his chair, looked away, then looked back.

It occurred to him that was the day of that other murder. He supposed he should have realised it was about that. He opened his mouth to speak, then closed it, then started on a halting reply. 'I… I came into town from Larmouth by train, getting here about one o'clock and went for a stroll along the seafront. Then… yes, that's it. Yes, I looked at the sea for a while.' He thought for a moment or two, then continued, 'I spent time at the funfair, trying my hand at the rifle stall and the hoops. I had a candy floss and went onto the beach where I sat for a while looking at the sea. Then I walked along the seafront to stretch my legs.' He started to talk more confidently as memories of his movements flooded back. 'I did walk along the Ridges as far as the headland, turned, then wandered back, getting back to the seafront about four. I had a sandwich and tea at a café, and sat there for a while watching folk go by. Then I got my train at five and went back to camp.'

'Were you with anyone at any time?'

'No. I was by myself.'

'Do you have any witnesses to your movements?'

'Anyone might have seen me at any time. There were plenty of people around. It was a sunny day in Birtleby at the seafront. The people at the café should remember me. I was served by a girl about eighteen with curly dark hair. And I bought a train ticket at the station and I might have been seen getting on and off the trains.'

'Anyone else?'

'No one who comes to mind.'

'Did you follow anybody about that day?'

Pulteney said nothing at first, wondering how to answer the question, because he had found a female voice to trail after, as that was why he went for a stroll along the beach, but it might not be a good idea to admit to that.

'No.'

'Did you see Jane Dawson or talk to her at any point?'

'I don't know who Jane Dawson is.'

'A young lady about twenty, brunette, slim, wearing a brown jacket.'

'Doesn't ring a bell.' Though he did remember her and had a clear picture of her in his mind, not that he'd known her name.

'Did you murder her?'

Pulteney answered that question with no hesitation. 'No.'

He felt frustration build up in him, at his powerlessness, and at the contempt he was sure he saw in the attitude of the policemen. He bit his mouth in his effort to keep anger under control with a savageness that surprised him.

'We have a witness,' Walker said, 'who saw you walking along the beach after Jane Dawson just before the time she would have been killed, and another witness who admits to strolling along and talking to her, but says you were following on after them. Can you tell me anything about that?'

A witness? Pulteney cursed silently.

'I can't because I don't know anything,' he said, struggling with the words. 'It's ridiculous what you're suggesting,' he said. 'I didn't. There's a murderer out there. You should go after him.'

But when he looked at Walker and Blades he saw no sympathy. Walker said, 'We're charging you with the murder of Jane Dawson. Anything you say may be used in evidence against you. You have a right to a solicitor.'

CHAPTER FIFTY

Pulteney was not enjoying this view; he was staring at the plaster above the scarlet-sashed figure of the judge on his dais in the courtroom at Birtleby, where the Royal Arms were emblazoned, along with the Sword of Justice – the sword of which felt as if it were hanging above his own head. He was still wondering how he had ended up sitting here waiting for his own trial to begin but, after the inquest into the death of Jane Dawson, once the police had finished gathering further evidence, Pulteney had found himself charged with both her murder and that of Anne Talbot.

When Pulteney looked across at the jury, his impression was of a blur of self-righteous, portly, middle-aged men, but he did not dare look at any of them and thought it safer to concentrate on gazing at the oak floor in front of him, though he did glance at the judge, a white-wigged man with a ruddy, round face.

Below the judge's bench was a desk at which was seated a thin man with grey hair swept back, who was wearing a brown suit, and whom Pulteney took to be the Clerk of the Court. The man stood and addressed the jury.

'Members of the jury, please stand.' They did so with a promptness that alarmed Pulteney, as did the alertness in the way they shared glances with each other and returned the gaze of the Clerk of Court, who continued, 'Usher, please hand out cards and bibles.' When this had been finished, he said to the jurors, 'With the bible in hand, and reading from the cards, repeat after me, "I swear by Almighty God that I will well and truly try and true deliverance make between our sovereign King and the prisoner at the Bar whom I shall have in charge, and a true verdict give according to the evidence.'

This was words and form to Pulteney, and held little meaning for him, but the seriousness of the tone of the Clerk of the Court chilled him. The jury seated themselves and waited in silence, if not without the odd shift of legs or arms as the usher took back the bibles and cards and placed them on the ledge of the jury box.

'William Pulteney, please stand,' the Clerk said, and Pulteney forced himself to do so. 'William Pulteney, you are charged on indictment that on 19 August in Birtleby in the county of Yorkshire you murdered Anne Talbot. Are you guilty or not guilty?'

Murder by trial was what this felt like, the words of the Clerk a preparatory strafing for what was to follow. Pulteney stared at his feet as his hands gripped at the rail in front of him to prevent themselves from shaking. In the end, he was able to force himself to look up and back at the Clerk of Court. 'Not guilty,' he whispered.

'Please repeat that,' the Clerk of Court said, 'so that we can all hear what you are saying.'

'Not guilty,' Pulteney said, much more loudly; he barely stopped himself screaming.

The Clerk continued, 'Further you are charged on indictment that on 10 September in Birtleby in the county of Yorkshire, you murdered Jane Dawson. Are you guilty or not guilty?'

You are charged on indictment, Pulteney thought, was an odd way of saying you did her in didn't you, you murderous bastard, which was what this court official meant.

'Not guilty,' Pulteney replied, and this time there was no mistaking the clarity in the words or the defiance.

The Clerk of the Court turned to the jury and said to them, 'Members of the Jury, the prisoner stands indicted for that on 19 August he murdered Anne Talbot, and that he on 10 September murdered Jane Dawson. To both indictments he has pleaded not guilty.'

They were obviously listening, Pulteney thought, so they must have got that already. This man was putting on a drama. The Clerk motioned to Pulteney to sit, which he was relieved to do, and made no attempt to control his sigh.

Behind desks on either side of the court were seated two black-cloaked figures with curled wigs, the Counsel for the Prosecution and the Counsel for the Defence. One of them stood, a broad, well-fed looking man with a hooked nose and clear eyes. He opened his mouth to speak but was interrupted by the judge.

'One moment, Mr Simpson,' he said before addressing the jury.

The judge, who had introduced himself earlier as Mr Justice Johns, allowed his eyes to wander round his courtroom before resting them on the jury.

'A serious crime has been committed, and the evidence against the accused must be considered carefully, because the consequences for the guilty in a trial like this are severe. The punishment I am required by law to confer upon him would be hanging by the neck until dead.'

Pulteney was relieved to see that several jury members looked nervous when the judge said this. The words terrified him.

'Listen very carefully to the evidence you are about to hear and weigh it well. It doesn't matter that the police officers who have gathered the proofs must consider the defendant guilty because of them. What matters is if you do. You judge the innocence or guilt of the defendant, not them or me. How sound is the case you are about to hear? That is the question you must ask yourselves.'

Fair words, Pulteney thought, as the judge stopped and re-appraised the jury, and Pulteney considered that the form of the trial at least would be reasonable. All the same, he wondered about the prejudices that would lie beneath the surface. He looked at the jury and wondered what manner of men they were and what they might be guilty of themselves.

The judge said, 'I ask Counsel for the Prosecution to call his witnesses.'

From Pulteney's point of view, now began a pantomime.

Looking at the audience in the public gallery, he saw a mixture of people, male, female, middle-aged, young, well-to-do, and plenty of a common sort. He noticed, too, people he recognized from his own village, his brother, and one or two of the elders from the church, who looked as they did at services, self-righteous and intimidating. His father was in the gallery with his large grey head that seemed so precariously attached to the long neck, and Pulteney took in the condemnation in his eyes.

Mr Simpson stood and addressed the court. The hawk-like nose made him look predatory as he told them what he was about to prove: that Anne Talbot and Jane Dawson were murdered in a similar manner and with a similar instrument, and that, though there was no witness to the murder, there were enough to prove William Pulteney was present at the time and place of both murders. Also, there was found in his possession a weapon that would fit the unusual injuries suffered by both women, and there were signs that it had been used recently.

Pulteney's eyes drifted away from Simpson. One glance had been enough to take in his single-mindedness. Pulteney looked at some of the women in the public gallery. Weren't some of them from Whitney? Their normal cackle came to mind, but their stares were cold now.

Mr Simpson continued, 'I wish to call Chief Inspector Walker of Scotland Yard.'

Pulteney took in the steady eyes as Walker was presented with a bible and oath card, and he noticed that the theatricality of judicial costume and rhetoric did not intimidate Walker. In a clear voice, the inspector told the story of the investigation of the first body much as he had at the first inquest, only showing any tremor when he began to describe the scene at the discovery of the second body. Pulteney supposed he was more shaken by this because at the time he must have thought he had his murderers behind bars.

When Simpson instructed Walker to expand on what he found unusual about the second murder scene, Pulteney felt like screaming because Walker went on to enumerate so many points of similarity between the second and first murder, when Pulteney thought it might have been enough just to say that two young women were found dead on a beach at Birtley with their heads bashed in. But Mr Simpson assiduously encouraged Walker; he seemed to be making sure that even the densest member of the jury understood. Pulteney wished Simpson did not look so confident. Pulteney's glance went up and out of the arched window past the castellation of the structure outside it. There was a clear blue sky out there, and Pulteney's mind struggled with the concept.

'Would you explain how you assembled a case against Pulteney?'

Walker paused as if to collect his thoughts, then fixed a decisive look on Simpson, as Pulteney did his best again not to listen to what Walker had to say. Their case against him depressed him and listening to it only made him feel his stupidity in allowing himself to be manoeuvred into this dock, but his mind did attune itself to the words 'Christopher Fleming'. What was that? Walker had said Pulteney had been seen there by two witnesses, Andrew Hanson and Christopher Fleming. Chris? No. Not Chris. Chris wasn't testifying against him?

Then his mind focussed itself on the cosh that was brought forward in its plastic bag as evidence against him. It was his, an instrument useful for his protection he had thought when he acquired it, but which was now a weapon against him. As the usher passed through the jury holding the evidence bag, the jury peered at it. Pulteney had to admit it was an ugly weapon. Had Simpson described it as a wooden cudgel? That was an understatement. It was a trench club, of the kind made by pioneers for soldiers on night raids, a long wooden club with steel studs projecting from it. Pulteney supposed it did seem reasonable to assume someone with such a thing in his possession had a violent streak, even though he knew many soldiers had simply brought these back as souvenirs.

Some words spoken by Walker came across with a particular chill. 'It does show marks of use,' Walker said. 'There's a dent on its surface that shows it has met another object with considerable force, and that recently.'

CHAPTER FIFTY-ONE

Pulteney stared at Parker when he took the stand, and took in the coldness in the professional demeanour, and the distaste in the glance Parker gave him. Then Pulteney looked back at the floor, which, unremarkable as it was, held more appeal, and he didn't listen carefully. Pulteney had heard the police surgeon's description of the first body at the inquest, and this drift of words sounded similar: Parker was detailing lacerations, bruising, and the extent of damage to the cheekbones and forehead.

Pulteney did start paying more attention to Parker's account of his examination of the second body, but soon switched off even to that. 'The body was that of a young female in physically healthy condition till the blows that caused her death.' The words made Pulteney wince: a young woman who was perfectly healthy apart from being murdered. Parker made it sound such a waste of life, and the jury would lap that up. Pulteney did take in the identical nature of the injuries being described, but he concentrated more on stopping himself fidget. He was sure the way he shifted about and screwed his hands into the rail ahead of him made him look as guilty as the jury probably thought he was. He didn't want to hear any of this, or to be here.

'Do you consider the same implement could have been used in both cases?' Simpson asked.

That question made Pulteney sit up as the usher presented the cosh again. Parker's words as he looked at the cudgel in his turn were unnerving too.

'It looks suited to the purpose,' Parker was saying, 'well enough to have done the damage to both skulls without any help from the stone. I thought a stick with a brass top could have done the initial damage but then there were the lacerations. I was puzzled, but this answers every question. It's narrow enough, rounded enough, and sharp enough to explain every mark, though I tend to think in both cases a stone was used for the coup de grace.'

'So, this instrument could have been used in both cases?'

'Definitely.'

That sounded conclusive to Pulteney; he was surprised that it was thought necessary to call another doctor to the stand after Parker was dismissed, and he was dismayed at the continued punctiliousness.

The confidence in Langford's stride forward and the smug, educated tone in his carping voice grated. Hadn't there been a disagreement between Langford and Parker as to the time of death at the inquest? Pulteney was sure he remembered there had been but it seemed to be smoothed over now. After all, the evidence Pulteney himself had given at the inquest suggested he was definitely there or thereabouts when that murder was committed. And it had been Langford, not Parker, who had indicated that time of death, and he carried the clout of that great list of letters after his name. The words spoken by Langford that came across most clearly to Pulteney were: 'The damage to this young woman's skull was similar to that caused to Anne Talbot, indicating both that a person of similar strength had undertaken both crimes, and that the same implement had been used in both cases, something narrow with a bluntness which caused the initial damage, and something that also held sharp edges to explain the lacerations.' And the expression on Langford's face when he examined the trench club was as eloquent as what he said when he agreed that could have been the implement.

CHAPTER FIFTY-TWO

When Chris stepped forward to the witness stand, Pulteney felt a heaviness descend, as he had thought of Chris as his friend. Pulteney now stared at him with wonder. Chris had a fixed expression on his face and Pulteney noticed that he avoided looking in his direction. Pulteney reflected that, though Chris had never been a person who liked standing out in a crowd, he could hardly avoid it now.

Simpson addressed Chris. 'Would you describe what you know of William Pulteney's movement on 19 August and how you came to know of them?'

Pulteney noticed that Chris looked straight ahead without looking at Simpson either, and there was something mechanical in the way he spoke, almost as if this was something he had learned by rote.

'I was in his company that afternoon. We were walking along the seafront and William noticed a group walking along and chatting with each other. There were three of them, two men and a young woman. William said, "Why don't we follow them and see what they get up to?" I said, "Why? What do you think they're going to get up to?" but he said, "I don't know but it'll be a laugh and will help pass the time." We followed them but I wasn't keen on it. It was William's idea and, after a while, I told him I was going to leave him to it and I did.'

Simpson enunciated his question carefully.

'Do you know who these people were that he was following?'

The expression on Chris' face didn't change; his demeanour suggested he only had interest in presenting facts.

'At the time, no. They were strangers to me, though William said he'd seen the young woman about the day before. It was on the Saturday that I read in the paper about the body found at the Ridges and thought it sounded like the young woman, so I got in touch with the police.'

'And you told them you'd been in company with William at the time you'd seen her?'

'Yes, and it was after I'd told William I'd done this, that he got in touch with them.'

'Because his name would have come up anyway?'

'I suppose so.'

Chris said he was sure the young woman was Anne Talbot because of the clothes she was wearing, her black bob of hair, and her build, and that she was in the company of the two men later identified as Harry Barker and Bob Nuttall.

'Did you see these young men committing any violent act towards Anne Talbot?'

'No.'

'How did relations look between them when you saw them?'

'They were chatting in a friendly way and laughing.'

Simpson continued, 'And can you tell me anything about Pulteney's movements on 10 September, the time of Jane Dawson's murder?'

Chris looked thoughtful as he replied, 'I wasn't in his company that day but I did see him and thought he looked suspicious.'

'Why?'

'He was following on behind a couple.'

'What did you do?'

'I tagged along behind to see what was what. He followed Jane Dawson with a young man along the Ridges. I lost sight of them after that. If I'd followed them any further I'd have been seen.'

Hoggard, Pulteney's defence counsel, had also asked some questions of previous witnesses though not many, and Pulteney thought he had given the impression of being ineffectual and not worthy of attention, but Pulteney paid heed to him now. It would be useful if Hoggard could cast doubt on Chris. Hoggard did draw himself up in an attempt at adopting an imposing manner.

'How are you sure this was Jane Dawson?'

Pulteney did think that question might be promising.

'I was shown a photograph. The police gave me the name of Jane Dawson.'

'So, you knew this was the young woman Pulteney had been walking behind because the police told you this was the victim?' Hoggard said.

Chris looked flustered for a moment, then answered, 'It was the same person. I recognized her.'

'Yet in your original statement you said the young lady was wearing a check skirt and a blue jacket, and Jane Dawson was wearing a black skirt and a grey jacket.'

'I was mistaken.'

'And if you were mistaken about that you may have been mistaken about the identity of the young woman?'

Pulteney had to give Hoggard some credit for making a half-decent attempt at flustering Chris, but Chris looked defiant enough when he replied, 'The hair was the same and the build. It was her.'

'Did you have a clear view of the face?'

'Reasonably.'

'From how far?'

'I didn't have a measure with me. Sixty yards maybe.'

'As much as that?' Hoggard paused and swept a look around the court as if in triumph.

The look Chris gave him in return was dismissive. 'About that, yes.'

Now the judge spoke to Chris.

'Are you sure it was the same person?'

'As sure as I'm standing here.'

This made Pulteney certain the judge wanted the guilty verdict and his heart quailed again. Then Chris stood down from the stand.

'Next, I would like to call Andrew Hanson,' Mr Simpson stated.

The young man who stepped forward to the stand seemed insubstantial, as if where he stood stripped him of any certainty he might normally have held. He did look smart in his soldier's uniform, with his hair cut *en brosse* but, as he gave his name and took the oath, his voice held a quaver.

Simpson rose and spoke. 'Please describe your movements on the afternoon of September the 10th.'

Pulteney watched him with interest. He recognized the man but didn't know him, or what to expect from him.

Andy shifted from one foot to another and said, 'That afternoon I went walking with a young lady called Jane Dawson along the Ridges. I was with a mate, George Wilkinson. The lady was later found murdered there, though when we left her she was healthy and happy.' Then he paused and looked around in a way that suggested he didn't expect anyone to believe him.

'Please continue,' the judge told him.

Hanson drew a long breath and, making what looked like an effort, continued, 'We noticed a sailor going along behind us and Jane didn't like the look of him at all, so George and I took a gander at him, and he did look odd.

We thought he was following us, and we wondered why. But he must have turned back because later when we looked he had gone. So we went on along the Ridges, had a chat and a laugh, and then George and I left her as we had to get back to base.'

'But she didn't go with you?' Simpson said.

Andrew looked across to the jury as if taking them in for the first time. He studied the nearest member of it to him, a large man with a moustache, enormous, unruly eyebrows and an open stare.

Then Andrew continued to speak. 'She stayed in Birtleby. It's the opposite direction but she would have been able to make her own way back.'

'And do you recognize the sailor that you saw that day anywhere in this courthouse?'

'Yes.'

'Point him out, please.'

Without hesitation, Andrew pointed to Pulteney, who once again wished he was anywhere but there. Pulteney looked across at Hoggard who now stood, ready to ask his questions, and Pulteney made a silent prayer.

Hoggard spoke to Andrew with a courteous authority. 'Is there any doubt in your mind that the sailor you saw following you that day was William Pulteney?'

'No.'

'How far away was he when you first saw him?'

'About fifty yards.'

'That's a reasonable distance. You're sure you could see his face clearly?'

To Pulteney's chagrin, as Hanson looked back at Hoggard, he didn't look daunted, but rather as if he might be gaining in confidence. 'Clearly enough, and I could see his height and general build as well.'

'Could it not have been any tall, gangly man dressed in a sailor suit?'

'When I was asked to pick him out in an identity parade, I did so.'

'William Pulteney told me he was nervous on the day of the identity parade. Was that a factor in helping you decide which one was the sailor who had been following you?'

The question seemed unlikely to be helpful to Pulteney and he wasn't surprised that the judge decided to intervene. 'It is sufficient for the witness to have picked out Pulteney at an identity parade. At a trial, we are presenting facts to the jury; you are trying to extract an opinion, and a hazy one at that. I have no doubt all of those involved in the witness parade were nervous.'

Pulteney gave Hoggard credit for his effort but not the result.

'No more questions,' Hoggard said as he sat down.

The judge told Hanson he could leave the stand and he did so. Simpson rose, and said. 'The Crown would like to call Dr Martin Coombes of the Leeds Asylum, a well-respected alienist.'

Pulteney froze when he heard this as his memories of his interview with Coombes were clear. The jury looked with curiosity at this specialist in criminal pathology who was being brought forward by the prosecution. Dr Coombes was a tall man with a sweep of grey hair, and sharp, dark eyes. He stood and surveyed the court before allowing his glance to settle on Simpson. Pulteney's mind went back to the personal nature of the questions he had been asked by him, and noticed a thinly veiled impression of contempt as Coombes glanced across at him.

Simpson addressed Dr Coombes. 'You examined the accused, William Pulteney, on 5 December?'

'That is correct.'

'And what were the conclusions you drew from that examination?'

Coombes spoked quickly and easily. 'He gave the impression of a slowness which would be consistent with the term backwardness. This fits in with reports from his school which describe him as that. He also gave the impression of knowing clearly the distinction between right and wrong, and of being mentally competent.'

Pulteney did object to the description 'backwards' even though it was how the school had categorized him; he had always thought they had done that to cover up the laziness of the teacher.

'Did he give you the impression he could be capable of the type of crime he is accused of?'

'Capable of it. Yes. In conversation, he showed indications of a strong but unfulfilled passion for women which, during the examination, exhibited itself as an anger against them. He has had no successful relationships with women. My impression is the frustration that has built up in him over this has turned to a deep-seated rage. Also, I would define his personality as inadequate. He is over-dependent and brittle. With the personality type he has, and his limited intelligence, he could conceivably lose control. This might well result in violence towards women.'

Pulteney thought back to that interview. He had resented Coombe's questions and allowed them to anger him; he remembered shouting at Coombes something about him being a charlatan, and then Pulteney had made uncomplimentary comments about women such as Anne Talbot being no better than they ought to be; he wished he hadn't. His father had tried to din into him the importance of keeping his temper.

'You say he is capable of such a crime. Did Pulteney confess to committing it, or admit a desire to commit one like this?'

'No, I wouldn't have expected this even if he had done such a thing.'

'Are you satisfied with the proofs behind your statement?'

'All mental evidence is an opinion – it is the nature of it - but I have examined him, and I am satisfied he has the character type to have committed such a crime.'

'No more questions.' Dr Coombes was dismissed. 'That is the case for the prosecution,' Simpson said.

Pulteney looked at Simpson's face and supposed it was a good idea from Simpson's point of view to give the impression of a person who believes he has presented a winning argument, which he probably had.

'We will next hear the case for the defence,' the judge said. 'But there will not be time to hear it today, so we will break till tomorrow morning at the same time. The jury is cautioned not to read newspapers or discuss the court case with anyone outside the jury. Courtroom dismissed.'

A hubbub burst over the court as people commented on various aspects of the case, and Pulteney found himself led to a waiting police van and the subsequent familiarity of his cell.

CHAPTER FIFTY-THREE

When court resumed, the judge asked Hoggard to begin presenting the case for the defence. Pulteney could see that Hoggard possessed none of the confidence that Simpson had. There was a long hesitation before beginning his questions, and the occasional waver in his voice when he did.

Hoggard began by recalling Dr Parker to the stand, and tried to elicit from him the opinion that there were differences in the injuries received by Anne Talbot and Jane Dawson: that it could be interpreted that Anne had been struck on the face and fallen back before a large stone was dropped on her, and that Jane Dawson had just been hit several times in a frenzy by an attacker using one instrument, and that this attacker must have had greater strength than Anne Talbot's assailant.

Parker's unflustered reply had been that with the same instrument and the same assailant there would still be differences in the injuries received due to the reactions of the victims, the manner in which the attacker had come across them, and even the mood or determination of the assailant at the time, which he thought would cover any differences here. Pulteney noticed that Hoggard, having failed to land any blows on Parker, did not call Langford as a witness, but instead called Pulteney forward.

Pulteney advanced to the stand. He had been warned beforehand that this would happen, had questioned whether it was necessary, and, after acquiescing, had awaited the ordeal with nervousness.

After Pulteney was sworn in, Hoggard rose and gave him a reassuring smile before proceeding to ask, as he had warned Pulteney he would, 'Did you kill Anne Talbot?' Pulteney's reply was an emphatic no. When Hoggard asked him if he had killed Jane Dawson, Pulteney insisted again, 'No.'

The judge gave Hoggard a supercilious look. 'As the witness has already pleaded not guilty, I'm not sure that was necessary, Mr Hoggard.'

'As you please, m'lud.'

Pulteney thought saying he had not killed anybody had been worth repeating, as it had made him feel better; though not a priority of the judge, he supposed.

Hoggard continued with his questions. 'It has been stated you were in the vicinity at the time of Anne Talbot's murder. What is your reaction to that?'

'I made a statement saying I was on the Ridges on the afternoon of the Thursday, and, yes, I did see a woman who looked like the one they said was murdered.'

As Pulteney glanced round the court, he took in his father's expression and resolved not to look in his direction again. He also noted his brother's stare, curious but cold, and the sneers of the normally jokey fishwives whom he'd known all his life.

'Did you see anyone else with her?'

Pulteney hesitated. He wondered if he looked as he felt, once more, the small boy accused of scurrilous things.

'I saw two men, who I later learned were called Harry Barker and Bob Nuttall.'

'What were their relations with the victim as far as you could see?'

'They were walking along, having a good time, laughing and joking. They looked overexcited and I thought they might have had a lot to drink.'

'Tell the court what you saw happen.'

Pulteney gave the same account that he had given at the inquest.

He kept his eyes on Hoggard and away from the gallery for the most part as he spoke, though he found he couldn't stop himself shooting a glance at his father, but there was no reassurance there.

'We will now come to the day of Jane Dawson's murder. Why were you on the beach?'

'I often go for a walk along there.' Pulteney hesitated, thought he'd better put more confidence into his speech and attempted to do so as he said, 'A lot of people do. It's supposed to be good for your health.'

'As you were doing this, what did you see?'

'A group of three persons was walking ahead of me into the dunes, a young woman I was later told was Jane Dawson, and two soldiers I was later told were called Andrew Hanson and George Wilkinson.'

'We've seen one of these soldiers on the witness stand here?'

'That's correct. Andrew Hanson.'

'What were the relations in this group as far as you could see?'

'They were having a good time together – up to a point.'

'What point was that?'

'Two of them went ahead together, George Wilkinson and the young lady, leaving Andrew Hanson by himself. Then an argument started between George Wilkinson and Jane Dawson, who shouted at each other.'

'Did you make out any of the words?'

'No.'

'But the voices were angry?'

'Yes.'

Again, Pulteney glanced round the public gallery, but there was still no sympathy in the reactions of those seated there.

'Then what happened?'

'I didn't want to know about any argument and turned back.'

'That was the last you saw of any of them?'

'Yes.'

Pulteney thought his father's face reminded him of a statue, and he realised why: his father didn't dare allow his emotions to show because of the amount he was suffering.

'In both cases, the victim found herself alone with one of the young men and you lost sight of her after that?'

Though Pulteney now looked at his feet, there was defiance in his voice. 'Yes.'

'And there was a particularly noisy argument between Jane Dawson and Andrew Hanson?'

'That's correct.'

'So, it's possible Anne Talbot was murdered by Harry Barker and Jane Dawson by Andy Hanson?'

Pulteney felt hopeful for a moment as he answered, 'Yes.'

At this, Hoggard sat down, as he had finished with his questions, and Simpson now stood up. His stance was aggressive.

'Are you in the habit of following couples into lonely spots to watch them?' he asked Pulteney.

'I don't do that.'

'That is what you have stated you were doing.'

'I didn't say I was following them to see them doing anything.'

'Is it not true that part of the beach has a certain reputation?'

Pulteney's voice shook as he answered, 'Not that I'm aware of.'

'Were you following these couples in the hope of getting information you could use to blackmail them?'

'No.'

'So, you were following them for prurient reasons?'

Pulteney said nothing at first, baffled by Simpson's cleverness, then said, 'No.'

Simpson continued his questioning. 'Do you have a girlfriend of your own?'

Pulteney paused as he became aware of the stares of the fishwives. Then he forced himself to reply. 'Not at the moment.'

'So, you have unfulfilled desires?'

'That's common among young men till they settle down,' Pulteney replied.

'But it leads you into following young women with their young men into lonely places?' Simpson continued.

Pulteney said nothing this time.

'You do have to answer the question,' the judge said.

'Just for something to do,' Pulteney said.

'In your statement regarding Anne Talbot you told the police you followed Anne Talbot, Harry Barker, and Bob Nuttall to see what they would do. Is that correct?'

'Yes,' Pulteney said.

'Why were you following Jane Dawson, Andrew Hanson, and George Wilkinson?'

'We just happened to be going in the same direction.'

'You again happened to be going in the same direction of a young couple when they went to a lonely spot in the dunes?'

'Yes.' As Pulteney looked at the jury, he gained the impression they were looking at him as if he were some sort of exhibit. 'And I didn't follow them all the way there. I stopped and turned back.'

'You claim?'

'I did.'

'And have no witnesses to that effect?'

'No.'

Then Pulteney was told to sit down. Any lift in mood he'd felt after Hoggard's questions had now gone.

Simpson had made him look stupid and guilty just as he'd expected.

'Have you any more witnesses for the defence?' the judge asked.

'Yes, m'lud,' Hoggard replied. 'I would like to call Edward Mountjoy.'

Pulteney hadn't been warned about Mountjoy and, judging by the look on his face, neither had Simpson. Pulteney stared at the new witness. The man who came to the stand was middle-aged, with pale skin, and fair hair starting to tinge with grey. He wore a brown suit and waistcoat with a strikingly heavy gold watch chain hanging from a pocket, and a gold ring set with a large diamond.

'Please describe your occupation,' Hoggard asked him.

'I am a jeweller, and I own a shop on the shore road at Birtleby.'

'Was Anne Talbot a customer at your shop?'

'She was. She came in on the Wednesday and had a gold-plated pencil laid to the side for her to collect later that week. She had this wrapped as a present for a gentleman friend and wrote out a card to be given with it.'

Some of the jury gasped, all gaped, and even Justice Johns looked surprised. 'You have these exhibits ready to show the court?' he asked Hoggard.

'Usher, would you show these exhibits to the jury?' Hoggard asked.

As they were passed around, jury members peered, one tutted, one nodded, and one frowned. Justice Johns then perused the pencil and card and wrote a sentence or so in his notes.

'Who is the card addressed to?' Hoggard asked Mountjoy.

'A man called Jean-Michel.' Pulteney doubted whether this would change anything, but he was glad something resembling evidence was being put forward in his defence. He looked across at Walker who looked merely puzzled. Mountjoy continued, 'She said he was an uncle.'

'When did she say she would be calling for the gift?' Hoggard asked.

'In a couple of days.'

'Why did she not take it with her?'

'She said she wanted it kept somewhere safe as she was staying in lodgings.'

'Did she say anything about this Jean-Michel?' Hoggard asked.

'Only that he would be arriving in Birtleby later.'

'Where are you leading with these questions?' the judge asked Hoggard.

'I wish to show there is not only an argument Barker may have killed Anne Talbot, and that Hanson may have killed Jane Dawson, but that there is yet another suspect, this Jean-Michel, whom the police should have made the subject of further inquiries.'

'Thank you, Mr Hoggard,' Justice Johns said. 'You may continue.'

'Did she say where Jean-Michel would be travelling from?'

'Leeds.'

'You don't know the address?'

'Did she give any more details about him?'

'No, but she spoke of him with fondness.'

Now that Hoggard had finished with his questions, Simpson rose. 'To sum up, you can't describe this Jean-Michel as you never met him, you don't know his address, so that it's impossible for us to trace him and question him about anything, and, for all we know, he may be spurious.'

'It was my impression that he did exist and meant a lot to Anne Talbot,' Mountjoy replied.

Pulteney thought it a good idea on Hoggard's part to suggest other lines of inquiry, but it might have been more useful if he could have placed some doubt on the evidence produced by the prosecution. Pulteney felt no more hopeful than he had at the beginning of this.

'Have you any more witnesses, Mr Hoggard?' the judge asked him.

'No, m'lud.'

Pulteney's eyes were drawn to an individual seated in the front row of the jury. This was a man aged about forty who wore a neatly pressed, blue serge suit of a common type; his tie and shirt were nondescript, and Pulteney noticed he wore no ring and carried no watch chain, but what was most striking was the expression of revulsion on his face as he stared at Pulteney.

CHAPTER FIFTY-FOUR

The judge looked round the courtroom to make sure of silence. 'Mr Simpson, would you make the closing speech for the Prosecution?'

Simpson rose and Pulteney, who hated the lawyer's looming figure, stared at the floor again.

'The case for the prosecution is simple,' Simpson said.

Pulteney thought it probably was. He did his best to blot out Simpson's address from his mind by thinking of something else but the only thing that came to mind was the sound of guns when he had been at sea during the war. Between their booming reverberations and the machine-gun rattle of Simpson's words, Pulteney could find no comfort at all, and concentrated on chewing his lip and pressing his fingers and thumb into the rail in front of him as he leaned forward, his head bowed, unaware of the strange sight he presented. Pulteney noticed Simpson had no problem delivering his spiel: the alienist's opinion of Pulteney; the weapon in Pulteney's possession; and all the witness statements that placed him at the scene of both crimes. Pulteney listened more when Hoggard started speaking as he hoped for comfort somewhere.

Hoggard's arguments seemed to focus themselves on the circumstantial nature of the prosecution's evidence. As he pointed out, though they may have proved Pulteney was in the general area where the crimes were committed, that didn't prove that he committed them.

One or two jurymen nodded at this, which momentarily cheered Pulteney. Was Hoggard going to be convincing?

'My client's character has been maligned. It has been argued he is "odd". This is the only motive presented and it hardly amounts to even that. It is more a suggestion the jury should show bias, which is strange. At school, he was indeed classed as backwards, of which there is a normal percentage in the population, but it means no more than that my client had difficulty with reading and counting. It also classifies him as someone who would have more difficulty than articulate members of the population in denying charges of which he is innocent, such as the ones he is charged with today.'

Hoggard looked at the jury with a persuasive smile on his face but, as far as Pulteney could see, they just looked back blankly.

'As far as his relations with women are concerned, as we all know, women are fussy, and he is not prepossessing, so it proves nothing to say that he is not in a relationship with a woman. My client happened to be going for a walk along a beach for the good of his health. Who has not done that? And if someone else happens to be going the same way, they are; it is not a crime to be walking in the same direction as someone else.'

This sounded convincing to Pulteney but not to the jury, he noted. The members of it who had been starting to appear sympathetic to Hoggard now started to look doubtful. Most of what Hoggard had said struck even Pulteney as verbiage but Pulteney had to admit that Hoggard continued to do his best.

'When we consider Anne Talbot herself, what can we say about her? A young woman not yet eighteen, on holiday by herself in a place unknown to her. Behaviour like that makes herself a target to anyone, and did draw the attention of a few young men, some of them quite undesirable, so why are we just focussing on my client as a possible murderer? Could she even have come to Birtleby to meet someone? This Jean-Michel, for instance. The police have not followed up other more obvious leads and perhaps, if they had, my client would not be sitting in that dock now.

'Jane Dawson was also notorious for her flirtatious behaviour with young men. Who's to say one of them wasn't so undesirable as to be her murderer? The prosecution has not proved Pulteney did commit these crimes. They have only proved he may have done. I have shown that others may have done. Prisoners should be found guilty if the facts fit the case but there are no facts to consider.

'Consider where the burden of proof lies in these cases. The prosecution must prove its case beyond reasonable doubt. The defendant does not have to prove his innocence, which is presumed unless proved otherwise. I urge you to consider that there is doubt here and ask you to find William Pulteney innocent of these crimes. I here conclude the case for the defence.'

At this, Pulteney's counsel resumed his seat and a burst of whispering spread round the court. The judge raised his gavel and asked for silence. He perused his notes, glanced round the court, rested his eyes on the jury and began his address.

Pulteney did not listen to his preliminary ramble, which seemed to consist of a stream of formal words that made empty patterns in the air, though he suspected they could serve well enough as rope to hang him with.

Justice Johns then summarised the case for the prosecution, which had been too clear already as far as

Pulteney was concerned, before starting to outline the arguments for the defence. Pulteney did pay careful attention to that.

'Defence counsel has suggested there are three other suspects who may have committed at least one of the crimes, yet none of the facts he has presented to suggest this are conclusive. We have heard the prosecution present a case against William Pulteney, and that is what we must consider on its own merits.'

He did not mention any of Hoggard's other arguments, as if he didn't think them worth considering, and instead referred to the prosecution's case again.

'This is a case based on circumstantial evidence. Unless someone witnesses the murder itself, which is not usual, that is all any case for the prosecution can be based on. What we must ask is whether the requirements for circumstantial evidence have been met.

'Prosecution has produced a motive for committing the crime by producing testimony from a renowned alienist on William Pulteney's pathological feelings of unexpressed rage towards women; these show a propensity for a crime like this, and that we can consider in itself motive.

'He has committed acts indicative of a guilty conscience or intent through his habit of following young women, in particular courting couples.

'He has made preparations for the crime by having in his possession an implement which is exactly suited to the injuries suffered by these young women.

'We know he had the opportunity to commit the crime as it has been proved he was there or thereabouts at the time of these murders.

'He has no adequate explanation for suspicious circumstances in which he was found, namely being in a lonely place in order to follow young women for his own reasons.

'It can be argued he has made an indirect admission of guilt through accusing others of one of the crimes, who have later been found innocent of this.

'The evidence presented by the crown does adequately meet the requirements of circumstantial evidence in these ways so that, if you, as a jury, wish to pronounce him guilty, there is sufficient proof for this in the eyes of the law, but it is up to you now, as the jury, to decide.'

The judge stopped talking and Pulteney became aware of the silence there had been from everyone else in the courtroom. A chair creaked. Someone coughed. When the usher started leading the jurors away to the jury room, the noise of chairs being pushed back and of feet tramping seemed enormous.

CHAPTER FIFTY-FIVE

It might have been necessary to continue the next day but, as the jury only took thirty minutes to reach a conclusion, court resumed when they returned. When Pulteney looked at them to try to sense their general mood, he could see they were pleased they had reached a decision. There was also an air of seriousness about them that was intimidating, and Pulteney didn't think they would have found him innocent so quickly.

The judge spoke to them. 'Foreman of the jury, do you have a verdict for this court?'

The foreman stood and faced him. This was the individual from the front row whom Pulteney had noticed staring at him. Pulteney noticed the tightness of the blue serge suit the man wore, as if he dressed rarely in this, presumably his best suit, and he'd put on weight since its last outing. The expression on his face suggested he found it just as difficult to fit into the restrictions of his role in this court.

'In answer to the charge of the murder of Anne Talbot against William Pulteney, how do you find the defendant?' the judge boomed.

Speaking as loudly and clearly as he knew how, the foreman replied, 'We find the defendant guilty.'

'In answer to the charge of the murder of Jane Dawson against William Pulteney, how do you find the defendant?'

'We find the defendant guilty.'

The foreman glanced across at Pulteney who noticed the previous stare of dislike had changed to one of pity, which Pulteney thought, on the face of it, no improvement. Pulteney noticed the rest of the jury avoided looking in his direction. The audience in the gallery stared at him. His father looked away when Pulteney glanced at him.

The judge spoke to Pulteney. 'William Pulteney, you stand convicted of the murder of both Anne Talbot and Jane Dawson. Have you anything to say why sentence of death should not be pronounced upon you according to law?'

Pulteney looked back at him. He was helpless, as helpless as he had felt on his ship when it had shaken with the force of a torpedo, and he knew well there was no point in saying anything at all.

'I will now pass sentence,' the judge said. He reached for his black cap and put the square of cloth on his head.

'William Pulteney,' he said. 'You have been convicted of foul and brutal murder. Your defence has been demonstrated to be untrue to the satisfaction of the jury. You must prepare yourself to undergo the penalty which the law enacts for such a crime as you have committed.

'My duty is now to pass upon you the sentence of the law. That sentence is that you be taken hence to a lawful prison and thence to a place of execution, and that you be there hanged by the neck until you be dead, and that your body be afterwards buried within the precincts of the prison wherein you shall have been last confined before your execution, and I direct that this shall be carried out at

Linfrith Prison. And may the Lord have mercy on your soul.'

CHAPTER FIFTY-SIX

As Pulteney had asked for him, the prison chaplain, Peter Martin, visited him in his cell, and sat in a chair opposite him, a look of Christian concern on his face. The sympathy did not look genuine to Pulteney who would not have expected it to, as he had been found guilty of murder. It wasn't as if this man knew him, and, to Pulteney, Martin looked as if he came from a different world; there was a softness to his skin that suggested an easier life, and an expression on his lips that suggested becoming fat had been a pleasant chore. Pulteney did not care what the man was like, though, as there were things he needed to say, and it didn't matter whom he said them to.

'Do you feel the need to confess?' Martin asked.

Pulteney supposed Martin wanted him to admit to the murders, for the good of his soul, and he considered this. As he did so, his thoughts flashed back to Maggie, and he felt guilt about her again.

'You've to meet your maker,' the reverend said. 'He already knows everything but it's never too late to repent.'

'Repent?' Pulteney said. His mind was not taking anything in, and he repeated the word. 'Repent.'

'You do need,' the chaplain said, 'to seek forgiveness, particularly for such crimes.'

'I've always believed,' Pulteney said.

'I'm glad to hear it.'

'I prayed every night, even on the battlecruiser in the convoys, especially on the battlecruiser.'

'God listens.'

'I attended services regularly and never took the name of the Lord my God in vain. The only time I didn't respect the Sabbath was in naval service when they gave you no choice.'

'War doesn't stop for Sundays.'

Genuine pity appeared in the chaplain's face, Pulteney thought, or was that an illusion? Pulteney directed his gaze away.

'There was a girl once who accused me of attempting to rape her. I suppose I wanted to, and I regretted it then and I regret it now. I repent.'

The chaplain's eyebrows were raised.

'I didn't mean to,' Pulteney said, 'and I would have stopped even if she hadn't walloped me one, at least I think I would have. I like to think so.' It was what he had always tried to tell himself.

'God is listening. He welcomes those who repent.'

'I believe in God and I believe in Jesus Christ. I didn't believe in the war but you find yourself caught up in that. God might forgive us for what we did in that, though I doubt it.' Pulteney's speech came to a halt.

'And Anne Talbot and Jane Dawson, do you not feel the need to repent for what you did to them?'

The chaplain spoke with a carefully managed tone, which Pulteney thought might be annoying if he did not feel so guilty and have such need to keep on talking.

'They were beautiful,' he said. 'Their voices and faces were so clear and so young, but they were like a mirage, an illusion you followed as you'd never known beauty like that in your life.'

'Yes, my son.'

'But you don't see it. You don't get it.'

'God understands, my son.'

'You'd need to understand what war's like.'

'We all know about the war.'

'That's it. You think you do but you can't if you've never been there. It's a different world, and the feelings you go through are dreadful. There's none of the hope that shone in those girls.'

Pulteney could sense a repulsion in the chaplain but he saw him control it, though Pulteney didn't mind this, because it echoed the repulsion he felt towards himself.

'But I don't...' Pulteney said. He looked back at the chaplain with wonder. So much of life had become incomprehensible but he did have an understanding of himself, and knew what drove him most was a need to conform to what was expected of him. That was why he had joined the navy in the first place. It had been hell at home with all those reminders of his guilt about Maggie that his father kept on putting in his way. Pulteney hadn't fitted in at home anymore and that had told him how much he needed to, and that was why he had found life in the bowels of a ship a comfort even in wartime. Then Pulteney realised that he would do what this minister wanted him to because, whoever this unknown chaplain might be, Pulteney realised he needed someone to show him that forgiveness was possible, and that they accepted him.

'I confess,' he said. He spoke slowly at first, but the words rushed out in the end. 'I followed them and killed them and I regret it. I repent. I ask the Lord Jesus for forgiveness.'

But when Pulteney looked in the eyes of Peter Martin, there was neither forgiveness nor acceptance there, though Martin spoke the words his training had dinned into him, not that Pulteney listened to them. Pulteney supposed he was as ready as he was going to be. When they came to fetch him for his hanging he would face it as well as anyone ever did.

CHAPTER FIFTY-SEVEN

Bob was in the outhouse at his parents' house with a saw in his hand as he worked on a piece of walnut. He was making one of his decorative boxes. He didn't often have walnut to use but a friend of his father had given him a couple of pieces. It was Bob's favourite timber because of the warm tones that could be induced in it when it was polished up. The girls he and Harry had chatted to, and appealed to, or offended, never saw this side of him, the careful person who crafted boxes. Bob had gained his feel for wood long before his war, when he had worked as an apprentice in a boatbuilder's yard in Birtleby, a hub full of the chatter and ribaldry of men at work, and the skeletons of what would become working fishing boats. With the collapse in fishing after the war there hadn't been enough work.

Bob missed working in the boatyard; he yearned for the smell of fresh timber, the company, and the wage. There were no openings in other yards but he often busied himself now making objects he could sell. He was fortunate his father had a friend in town who owned a shop, and Bob could place the things he made there. When they were sold, this gave Bob extra pocket money. He didn't advertise the fact he did this, as if being creative was something to be guilty about, but he enjoyed his moments of peace in this brick outbuilding with its small windows and its earth floor. He was so engrossed this morning he didn't notice at first the stranger striding through the open door.

He was a short, plump man with a strong-looking face, a thick, bristling moustache, and a bald head. His face held a warmth which Bob responded to.

'Robert Nuttall?' the man asked.

'Himself,' Bob replied as he placed the saw on the bench.

'It's good to meet you,' the man said, holding out his hand. 'Alexander Cross.'

As Bob proffered his in return, he noticed the man's eyes wander around before lingering on one of the finished boxes.

'You've a feeling for wood.'

'It's good of you to say so.'

'I've seen your work around and was talking to your father. He said you'd be down here.'

'He didn't mention anyone was coming around.'

'I was sorry to hear about your troubles with the police. They make dreadful mistakes.' Bob doubted if there was anyone in the country who hadn't heard about the Birtleby murders. 'I'm glad you were released and they got the man responsible. He'll hang for it.'

'So he ought. It was a dreadful thing to do to young women.'

'An odd fellow. I'm surprised the police ever listened to anything he said.'

'That's what I thought.'

'And so soon after you'd got back from the war. That was terrible. But at least you made it back. So many people lost someone out there. You were in the trenches?'

'Yes.'

Bob thought back to the mud and the shells and the bullets and the impossible wire.

'I lost my son on the Somme,' Cross said.

Bob thought of the men walking beside him with their rifles at the ready, only to be mown down like wheat.

'You were at Shaw's, the boatbuilders in Birtleby?'

'For a while. I didn't finish my apprenticeship before I was called up.'

'I could take you on,' Cross said, 'as a joiner's mate, to learn the trade with me.'

'I'd like that fine,' Bob said.

Then, unbelievably, they were talking about money and the time he'd start.

After the man had left, Bob returned to the box but couldn't concentrate on it because of an emotion he had forgotten, which was excitement. He wondered at the relaxation in his muscles, as a tension he hadn't realised was there, left. Something was over, and something was beginning. He put his saw away, and paced the workshop in glee.

CHAPTER FIFTY-EIGHT

Bob had arranged with Harry to meet him outside the Victoria, and he found him there, smoking his habitual cigarette and gazing out to sea. The boom of waves and the spit of spume were a backdrop to every part of life in Birtleby. Harry grinned at him and Bob grinned back.

'A while since we've been here,' Harry said.
'We can't avoid it forever,' Bob replied.
'Shall we go in?' Harry said.
'Your round is it?' Bob replied.
'I thought it was yours.'

They strode in, in their grey suits; Bob with his cap, Harry wearing his felt hat, Bob flourishing his brass-topped stick. Elspeth was behind the bar, and her eyes turned away from theirs when she saw them. Bob gave her a grin.

'The non-condemned men would like a pint of Guinness each. And would you like an Abdullah?' Bob boomed, proffering a nearly full pack.

It was out of character for Elspeth to blush but she did. Bob thought it maidenly but didn't comment.

'And would you like a port wine yourself?' It was Harry's turn to beam at her.

Elspeth looked at him with eyes that narrowed but this was momentary.

'Don't mind if I do,' she said. 'Not that I'm supposed to drink with customers when I'm serving but I'll be friendly,' she said.

She poured the drinks as Harry planked himself on a bar stool beside her and Bob did the same.

'Haven't seen you in here for a while,' she said. 'I'm glad you were released.'

'I'm sure you are,' Bob replied, and the kindness in his tone surprised him.

'We thought you'd done it.' She looked away when she said this, then turned her eyes towards him. 'I should've known better.'

'Yes,' Harry agreed.

'Somebody did,' Bob said. 'It just wasn't us.'

'He'll swing for it now,' Elspeth said. 'And thank God for that. Fancy it being the sailor who identified you.'

'Who else would it be?' Bob said. 'If he'd put us away, he was in the clear.'

'And then to do it again. He must be stupid.'

'He's not the full shilling, or so I've heard,' Harry said.

'I'm so sorry,' Elspeth said. 'I was on that witness stand at the inquest. That could've gone wrong for you.'

'It did,' Bob replied. 'Just as well for us he's a murdering maniac who couldn't stop.'

'Not just as well for that Jane Dawson.'

'No.'

'We were all so afraid,' Elspeth said. 'And it turns out we were right to be. He did it again. It could've happened to any of us girls.' There was a pleading in her voice and eyes as she said this. She sipped her whisky splash and looked across at the two of them: young men with long limbs and wide shoulders, and troubled eyes from the war like so many. Bob considered her.

'I'm a young man with a future,' he said.

'Are you?' Elspeth asked.

'What do you mean?' Harry said.

'I've a job. Don't look so surprised. I thought your eyes were going to pop out of your face then, Harry. It's true. I've been taken on at Alex Cross the joiner's in Blackforth. He'd seen my woodwork around, and heard all about our case, and must have felt a pang of sympathy. Fancy that. Everyone was treating us like pariahs.'

'That's good,' Elspeth said.

'Jammy bugger,' Harry said, 'but I'm pleased for you. I wish I could be so lucky.'

'When do you start?' Elspeth asked.

'Monday.'

'So, you're celebrating,' she said.

'Yes.'

'Never mind, Harry,' she said. 'Maybe someone will take pity on you too.'

'I've tried all the estates round here. There's no work for half-trained under-gamekeepers.'

'There ought to be sympathy for you now,' Elspeth said.

'I haven't noticed much.'

'You didn't do it,' she said. 'Now they've got the man who did it, people will look at both of you differently.'

'Some false sympathy maybe but it won't last,' Harry said.

'Cash in on it while you can.'

'I suppose,' Harry said.

'So, thanks, Elspeth,' Bob said.

'What for?'

'For getting me in bad with the police. I'd still be hanging around looking for work otherwise.'

Now Elspeth did blush. 'You believe in making a girl suffer,' she said.

'When she deserves to,' Bob replied.

'Which you do,' Harry agreed.

'I am sorry,' Elspeth muttered. 'And I've said so.'

'We don't mind how often we hear it,' Bob said.

Harry looked as if he was to be making up his mind about something. Then he said, 'Agreed. Mind you, you had us worried. It was a close-run thing.'

'I know.' Elspeth drew in her breath sharply.

'But you told the truth,' Bob said, 'not one word of a lie, not like that Nancy Harland.'

'I'd wondered about that,' Elspeth said. 'She was a bitch if she made that up.'

Bob looked at Elspeth thoughtfully. The anger he had felt towards her at one point had gone. It was strange how easy it had been to forgive. He hadn't expected that. He pondered the shine in Elspeth's auburn hair and the softness in her skin. Women and he lived in such different worlds and, though he was fascinated by theirs, it had always been so out of reach. Every time he'd tried to make friends with women he seemed to annoy them or they angered him, and he had been furious with Elspeth this time but that fury had gone. Something in him felt as if it was healing. He supposed women had the right to be suspicious and Elspeth deserved his forgiveness. There were dangers in their world that men didn't have to think of. He reached forward with his glass to clink it against hers.

'To the future,' he said.

And Harry did the same.

'The future,' Elspeth said.

'It can't be any worse than the past,' Harry said.

When Bob looked at Elspeth, he realised he must be the typical picture of any young man looking at a desirable young woman. He grinned at her and she grinned openly back. The over-excitement of things got to him, and a thought occurred.

'I know you've never liked the look of us,' he said, 'but I don't suppose you fancy the Hippodrome with me tonight, do you?'

CHAPTER FIFTY-NINE

The quiet lap of waves, the sound of breeze stroking long grasses, the sweet sharpness in the scent worn by the young woman next to him: Bob gloried in it all. He had been to the Hippodrome with Elspeth and enjoyed it. The film had been good and the company of Elspeth better, and she even agreed to a walk along the beach with him. They strolled in the half-light of evening, sharing quiet words and warm glances.

'That Charlie Chaplin isn't half a laugh,' Elspeth said.

'Considering what he has to put up with.'

'Haven't we all?'

Bob looked at her mouth and thought he would enjoy kissing it, but it might be better to leave it till later.

'I didn't know you made boxes,' Elspeth said.

'It's a hobby.'

Bob was wondering about Elspeth. A full life flowed beneath those eyelashes but she didn't allow much of it to be glimpsed in that bar in the Victoria. He supposed it was natural for her with the number of men passing in and out of there, but Bob had often wondered why she was as guarded as she was. He supposed lots of people had been hurt in the past and most of them didn't want to talk about it, but he wondered what it was with Elspeth.

'I'm honoured,' he said.

'Are you?'

'You don't go out with men much.'

'It has been known,' she said.

'How did you get your job at the Victoria?'

'I was in service but you have to work so hard and you never get any time to yourself, and I knew a girl who worked at the Victoria, and I thought why not?'

'Where were you in service?'

'Wapping House.'

'Oh, that one.'

'It was a full house, with a husband and wife and her mother, and a couple of grown-up sons. It was time they left the nest.'

'Paw at you, did they?'

'Got it in one. I thought it would be safer with men at the Victoria because at least I could keep the bar between me and them.'

And she said it lightly, and if there was anything to tell she would talk about it if she wanted to. Women lived in their own world, men in theirs, and how much did they really know about each other's? You're thinking too deeply, he thought. Make the most of the moment. Walk this beach. Talk with her. Laugh with her. Work up to that kiss. His eyes lingered on her auburn hair as it caught the setting light of the evening sun.

It was a good kiss, and he took care not to go too far.

CHAPTER SIXTY

It was the kindness of Martin that struck Pulteney as he sat with him all night, though when Pulteney noticed the sky beginning to lighten behind the barred window, it was relief he felt. It would not be long. Martin had prayed with him and prayed for him, and there was just the deed to be done. Pulteney hadn't found Martin a comfort. Dying was a lonely business, there was nothing to be done about that, and there was no one lonelier than the convicted murderer. But death was what everyone came to in the end.

Pulteney thought of Anne in her green coat, swinging her way along the path with her two young men, blithe in her ignorance of her loneliness. He thought of the lightness in her stride, and the laughter she had thrown behind as she strolled to her battered death.

He thought of when he had watched Jane Dawson at the beach, running her hand through the water as she strode through it. If she'd known how close death was, would she have behaved differently? She was basking in life and her joy in it. What was there to change?

Pulteney looked across at Martin, his hands together, his head bowed in prayer for Pulteney's soul. Then

Pulteney looked at the barred window and the sky behind it and thought it would be good if he could walk out into the air.

He remembered once before when he had known he was going to die, though he had escaped from it then. It was when he was on convoy duty in the Atlantic and his ship had been hit by a torpedo at night. He had been in the heat and sweat of the boiler room as he stoked the engine, and the torpedo had thundered into the hull but, fortunately, breeched a different chamber. An officer had hauled him forward and yelled at him. Pulteney had dragged himself through the next chamber, then on up onto the deck where wind and spray whipped at him. It was a freezing night with waves pounding over the ship. The ship had lurched and keeled over, and Pulteney and other sailors had tumbled into the waves, where the cold sliced through him like steel. He thrashed about and, as he did so, his arm met a leg. Then he realised there was a wooden spar and a sailor clinging onto that. Pulteney wound his arms round him to pull himself up onto the support but there wasn't room for both, and they'd kicked and pushed and hauled at each other till both might have lost hold of the spar, but then Pulteney had it to himself and the other man was thrashing about in the water further off. The man drowned. Pulteney knew that, and that he should have died too in water as cold as that. He didn't expect to survive longer than five minutes even with a spar to keep him afloat. He had been counting down his life in minutes in his mind, when a lifeboat picked him up. So he'd felt he had known he was going to die, as he did now. And he had known he deserved it then, as he knew that he did now, just because of what he'd done to the other sailor on that spar.

The sky continued to lighten behind the bars. It would soon be time.

Anne Talbot's voice sung once more in his mind. Then Jane Dawson's. He would have followed those rivers of joy anywhere. They had promised the things that had been taken from him: peace, innocence, and the lightness of joy. He wouldn't have hurt someone who owned a voice like that; and he hadn't. He'd followed Anne Talbot and Jane Dawson, but despite his confession, he hadn't killed them.

The door opened without warning and two warders came in, put his hands in handcuffs behind him and a hood over his head. They hauled him through the door and across the passageway to where the scaffold had been prepared.

EPILOGUE

You see her standing in the dunes. The chance is there and you know you will take it. The way your emotions surge before one of your slayings is terrible and you need the release of your kills, though the relief of that will only last a short time before the anger begins again and slowly works you up to the next murder.

If you'd been able to adapt to peace you wouldn't be like this, but you are. You supposed it was the same for everyone to a greater or lesser degree: the memories of war were inescapable and were what made you the person you now were.

It had been Pulteney who'd talked of the music in young women's voices when you and he had followed them along the seafront. It had become a fascination for you too, like the sirens in the story that had drawn sailors to their deaths with the hypnotic qualities of their singing, except Anne's voice had been so lovely you had to kill her – to prevent her gaining the knowledge that killed innocence.

Murdering Jane Dawson was as unavoidable as killing Anne Talbot; something else decided her death for you.

Now this other opportunity has come, and you can't resist. After all, you got away with two. And you'll get away with this because you are who you are – Chris. That is how you feel.

A woman on her own swings her way along the path leading away from the beach as she parts with her young man. She's pretty. Light plays on her short, auburn bob from the evening sun, and you tell yourself you might turn away, but she is singing. It is a music hall tune, a song of misplaced love, which she sings with a real tenderness despite the sentimentality of the words. Her voice strikes its note of truth as you follow her further into the dunes where the waves provide their quiet if incongruous rhythm. It's a beautiful voice, full of youth, loneliness, hope, and despair, and you feel such a need of it, and such an ache for the softness of the flesh that carries it. You would follow its sound anywhere. Where was it when the shells crashed, and the bodies fell, and you heard the sound of death, not soft but booming? War was such misery, such a contrast with that quiet femininity. But that fills you with fear because there is such fragility in its lightness. How do you protect that from shell and bullet, from pain and blood? You feel the need to keep it safe.

You creep closer, listening to the notes as they lift into the breeze.

When her face turns towards you, you catch the look of fear. Why do you know only one way of saving her from that?

You lift the marlin spike.

ACKNOWLEDGEMENTS

Thanks to Andrew Greig and Michael Malone for their comments and encouragement, and to the Brodie Writing Group.

If you enjoyed this book, please let others know by leaving a quick review on Amazon. Also, if you spot anything untoward in the paperback, get in touch. We strive for the best quality and appreciate reader feedback.

editor@thebookfolks.com

www.thebookfolks.com

Also featuring Inspector Stephen Blades:

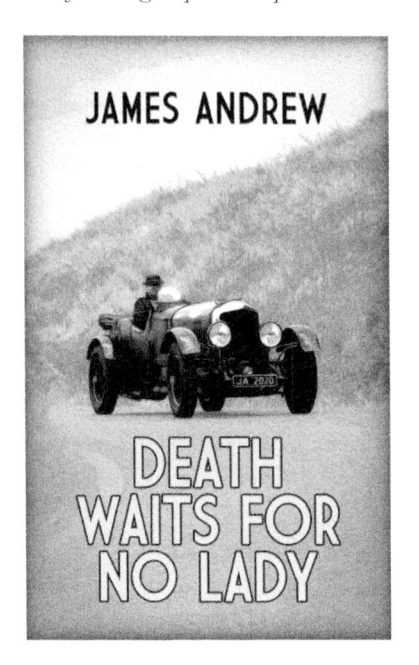

BOOK 2

When a parlour maid finds her wealthy mistress dead, Detective Blades is called in to investigate. The lady of the house's lifestyle has changed considerably following the death of her father, so the police focus on her many apparent suitors. Which of them could have wanted her dead?

Available on Kindle and in paperback from Amazon.

JAMES ANDREW

THE RIDDLE OF THE DUNES

BOOK 3

A woman is killed near the beach. There is little evidence. But the crime bears the hallmarks of several similar murders some time ago. The trouble is that the man supposedly responsible was sent to the gallows...

Available on Kindle and in paperback from Amazon.

BOOK 4

When a young woman is reported missing, Inspector Blades pulls out all the stops to find her, despite knowing deep down that she's been killed. He must find a man seen carrying suitcases near her last known whereabouts, and unravel a mystery to find the killer.

Available on Kindle and in paperback from Amazon.

Printed in Great Britain
by Amazon